An excerpt f
To Tame A C.......

"Do not become peevish again, Josephine. You remember what happened, oh, five minutes ago." The wretched thing went back to smoothing her skirts again, while he thought what a puzzle she was. "My dear, you must admit that you felt better after I spanked you. Expiated and all that. It would have been the end of the whole matter, if Baxter hadn't found us on the way back."

"But he did find us."

"Yes, and I married you, which he wanted from the beginning. It has happened and we must resign ourselves to it. Come here, would you? Stop picking at your skirts." He hauled her onto his lap and clasped her restless fingers in his. "Listen to me. There are men with whom you can feel safe, and men with whom you decidedly cannot. I promise you will always be safe with me, no matter how aggressive and wild you imagine men are. That's not to say I won't demand my marital rights."

She stiffened in his arms. "What does that mean? That you'll spank me whenever you like?"

He laughed, then sobered when he saw her expression. "Oh, my sweet, confused girl. Do you think we've been talking this entire time about spanking?"

He watched the flush spread across her cheeks. "I don't know. I'm sure I don't know what we've been talking about." She tried to escape his lap, but he pulled her back and circled her in his arms, and made her face him.

"Do you even know what marital rights are?"

"I don't want to know," she said, shrinking back from him.

"I suppose you believe they involve wild humors. Whatever the hell those are." He shouldn't curse. He should look at her innocence as an opportunity. Above all, he mustn't frighten her any more than she already was.

To Tame A Countess

by

Annabel Joseph

Other erotic romance by Annabel Joseph

Mercy
Cait and the Devil
Firebird
Deep in the Woods
Fortune
Owning Wednesday
Lily Mine
Comfort Object
Caressa's Knees
Odalisque
Command Performance
Cirque de Minuit
Bound in Blue
Master's Flame
Burn For You
Disciplining the Duchess
The Edge of the Earth (as Molly Joseph)
Waking Kiss
Fever Dream
Training Lady Townsend

Erotica by Annabel Joseph

Club Mephisto
Molly's Lips: Club Mephisto Retold

Coming soon

My Naughty Minette
Under A Duke's Hand

For Mrs. Shaffer and Mr. Ed,
who encouraged me to write without fear.

Chapter One: Lady Maitland

England, 1793

The Earl of Warren let his mind drift as his younger sister rambled on in a cheerful voice. Wilhelmina—or Minette, as everyone called her—could carry on a conversation for hours, no matter if the other person participated in the exchange. He had the questionable fortune to be sharing a carriage with her on a day-long journey to a friend's home in Hertfordshire.

"Will we be there soon?" Minette perched on the edge of her seat, craning to look out the window.

"It's at least two more hours, love. Perhaps you should rest."

Minette was as likely to rest as an overstimulated puppy. The nineteen-year-old woman was as tiny as he was large, and possessed of boundless energy. They shared the same riotous blond curls, courtesy of their late mother, although such hair suited his vivacious sister far better than him.

"I can't rest," she said. "I am far too excited to see my friends again. Calliope will be there, and Lucy, and Helena, and Prudence, and Melinda and Belinda…"

She went on to name about a thousand girls her age, while Warren thought what a torment this house party would be. It was already early spring, so social duties loomed on the horizon. After a week in St. Albans as the Earl of Baxter's guests, everyone would swarm to London for the start of the season, to plan their balls and dinners, and match up their young Melindas and Belindas with husbands.

Warren himself was a prime matrimonial prospect. He was an earl, for one, and excessively rich, for another. He was also considered handsome, with well-formed features and unusually vivid blue eyes. He was so eligible, in fact, that mamas and papas tended to overlook his rather sketchy bachelor activities and his association with a group of gentlemen known for lascivious pursuits.

"I'm sure your friends will be happy to see you again," he said when she'd finished listing their names off. "And which gentlemen will be there? Any you are sweet on?"

"Warren! I'm not sweet on anyone, and if I was, I wouldn't tell you."

"Just behave yourself, all right? I won't hover over you, but I expect you to stay out of trouble. No going off alone with any gentleman. No flirting or sending correspondence."

"I wouldn't," she said, looking shocked. "I shall spend my time with my companions. We've made a pact to stick together and watch out for one another's interests."

Funny, but he had made the same pact with his friends several years ago. As only sons, the four of them had long been hounded by expectations of marriage and duty, but so far, only the Marquess of Townsend had fallen. The Earl of Augustine, the Duke of Arlington, and Warren continued to enjoy their bachelorhoods, and their "interests" were nothing at all like those of Minette and her friends.

"What are you going to do at the party?" she asked him. "Will there be any ladies you are sweet on?"

"I sincerely hope not, since I plan to stay in the card room and drink."

Minette shot him a scandalized stare, but he meant what he said. One hadn't much opportunity for sensuous pursuits at a quality function, unless one wanted to try one's hand at seducing innocents, any number of whom would be at the party. But that had never been his style.

"I hope you're joking about cards and drinking," said Minette. "How horrified I would be if you were so rude. Lady Baxter had matched the number of ladies and gentlemen perfectly until your friends decided not to come, and so you must socialize and make conversation, and dance at the evening entertainments, and be a charming person for the sake of your hosts. In particular you must be kind to Lady Maitland, since she is the Earl of Baxter's ward."

"Baxter has a ward?" Warren asked, interrupting her mid-prattle.

"Yes, her name is Lady Maitland, and all of us think she is ever so mysterious and sad."

Warren could sense a long story unfolding, and braced himself to endure a quarter-hour's worth of details. "Why sad?" he asked when she looked at him expectantly. "Please tell me all about this Lady Maitland. Don't leave anything out."

Minette leaned forward, clasping her hands. "Oh, where do I begin? She has been to places all over the world, for a start, because her father was an avid traveler in addition to being a baron. She only came back to England a short while ago. She made her curtsy to the queen the same day I did, but she was all in black, can you imagine it?"

He tipped his hat forward over his eyes. "No, I can't."

"It was because both her parents died suddenly. I don't know how, and of course no one would talk about it. Perhaps they were bitten by poisonous vipers in some jungle, or murdered by Cossacks. Or set upon by cannibals."

"My goodness, Minette." He was fairly sure this was all made up.

"But her mourning dress was the finest thing," his sister went on. "With just a touch of ribbon, and elegant puffed sleeves. She was the most pale and tragic young woman and she had the smallest sort of hands, and gloves with a black pearl at each side. All of us wanted to be as pretty and dignified as her. During the audience, the queen said she must set about to be married, and soon, for she's inherited her father's barony."

He pushed his hat up a smidge. "Who are we talking about?"

"Lady Maitland! Her given name is Josephine, which I suppose I am permitted to call her, since she is mostly my friend."

"Mostly?"

"We exchanged a few words while we waited to see the queen, and she told me her name was Josephine, so that means we are friends, doesn't it?"

"All the world is your friend, my dear. Including this Josephine, I'm sure."

"But her official name is The Right Honorable Lady Maitland and she is a poor orphaned baroness who is all alone, without a mother or father or husband or anyone at all to look after her except for Lord Baxter who is some distant, distant, distant cousin. Isn't it the saddest story you ever heard?"

"She can't be a baroness with no husband," he said, sinking back beneath his hat's brim. "Only men have titles, and those titles are passed along to male issue when they die."

"She's got a title," Minette insisted. "I suppose there was no one else to have it." She placed a finger aside her gently pointed chin. "It doesn't seem fair, though. None of the rest of us young ladies have titles."

"You'll get a title if you marry the right sort of chap. Why didn't you accept Lord Bancroft when he offered? Or Lord Everett? Both were perfectly adequate prospects."

"Perfectly adequate," she said glumly. "And perfectly boring."

"You say boring. I say steady."

Minette pulled one of her thunderous pouts. "Why are you so eager to marry me off? Do you want to get rid of me?"

"Not at all, but you know how the marriage market goes. The longer you're on it, the less appealing you are."

"I had more suitors than Bancroft and Everett. Many more."

"I know." And she had rejected all of them for the most buffle-headed reasons. Too short. Crooked nose. An excessive fondness for chamber music. "I have every hope you shall eventually make an excellent match," he said. "In the best case, you'll choose someone we both esteem."

"I don't know how that will be possible, when you hate all the gentlemen I like, and I hate all the gentlemen you like. What's worse, all the gentlemen whom I least admire seem to want me the most, while the ones I admire most don't want me at all."

"Because you chatter too much," he said *sotto voce*.

"What did you say?"

"Nothing. Listen, I was up quite late. How about letting your brother get some sleep?"

"But who shall I speak with to pass the time? Why didn't you let Mrs. Everly ride with us? Then we could have conversed while you rested."

Just what Warren needed, the stodgy Mrs. Everly droning in his ears. "There was more room in the baggage coach," he said. "Now hush."

The truth was, his aged valet and Minette's hired companion were fond of each other, and had precious little time alone, and so he had suggested they ride together in the other coach. Warren was sensitive to such things, to longing and hope and attraction, though he was not a particularly romantic man. He'd been ten when he became the Earl of Warren, and had learned to go about life in a very particular way.

And that particular way did not involve fawning over women.

He was more concerned with getting Minette happily married. His sister had never known their parents, who had died in a carriage accident soon after she was born. He wanted Minette to have a family and a sense of belonging beyond what he could give her—which, despite his best efforts, was not very much. He brought her to parties like this to increase her chances of finding a compatible partner. His friends Lord Augustine and the Duke of Arlington had been supposed to come too, but absconded at the last moment to Bath, to chase after some actress's skirts.

"Warren," she said, stifling a yawn. "Will you sit over here so I can lean on your shoulder?"

"Ready to rest now, are you?"

"Don't tease!" she whined. "Will you?"

"Of course, mopsy."

She scooted over and he switched to the front-facing bench, slouching down and propping his feet on the opposite cushion. When he'd slouched enough for her head to reach his shoulder, she settled against him in the same fashion she had since she was two or three years old. As a child, Minette had often wandered about in the throes of slumber—sleepwalking, they called it. During those night-roaming years, she had slept beside him a lot.

"All right?" he asked.

"Yes." A brief pause. "I feel nervous about this party."

"Why?"

"I don't know. I suppose I'm always worried when I'm out among company. I'm afraid I'll say the wrong things and everyone will come to hate me, and issue me the cut direct next time I'm around."

He chuckled. "Everyone loves you, silly. And even if everyone hated you, I would still love you and let you live at Warren Manor for the rest of your days."

"Would you?"

"Well, in your own secluded wing."

Minette batted him on the arm. "I hope you're sweeter to your lady friends than you are to your sister."

"I'm not, unfortunately. I'm only ever sweet to you."

She thought he was joking, but he wasn't.

Unfortunately.

"Go to sleep, will you?" he said, patting her curls. "I'll wake you when we're there."

* * * * *

The Baxters' house party was even grander and more crowded than Warren expected. With sixty guests, he understood why they'd only been invited for a week, as opposed to the typical fortnight. There was the usual mix of married couples and single guests looking for prospects. Since the latter outweighed the former, the party took on an air of flirtation from the start.

Of course, his sister was in heaven. Since she was beautiful, sweet, and naturally cheerful, men flocked to her and competed for the smallest scrap of her attention. And because she attracted so many men, swarms of young misses also surrounded her to benefit from her social success.

Warren watched all of this with a jaded eye. He was eight years older than his sister but he felt two decades older most days. As for the other young ladies, they seemed to grow sillier every year.

The second evening, the Baxters set up a great revelry in their ballroom which he attended out of social obligation more than anything else. He danced with three of the unattached women, again, out of social obligation. The first chattered on nearly as effortlessly as Minette. The second two he chose for their wallflower qualities, so they were much quieter.

At the end of the third dance he considered his social duties discharged and headed to the card room where the gentlemen—and some of the older ladies—gathered to play, drink, and smoke. He'd just settled into a hazy corner with a glass of port when he heard his name.

"Warren? Why, it *is* you. What have you been up to, you filthy beast?"

Warren frowned at the Earl of Stafford. "Do you mind piping down? I have a reputation to preserve."

"We know your reputation, Wild Warren," the man replied, arching a dark brow. Someone had long ago joined Warren's hated first name and his title to create the moniker. He forgot how much it irritated him until now.

Stafford, who loved to irritate people, sat beside him without waiting for a by-your-leave. The earl was an Oxford classmate who had long run in the same debauched circles as Warren and his friends, but none of them liked the man. He was unpleasant at his best, and downright degenerate at his worst. He waved a be-ringed hand toward the ballroom doors. "Why aren't you out there putting a sparkle in the eyes of the unmarried guests?"

"There's enough sparkle on your fingers already, old chap."

Now Stafford was the one whose lips twisted in irritation. "Ha, you're a funny fellow. How is your sister? What's her name? Winnie? Minnie?"

"Minette," Warren said, looking about for some avenue of departure.

"Pretty thing. Such a smile, and those curls. She's got to be marrying age now, yes?" The man's handsome features twisted into a leer. "I wouldn't mind courting her, young as she is. She's got the famous Bernard breasts."

With that outrageous remark, Stafford managed to insult both Warren's sister and his late mother. It wouldn't do to brawl in his host's home, but if Stafford didn't move along soon, Warren might lose his composure and plant a fist in the man's face. "If you so much as look at my sister, I'll kill you," he said in a low voice. "I'll kill you slowly and painfully, with great amounts of torture. That is a promise, Stafford, not a threat."

The earl threw back his head and laughed. "I'm only joking, dear boy. Deliver me from overprotective brothers. No, I've got my eye on

13

someone else. Only reason I'm here at this damned boring party, you know."

"Damned boring? You're happy enough to drink Baxter's wine, though, aren't you?" Warren liked Baxter, and thought Stafford a preening, self-concerned arse.

"Oh, Baxter's a grand sort," the man said with another wave of his rings. "At least, I'll let him believe so while I'm paying my addresses to that daft chit he wants to marry off."

"I've no idea what you're talking about," Warren said. "Are you drunk?"

"I'm speaking of Baxter's ward, man. The Baroness Maitland. She's looking for a husband, and I'd be as happy as anyone else to get my hands on her fortune."

Ah, the pale and tragic Lady Maitland. Even more tragic, to be courted by Stafford. "I'm sure you're not even in the running."

"Oh, I am," Stafford said with a smirk. "I can be charming enough when I need to be. Even charming as you, Lord Warren, and I've not much competition in this case, since the girl is so strange."

"If she's strange, why do you want to marry her?"

"Money, of course. And she's titled too, a baroness in her own right. Her father passed down everything—fortune and title, and a parcel of property not so far from yours."

"Maybe he thought her too homely to find a husband."

"Homely? No one could call her that. She's got beautiful auburn hair, a slim little waist, and great, big, bountiful—"

Warren pushed down the man's hands as he sketched curves in the air. "Be that as it may, do you really want a daft woman having your children?" The Stafford line was already mentally thin, though Warren didn't say so aloud.

Stafford shrugged. "I've looked into all that. She's not insane or anything, only a bit rough in manners. She grew up in foreign parts, so what do you expect? I can always have someone else raise the children if she's a hassle, and stow her in Bedlam. Out of sight, out of mind."

"What a detestable fellow you are."

"Detestable? I call it practical. Don't tell me you wouldn't do as much."

"I wouldn't do as much," said Warren. "I'd never put a woman in Bedlam."

Stafford gave him an arch look. "That's rich, coming from you. Everyone whispers about your wicked and unnatural proclivities. Word is, you drove one of Madame Cecilia's girls mad."

"Drove her mad with pleasure." It was a well-passed-about myth that he had broken Mary Branham's mind, but it wasn't true. The poor lass had been broken to begin with. He'd only set her up in a cottage in Cornwall so she wouldn't have to sell her body anymore.

Stafford took another gulp of port. The man was considered handsome but wouldn't be much longer, if he persisted in heavy drink. "Be sensible, Warren," he said. "Daft or not, Baxter's ward has money. Why marry a poor woman when you can marry a rich one? The Maitland property's not much, but there's enough in the bank to keep a gentleman in cards, wine, and women for the rest of his life."

Stafford deserved to be heartily beaten. Daily. It was only his title and influence that allowed him to move in polite circles. And if Baxter had invited him here, he must—for some unfathomable reason—approve of Stafford as a suitor for his ward.

"Perhaps I'll marry her," said Warren. "Steal her from your clutches."

Stafford laughed. Warren's reluctance to marry was a well-known fact.

"So when's your wedding to this Lady Maitland?" Warren asked. "I'll want to be looking about for an appropriate gift." *Like a pistol for her to blow her brains out.*

"We'll wed as soon as I can get the woman to accept me. She's not crazy to marry but I can romance her, at least until she's under my thumb."

"And then?"

"And then I'll do what I like, won't I? And with a great deal more gold in the bank."

It was a bleak picture, this Baroness Maitland languishing with an arse like Stafford for a husband, especially when she didn't want to marry in the first place. He hoped she was a strong woman with a resilient heart.

Warren stood to excuse himself, having endured enough of Stafford for one evening. "I wish you a pleasant night. And good hunting with Baxter's chit."

"Good hunting indeed." Stafford raised his glass, rings glittering as bright as his ingratiating smile. No wonder the man needed money. He wore more jewels than a king's whore.

Warren left the card room, feeling unnaturally tense around the shoulders, as if his coat was too tight. He decided to check on his sister, although he knew the stalwart Mrs. Everly was looking after her. Friends greeted him as he walked toward the ballroom. No matter his private exploits, he was generally liked and respected by the *haute ton*, and maintained a faultless public image for Minette's sake, and for his Parliamentary career.

As expected, his sociable little sister was surrounded by friends, having a fine time. He watched her for a while, then skirted the shadows of the ballroom, lest some ambitious young woman come fluttering about to beg for a dance. He paused by a line of tall potted plants, thinking how grand it would be to hide in them and jump out at tottering dowagers, if only there were tottering dowagers around.

But there was only a young woman in a black mourning gown, peering out from behind a cluster of yellow-green leaves. He stopped and looked again.

Yes, my goodness. This could only be Lady Maitland, that daft and tragic figure of Minette and Stafford's tales. She had disappeared behind her leafy fortress, but not before he noted thick, glossy auburn hair and a mouth made to be kissed.

He was always up for a lark, and this promised to be a good one. He looked around to be sure he was not observed, then set off with a jaunty sense of purpose to flush out this exotic bird.

Chapter Two:
Unwilling

Josephine had hoped hiding behind the potted plants would protect her from sociable advances. She'd only agreed to come down to please Lady Baxter, who believed Josephine's parents watched over her from heaven, and would not want her sitting alone in her rooms. Josephine had *not* agreed to change out of her black gown. Black handily repelled lighthearted people and lighthearted conversation. She didn't wear it to mourn, and honestly, she didn't believe her parents could be looking at her from anywhere but the deepest depths of hell.

Unfortunately, the black gown and odious plants had both failed her, for a tall, smiling gentleman was headed her way. He was exceedingly blond, even viewed through the black netting of her fan. When he drew closer, she caught a glimpse of piercingly bright blue eyes.

What was she to do? She could continue to hide and hope he didn't find her, or step out and make herself known, but that might require speaking to this stranger, and Josephine hadn't any desire to do that. She dithered so long that he came upon her unexpectedly, so she startled and then stumbled. She was obliged to grasp at large, waxy leaves to keep her feet.

He reached to steady her too. "Why are you hiding?" he asked. "Shall I rescue you?" His hands closed on her waist, a strong, warm pressure that startled her nearly as much as his unwelcome appearance.

"I don't need rescuing," she said.

But he had been joking. A corner of his mouth turned up in a lazy smile. He was a charmer, she could see—and therefore not to be trusted. The one thing Josephine had learned in her wretched life of traveling was to read people, particularly when they might pose a threat. His direct gaze unsettled her so much she looked away, but not before she noted strong, noble features and a chiseled jaw. Though his hair and eyes were light, his complexion glowed golden, as if health and contentment spilled from his very soul.

"I'm perfectly fine now," she said. "You may release me."

"Certainly I'll release you, if you're sure you won't tumble out of the trees again. Or the brambles, or bushes, or whatever these are."

What a mad person. They were obviously house plants, and she hadn't tumbled out of them, only lost her footing when he snuck up on her unawares. Her throat worked at the awkwardness of the conversation. "I am the Earl of Warren," he continued, when she failed to speak. "But we haven't yet been formally introduced to one another, so I wouldn't advise you to acknowledge my presence."

She raised her fan before her face and fluttered it. He was joking again, and giving her that expectant look, like he expected her to sally back. Perhaps he waited for her to say her name. She wouldn't give it to him, not here behind the plants, as she flushed rather furiously.

"Would you like to dance?" he asked.

"No. I would rather not."

"We can dance back here if you like, where no one can see us."

She became aware of the indelicacy of their situation, that she was not within view of others, and therefore alone with this man. She scooted from behind the plants to take a more proper and public position upon a chair against the ballroom's back wall.

"What a capital idea, Lady Maitland. Let's escape this overgrown jungle and have a bit of sun. You are Lady Maitland, aren't you? The esteemed baroness?"

Josephine could scarcely breathe. He had fetched a chair, setting it directly beside hers. When he sat, his right arm contacted her shoulder for a heartbeat of a second before he straightened. He felt very warm and...hard.

She did not utter a word, didn't even look in his direction. She stared instead at the swirl of the dance floor, her gaze going in and out of focus on a rainbow of pastel dresses and dark evening coats.

"My dear lady," he said at last, "it is customary in England to reply during conversations, perhaps even introduce topics yourself."

She brought her great black fan up between them as if it were some layer of defense. "I do not care to make conversation. And I was not raised in England."

"But you are here now, and shall be for the foreseeable future, I gather."

She hated him for his jovial courtesy and his smooth, steady voice. Fear and anxiety roiled inside her, an uncontrollable reaction to his closeness. She knew little of English gentlemen or their manners, except that they could not always be trusted. This one in particular seemed very threatening. Light, but dark. Humorous, but with a rather pointed edge. Her parents had warned her English society was peopled by vipers who poisoned one's soul. She stole a glance at Lord Warren, wondering if he was a poisonous sort of person.

As for him, he made an exhaustive study of her mourning dress. Or did he ogle her bosom? She held the fan so it shielded her chest.

"I would like to express my sincerest condolences to you, Lady Maitland, on the loss of your parents." He dragged his gaze back to her face. "It must have been a terrible blow to lose both at once. When my parents died, I hardly knew how to go on afterward. I was only ten."

It was hard to picture this cheerful man as a sad, orphaned child. It hurt her to even imagine it. "I'm sorry for you, if you loved them," she blurted out. "But I never liked my parents, and I don't miss them now that they're gone." There, that had shocked him into silence.

But after a moment he bent closer and asked, "Why didn't you like them?"

Josephine was embarrassed to have revealed so much, especially to this stranger. "My family matters are none of your concern."

"Perhaps not, but I'm curious. Did they beat you? Starve you? Deprive you of love?"

She needn't answer him, but some expectation in his tone had her searching for the words. "They...they put me in danger. They were very...selfish."

"They dragged you all over the place, didn't they? I suppose the reality was not as romantic as one might think."

There was no great sympathy or tenderness in his voice. He spoke matter-of-factly and yet she felt her throat close up with emotion, that someone might understand. "They didn't like England," she forced out, fluttering her fan again. One sentence. One fact that had ruined her entire miserable life.

"What places did you go?" Lord Warren asked.

"Wild, horrible places in India and Africa," she answered in a strained voice. "Hot places with insects and mud, and sickness, and violence, and people who distrusted us."

"Your parents liked these places?"

Josephine shrugged. She would never understand what had drawn her parents to their travels, or what had fed their desire to live outside civilized society.

"And now you are back in England after all," he said, making an obvious point.

"I wish I had died with them." She had thought the words so many times, but this was the first time she'd actually said them. It felt good, but awful. Tears clouded her eyes. She wished she could hide back in the plants. She had to escape this room, this conversation. This man, with his intent, disturbing eyes.

She moved to stand but he grasped her hand. "No. Don't go."

"I must."

"I've put you in a bleak mood and courtesy dictates that I cheer you up. Shall we have a dance after all?"

"I can't. I'm in mourning." Couldn't he see her black gown, her somber, unadorned fan? "And I don't like to dance."

"Everyone loves to dance."

"Not me."

"Because you don't know how."

She shot him an aggrieved look.

He shrugged. "You don't, do you? It's only natural, given your history." His noble features darkened in irritation. "Here, let's do something about this. I can't bear talking to you anymore through this blasted thing." To Josephine's shock, Lord Warren reached out and pried her fan from her fingers with all the casual insolence in the world.

"There, that's better," he said, setting it in his lap.

Josephine was flabbergasted. "You've just taken my fan."

"I'm afraid so." His exquisitely contoured lips curved into a smile.

She might not know the finer points of English etiquette, but she knew it wasn't proper for gentlemen to go about appropriating ladies' accessories at their whim.

"Give it back to me." They were the only words she could manage in her flustered state.

He shook his head and placed it on the floor beside him. "If I give it back you might hide behind it again, and we can't have that."

"Give it to me, please." She moved as if to reach for it and he took her wrist. It was the second time he'd put his hands on her. The third, if one counted peeling her fan from her fingers.

His gaze held hers. Light, and darkness. "I'll give you back your fan if you'll dance with me first."

"I've said I don't want to dance." She pulled away from him, or perhaps he let her go. She could still feel his heat where he'd held her. "If this is some bizarre form of courtship, you're wasting your time. I don't plan to marry."

He arched a brow. "That's rather subversive of you."

He mocked her. He seemed to find everything hilarious.

Josephine would have thought the situation could grow no worse, but then she glanced up and saw a horde of chattering females descending upon them, led by Lady Minette Bernard, who was the most annoyingly cheerful person Josephine had ever met.

"Oh, my dear Lady Maitland!" the woman exclaimed, leaning down to clasp her hands. "Or may I call you Josephine? Do you remember me from our audience with the queen? Well, your audience and then my audience. We certainly did not crowd before her together. Our pouffed-out skirts would have prevented it in any case." Minette erupted in peals of tinkling feminine laughter.

Josephine heard a soft sound from Lord Warren beside her. He had stood politely at the approach of the women and now regarded Minette with an exasperated expression that echoed what Josephine felt. Minette chattered on, oblivious.

"But how elegant you look tonight in your black. I must know your dressmaker. And when you come out of mourning, what a sparkler you shall be. Bold colors look ever so dramatic with dark hair. I have always wanted red hair, especially deep, dark auburn red hair like yours. It's so striking, and it makes one stand out, but my brother and I are blond as corn silk and always have been." Minette made a vague gesture toward Lord Warren and her precipitate approach made more sense. This babbling young woman was his sister, which explained why she was as overbearing as him.

"I do remember you," Josephine finally managed to reply.

"I'm so glad to hear it. Then we shall be Josephine and Minette from now on, and we shall call on each other in the mornings and be particular friends, especially now that you have made my brother's acquaintance."

Josephine didn't know what making her brother's acquaintance had to do with being "particular" friends, especially when both relationships had been forced upon her unwillingly. But she couldn't be ungracious in front of this great group of house guests, which had swelled to include some young gentlemen.

"Of course we shall be friends," said Josephine tightly.

Minette clapped her hands so hard that her blonde curls shook, then looked down beside her brother's chair. "Oh, dear Josephine, your fan is on the floor. Warren, do pick it up before you trample it." She turned back to Josephine. "It's grown so hot in here, don't you agree? But you look ever so splendid, as always. My hair goes wretchedly tangled in this kind of heat, but yours is smooth and sleek. Your lady's maid must converse with mine and share her secrets."

Josephine chose not to confess that she didn't have a lady's maid, since she seemed to alienate all of them within a day or two. She feared her daily care was a duty the regular household maids traded off as some kind of punitive measure.

"It has indeed grown uncomfortably hot," she said, standing and taking her fan from Lord Warren. "In fact, I'm not feeling well. I believe I shall retire."

This resulted in a chorus of such feigned agony and disappointment that Josephine grimaced. She glanced at Lord Warren, who gazed back at her with laughter in his eyes and a twitch in his lips. Yes, everything was hilarious to him. She didn't know why all the young ladies fawned over her and dragged along the gentlemen to give her soft-hearted looks. They considered her reclusive and mysterious, she supposed, when the truth was that she was miserable. Lonely, awkward, out of place, and unlikely to ever match their pretty manners and haughty miens.

"Please say you will stay and talk with us a bit longer," Minette begged. "All of us are tired of dancing, and you have been neglected, sitting here alone."

"I was sitting with her," Lord Warren broke in. "Am I of no consequence?"

"I'm sure that depends on who you ask," his sister replied with perfectly droll timing. "And anyway, Warren, I thought you only came here to drink and play cards?" This brought amused titters from the ladies and guffaws from the gentlemen.

"That, and find you a husband," he sallied back. "If I can find anyone brave enough to take you off my hands. Gentlemen?" He turned to the assembled young men. "Anyone?"

More laughter as Minette waggled a finger and glared at her brother. Josephine watched this curious exchange. She'd always been an only child, so their bantering and bickering fascinated her. Charmed her.

She did not wish to be charmed by him.

"Thank you for your company, Lord Warren," she said, breaking into their repartee. She looked around at the other guests. "I wish all of you a pleasant evening." Before they could complain or cajole any more, she walked from the ballroom and hurried down the hall, where the constriction of panic in her heart and the beating in her temples finally began to ease.

* * * * *

Warren watched for Lady Maitland the entire next day, even checked for her among the house plants. He wanted to be sure he hadn't ruffled her too badly in the ballroom, but the baroness was nowhere to be found. At least he knew she wasn't with Stafford, since the man dogged him at every turn, even inviting him out to a local flagellation parlor. Warren might have agreed to go if the invitation had come from anyone else.

Instead he dressed for dinner, submitting to the fussy exactitude of his aged valet. Starched shirt, cravat, pin, waistcoat and coat, and a comb dragged through his unruly hair. While his man fancied him up, Warren's mind turned on the conundrum of Lady Maitland. Now that he'd met her, with her great, innocent, green-amber eyes and her wary shyness, he couldn't allow her to go to Stafford. He'd kidnap her from the altar before he'd let that happen. All she had done was frown and glower at him in the ballroom, and yet he felt some impetus to protect her from that fate.

After dinner, he must go to Lord Baxter, who was an eminently reasonable fellow, and explain the reasons he must reject Stafford's offer for the lady's hand. He'd relate their recent conversation if he must, word for word, until he convinced him Stafford was an amoral and reprehensible worm. Baxter would forbid the match, Lady Maitland could avoid Bedlam, and Warren could sleep better at night, knowing he'd accomplished a selflessly heroic deed.

"Leave off, Henri." He shied from his valet's comb. "If you haven't made order of it yet, you never will."

"Yes, my lord." The elderly servant put down the comb, gave one last twitch to Warren's intricate cravat, then doddered away to clean up his grooming tools.

Warren headed to the dining room, wondering from whence this honorable and swashbuckling side of him had appeared. He supposed it had only been so long since a woman *needed* him. Oh, they wanted him. They always wanted him because of his money, his dashing looks, his talent at entertaining their fancies, his expertise in bed. But it had been a while since a woman needed him. And in this case, he could easily save Lady Maitland from marrying Stafford.

He only worried she needed more saving than that.

He fidgeted with the hem of his coat, feeling that tightness in his shoulders again. Surely there was a patient, earnest gent somewhere in England who could give this baroness the nurturing she required. Even if Warren was the marrying sort—which he wasn't—he had Minette to worry about, and his burgeoning career in Parliament, and a thousand other duties that eclipsed the importance of the eccentric Lady Maitland.

As soon as he walked into the dining room, he heard an all too familiar greeting. "Good evening, Warren. We meet again."

Jesus and the bloody devil. He might as well have Stafford on a leash. "Didn't expect to see you," Warren replied. "I thought you were going...elsewhere."

"I am, later. If you want to join me, the offer still stands."

"Not tonight." *Not ever, if you're going to be there.* He'd been to that flagellation parlor before, and it wasn't a great establishment. The women all seemed rather overused. He liked his whores like he liked his horses—fresh and frisky, with a piece of ginger in their arse.

"Seen the baroness about?" asked Stafford as some other guests walked by. Down the table, Warren could see his sister with Mrs. Everly.

"No, I haven't glimpsed Lady Maitland in some time. Honestly, I've been too busy planning how to steal her away."

"You're a howl, Warren, you really are."

"I'm perfectly serious."

Stafford studied his face. Pretty as the man was, he wasn't very intelligent. His smile darkened to a frown. "Now see here," he said, pointing a glittering finger at Warren's chest. "I was after her first. It's not the thing to move in on another chap's territory."

Warren shrugged. "All's fair in love and war."

"You know what I mean," he muttered. "And she wouldn't have you anyway. I saw you talking to her in the ballroom the other night, along with everyone else. She couldn't wait to get away from you."

"I haven't seen you talking to her at all," Warren replied in a bored tone. "Which makes me wonder if she'll have you."

"Like I said, there's no other competition."

"Except me."

"Blast, man, are you jesting with me? Because if you're serious—"

Warren held up a hand. Lady Maitland had entered the dining room, and was staring at both of them. Stafford followed Warren's gaze, and puffed out his chest when he located the object of his attentions.

She pursed her lips and turned away. Warren snorted under his breath. "Anyone can see she's wild to have you."

"She's no more wild to have you," Stafford snapped.

Warren ignored him, watching Lady Maitland instead. She looked even more agitated than usual as she slid into her seat. She clasped her hands in her lap and worried at her lower lip. *Never fear,* he wanted to say. *I'll protect you from this idiot. You have more options than you think.*

25

* * * * *

"Such crowds and noise." Baxter chuckled as he closed the study door. "Lady Baxter loves her house parties, but they can be a bother when a man wants a moment alone."

"I appreciate you taking the time to speak with me," said Warren.

"Of course. Anything for a friend."

Baxter poured a generous amount of port and handed Warren the glass, waving him to a chair near the fireplace. Warren sipped the rich liquid slowly, appreciating Baxter's fine stock. The men exchanged pleasantries and impressions of the past winter. Warren hadn't much to say for himself. He hadn't exactly been dissipated, but he had spent a great many hours at his gentlemen's club and favored brothels. Too many hours.

At last Baxter sat forward and fixed him with a frank gaze. "Enough polite talk. You asked me here for a reason. What is amiss?"

Warren took a deep breath. "I had hoped to have a word with you on the subject of your ward."

"Oh, thank God," Baxter burst out. "Absolutely. The answer is yes."

"The answer to what?"

Baxter's glass stopped halfway to his lips. "Haven't you come to ask permission to court her? I suppose it's too much to hope you'll marry her out of hand."

The conversation had taken an unwieldy turn. "Forgive me," said Warren. "You've misunderstood. I haven't come to ask for your blessing to court her. Or…marry her." He could barely get out the dreaded word.

"Then what have we to discuss?" asked Baxter in a curt tone. "If you've come to tell me she's been rude, or unsocial, well, that is simply her way. She was not raised in society, you see. She showed up on some boat after a months-long journey from God knows where. The very day I received the letter from the solicitors, the woman was on my doorstep with a trunk of black clothing and a sun-faded bonnet. We had to scramble to take her in, being the only family she had."

"You didn't know her parents?"

"I wish I had. A fascinating chap, the late Baron Maitland, and the baroness too, following him all over Christendom with their only child.

Unfortunately they had the poor luck to get killed during their travels. Murdered by robbers in some uncivilized corner of India."

"Goodness. How did your ward survive the attack?"

"By some stroke of good fortune, Lady Maitland was not at home when it occurred."

Warren digested this rather alarming information. "It appears the lady has had a difficult life."

"Indeed she has. So if she does not seem the thing to you, not gracious or polished as you would like, then—"

"Baxter." His reproachful tone silenced the man. "Do you truly think I've come to complain?"

The earl blinked at him a moment, then unruffled and took another drink. "Pardon me. I'm rather sensitive on the subject of Josephine. Er, Lady Maitland. My wife and I have come to care for her like a daughter. We're very protective of her."

"Of course you are. I'm here because I don't wish her life to become any more difficult than it already has been. She has this suitor—the Earl of Stafford. I know the man more than a little, not that I would call us friends. I want to tell you, with great and purposeful emphasis, that he is not an acceptable marriage candidate. He's a drunk and gambler of the worst order. He's heartless and self-absorbed, and notorious for his fortune-hunting exploits."

Baxter held up a hand. "Do you think I don't understand what manner of man Stafford is? Believe me, I do."

"So you will not allow the match to proceed?"

"I wish I could prevent it, but Josephine refuses to be reasonable and give any decent chap her attention. She insists she doesn't want to marry at all." The older man gave him a harried look. "Meanwhile, the king's breathing down my neck. His Majesty has taken an interest in the lady's well-being, and wants her joined to someone steady and respectable by summer. He is troubled by her current state of vulnerability."

The king was probably more troubled that this rich, titled young lady thumbed her nose at his orders to wed. Warren could see the strain around Baxter's eyes and mouth, and felt true sympathy for the man.

"Have you explained all this to your ward?" he asked quietly. "Have you explained what's at stake?"

"How am I to explain such things to a woman with so little knowledge of English ways? To a woman who does not care? She was raised in a jungle, for God's sake. Literally, in a jungle."

Warren reached to pour his host a bit more port. He feared the man would succumb to an apoplexy if he did not calm down. "So what is there to do?"

"You can marry her," he said gruffly. "I wish you would. You've no prospects or promises to anyone, have you?"

"No," he admitted.

"You're quite free to wed Lady Maitland—and such a fortuitous match. The king would approve, I'm sure."

Warren shifted uncomfortably. "You said he wished her wed to someone steady and respectable. I'm afraid that puts me out."

"You know what I mean. It must be someone of appropriate rank and wealth."

"It cannot be me," he said, a bit more firmly. "I'm sorry, but I'm of no mind to wed."

"And I'm of no mind to see Josephine joined to a jackal like Stafford," Baxter pleaded. "The man has waged a most impassioned campaign for her hand, even gone to the queen to make his case. You see how things are lining up for my unfortunate charge. If I was a single man I would marry her myself."

Warren believed he would. Their Majesties clearly didn't know what Warren and Baxter knew, that the Earl of Stafford was an all-around scoundrel.

"She's not going to marry Stafford," Warren said. "You can't allow that to happen."

"How am I to stay the man's hand when he wants her, and has the influence to take her? You're an earl too," Baxter persisted. "With more land, money, and friends than Stafford, and an ancestral seat in close proximity to hers. The king could not protest if Lady Maitland passed him over for you."

"I want to help, but I'm in no position to marry. Nor would I make a model husband, as you well know."

"You'd make a better husband than Stafford."

Warren stared down into his glass. Did he wish to play the hero? This was his moment to do so. Unfortunately, the heroic impulses were no longer there. "There must be someone else."

"There's no one else," Baxter said grimly. "She refuses to be courted, and has dressed in mourning long past the time she should. She says she wishes to wear black forever, though Queen Charlotte herself tried to coax her out of it. I believe she is trying to disappear."

"Disappear? Why?"

"I don't know. She doesn't wish to be noticed, or admired. She's been away from civilized people all nineteen years of her life, to the point where she's terrified to go about in society. Of course, people note her lack of social graces. There are some who already cut her, title or no. I don't know what to do. If Stafford ends up with her—"

"No." The word came out with rough emphasis, without conscious thought. But how was Warren to prevent it happening, without acquiring a leg-shackle himself?

* * * * *

"There you are!" Minette ambushed him outside his room. He could see she was still bright and animated from dinner. She preceded him through his door and settled herself on the end of his bed.

"Minette," he sighed. "Aren't you getting a bit old to hang about in a bachelor's room?"

"You're not a bachelor," she said, removing her gloves. "You're my brother, and there's talk that you won't be a bachelor much longer. Is it true you're sweet on Lady Maitland?"

He collapsed into the bed pillows and gave her a look. "How do these rumors start?"

"They start when you ask to speak to Lord Baxter privately. Everyone noticed you were in his study for ever so long a time. Did you ask his permission to court her?" Her eyes widened and she put her hands to her cheeks. "Oh my goodness, did you ask his permission to marry her?"

"Minette, darling, it's late."

"Lady Fairchild says you took away Lady Maitland's fan at the ball so you might gaze into her eyes. She says you very much intended to kiss her, and her in mourning. Really, Warren." But Minette's eyes shone with excitement. She grasped the counterpane and hugged it to her chest. "Do you love her? I must be the first to know. She's ever so pretty, isn't she? Just as I told you! What a lovely wife she would make, and you could help her smile again. It's so romantic. What did you talk about back there in the corner? I shouldn't have interrupted you, should I? The two of you might already be betrothed."

"We're not getting betrothed," he said in a definitive tone. "Are you the one who started all this gossip, young lady? I certainly hope not."

"I told you, it was Lady Fairchild. She said you were having a very serious conversation with the baroness at the ball, and that Lady Maitland seemed emotional. What did you talk about, Warren? Please tell me. Did you talk about lovely things? Did you try to comfort her, and then find yourself ever so incrementally coming to admire her, until you had to declare what you felt in your heart?"

Blast, he had to get Minette married before her silliness rendered her an impossible match. "Lady Maitland and I exchanged nothing but the most proper conversation. You may tell your flock of gossiping ladies that there is no romance between us in the slightest."

"But how poignant it would be, you and Lady Maitland falling in love after one emotional encounter," Minette said rapturously. "Everyone said Lord Stafford was to marry her but I couldn't believe it. You two are so much more perfect together. If you marry her, we shall be sisters-in-law."

"Do not dare say a word to anyone about me and Lady Maitland, or suggest to anyone that we have tender feelings for one another. She is not going to marry Stafford either, if you'd care to be useful and put that about." He nudged her off his bed and toward the door. "Where is your chaperone? You shouldn't be wandering the hallways alone."

Warren walked her to her room and left her there to plague Mrs. Everly. He thought of heading to the flagellation parlor, despite Stafford's presence there, but the only one he felt like punishing was himself. And Stafford, of course. He wondered if the man could be bought off his aims with enough money. At the very least, Warren might buy Josephine some time.

Josephine. Why did he think of her in familiar terms? They'd barely exchanged a quarter-hours' worth of words. He fell into bed early, feeling unusually cross and tired, and punched his pillow in frustration. He would think of likely chaps to court her as he drifted off to sleep. There had to be someone out there who didn't mind frowns and black dresses, and an unwilling bride.

Chapter Three:
Crimes

Josephine had the same dream in countless variations. Night after night, the tiger chased her, paws pounding ever closer until its hot breath tickled her neck. Every night she ran, sometimes in forests or meadows, sometimes in fallow fields or crowded London streets. One time she had found herself trapped on a ship with the tireless creature, running around and around the deck from stern to bow to try to evade him. In her dream she had jumped over the side to escape, and woken with a start before she hit the water.

The night before last, the tiger had stalked her through the Baxters' ballroom, weaving around waltzing couples to pin her with its gaze. It stilled and then crouched down on its haunches, preparing to spring. She ran from the ballroom and into the hall, down gilded and carpeted corridors, seeking shelter from the predator. As always, any escape routes were blocked. She ran until she was breathless, until her own rasping exhales were indistinguishable from those of the pursuing beast. She'd turned a corner and discovered Lord Warren and Lord Stafford arguing in her dream, in furious voices.

"I shall marry Lady Maitland," said Lord Stafford, waving an arm about.

"You will not," Lord Warren growled, "for *I* am going to marry her."

Neither one of them was going to marry her, not if she had her way. She wasn't some shrinking English miss, waiting around to be sacrificed to fate. She had packed a satchel with water and food, and a little money in case she needed it, and headed out in her sturdiest boots to take control of her life. If she followed this path through Lord Baxter's woods, she would come out along the main road, and then she could follow the church spire into Chapley. Once there, she would find a solicitor or banker to help her sort out her affairs. She had money and a title—she only had to figure out how to use those things to get what she really wanted: a small cottage somewhere, on the edge of a village, with a lady to cook and clean for her and chase visitors away.

She adored Lord Baxter, but he was rather too stuck on the idea that she must marry. Goodness, she hadn't come all the way from India on a stinking, pitching boat to be bullied into an unnecessary match. So what if she was an aristocrat? She didn't feel like one, and more to the point, she hadn't been raised like one, so she didn't feel disposed to marry. Aside from the obvious problem of men and their wild humors, she was sure to make a peculiar wife. She was regarded as an oddity by most of the Baxters' friends. People stared at her and whispered, and gossiped that she had grown up swinging from jungle vines.

She had never swung from vines, but she could navigate her way through a silly English forest to a village a couple miles away. And if she could find no help in Chapley, then she would have a note delivered to her solicitor in London, the one who had settled her inheritance when she'd first returned from India. She remembered him as a kind man, and he had spoken to her as a person, as the Baroness Maitland, not some English rose to be patted on the head. She'd written to the man once before, but Lord Baxter had refused to send the letter, offering to write on her behalf instead. He meant to be helpful, but he drove her mad. How vexing to have no access to her fortune, and no ability to steer her own fate.

Josephine paused to sit on a fallen tree and drink some water. That was one thing she knew from her travels, that one must take adequate refreshment along the way. How long had she been walking now? Strange, how a mile or two could feel so much longer on these winding paths. It was still early, gray and bleak and misty-cool beneath the forest trees.

With any luck, she could conclude her business in Chapley by mid-morning, and come home before there was any fuss. The maid never came tapping until noon or later, if she thought Josephine was still asleep. Lord Baxter would be unhappy, of course, that she'd taken these matters into her own hands, but her entire life was at stake. She felt the little cottage inside her like a burning flame, a desire so strong she could hardly bear it. Privacy, comfort, and protection from society's judging eyes.

If only it was not so still in these woods. After plodding along another half hour, she stopped and had a bit of bread. She hadn't brought very much to eat and was nearly out of water. Now and again, a quiet rustling made the hair rise on the back of her neck. *They're English woods, Josephine. No tigers here.* But she ought to have come to the main road by now. Determination warred with anxiety, so her knees gave a little shake before she got them moving again.

She was on the widest path, she'd made sure of it. It must be the path to the main road, although it twisted and turned more than she expected. What a fuss it would be if she didn't get home before her absence was discovered. Well, if Lord Baxter would only *listen* to her, rather than make her trod to Chapley on her own. When she arrived there—if she ever arrived there—she must be strong and assertive, the way her parents had been when they dealt with the natives abroad. She must pursue the matter of her portion and her barony, and how she might arrange things to make a marriage unnecessary. She would ask about her rights as a baroness, a title which, until now, had been a vague and indeterminate concept.

Rather like the location of the main road.

After another half hour or so, she stopped at a convergence of paths and looked around. She did not want to face the fact that she might be lost. If one was on a path, how could one be lost? But she was almost certainly lost. The path had curved back and forth so regularly, she couldn't tell if she'd been going in a straight line. Should she take a different path? That path might curve even more, and take her farther off course. She couldn't see Chapley's church spire from her location, or the house, or anything but thick woods and dense treetops.

After taking thorough stock of her situation, she slumped in defeat. What folly this had been. She had to find her way back to the house before she was discovered, or the Baxters would never trust her again. She must find some other way to contact her solicitor in London. She must communicate her dire circumstances, that a betrothal was imminent. Or perhaps she would try to speak to Lord Baxter again, and weep this time, and make such a scene that he would relent on this marriage nonsense. Yes, she would sob until the rafters shook. Men in England seemed to respond to that sort of thing more than reasonable letters. But which way was back? She had turned about so much in her confusion, she couldn't remember from whence she'd come. "Oh my mercy," she whispered. "What a coil."

She was lost in Lord Baxter's woods without the slightest sense of her direction. For all she knew, she wasn't even in Lord Baxter's woods anymore. She could be in *any* woods, with *any* sort of forest creatures making those intermittent rustling sounds. She began to walk again, only to have something to do besides utterly panicking. As the sky lightened, as morning dawned bright, the forest seemed to wake in a disquieting way. Now and again she heard crackling leaves or snapping twigs, and her heart stopped in terror. What else was roaming around in these woods? Deer? Boar? If she screamed, would anyone hear her?

"Oh, help me," she said out loud. "Help me, help me, what shall I do?" Behind her, she could hear a louder rustling, such as a larger creature might make. She was too afraid to turn around and face the threat. Instead, she ran in the other direction with all her speed and strength, like she did in her tiger dreams. The sound came closer and louder behind her, no matter how fast she ran. She imagined the scrape of claws, and hot teeth sinking into her throat. She cried in a frantic, choking way, without tears, without breath, and still ran until the pursuing creature caught her.

Its arms came around her, holding her, trapping her. "No," she cried, squeezing her eyes shut. "No! *No!*"

"There now," came a low, soothing voice. "Dear lady, calm yourself."

Josephine opened one eye, saw a plain collar and a muscular neck, and a tan leather coat and waistcoat. She blinked up into blue eyes wide with concern. "Lady Maitland?" Lord Warren muttered a soft oath. "What on earth are you doing out here?"

She pushed away from him, wiping at her tears, trying to compose herself. "Oh, thank goodness. I thought you were..."

She felt too foolish to say it.

"A wild beast?" He grinned. "I am merely a household beast who couldn't sleep and went out for a walk." He looked her over, head to toe. She must look a fright after her wild dash down the path. His gaze fell upon the satchel she clutched at her side. "Are you running away, then? Good God, woman. You're as daft as they say."

"I am not running away," she said, working to catch her breath. "And I am *not* daft."

"Like hell you're not. You gave me a start, I'll tell you." He put a hand against his chest. "A chap goes into the woods to find a spot of peace and—"

"Won't you help me?" she interrupted him. "I seem to have lost my way back to the house."

"Of course I'll help you, but you're a fair distance from the manor. Where were you headed at this hour?"

She looked down at her satchel and felt horribly silly at the plan she'd hatched. "I was not headed…anywhere."

"You were headed somewhere. Young ladies don't wander into forests unless they've somewhere pressing to go." He stared at her stubbornly, his arms crossed over his chest.

"Very well," she said, lifting her chin. "I was headed to Chapley, to take care of some business, but I've changed my mind now and decided to go another day."

He took her bag and looked inside. "Some bread and water, a handful of shillings, and"—he dug deeper—"a pair of velvet slippers. An experienced traveler, I see."

"I've traveled more than you have," she said in answer to his mocking gaze. "I can certainly walk into Chapley if I wish."

"No, you can't, because proper English women don't do such things. What did you want to do in Chapley?"

"That's none of your business."

"Humor me then. I would like to know."

He seemed partly irritated and partly kind. In fact, he seemed in a very odd mood, so Josephine answered him against her better judgment. "I wished to speak to a solicitor about my inheritance, because I'd like to buy a house. But I suppose I must write a letter about it instead."

"A letter is probably easier than running away."

"I wasn't running away," she protested for the second time.

"If you weren't running away, why didn't you go to Chapley with Lord or Lady Baxter in the comfort of a carriage, rather than blundering through the woods? And you have a house, you know. It's in Oxfordshire. It's called Maitland Glen."

"I don't want that house." She crumpled her skirts up in her palms. "I want a cottage, just big enough for me. I want it to be in some quiet town, with a garden and a...a little fence."

He stared at her as though she was quite ridiculous. She couldn't bear it.

"You said you wanted to know," she snapped, taking back her bag. "And so I told you."

"If it's just big enough for you, where will your husband live?"

"I don't want a husband." She emphasized this fact most clearly, since he was one of the gentlemen angling after her hand. "I don't need a husband, in fact. I have my own money, more than a few shillings. I just don't know how to get my hands on it yet."

"What of the crown's interest in you? What of the barony you inherited from your father? It's not just a title."

"I don't want to swan about in society and be some grand baroness. Haven't you been listening?" One of his brows rose. She supposed she was being very shrill. "I only want to buy a cottage somewhere, you see, and live alone. It's all I want in the world, and no one seems willing to help me do it."

"Because you can't," he said with air of exasperation. "Perhaps, being raised outside of civilized society, you don't understand why you must marry. You are very rich, with property and tenants which your title obliges you to manage."

"And that requires marriage...because...?"

"It requires marriage because you're young and unprotected, and slightly daft, if you want to know the truth."

"I am not daft," she cried. "I wish you would stop saying that."

He held up a hand as if to calm her, or concede the point. "Daft or no, the king wants you to take a husband to manage your barony. Preferably a man of greater consequence, so his title will take precedence over yours."

"I'll lose my title if I marry?" she asked, shocked.

"No, you'll still have it, but your husband will have the power. Like most men, the king prefers not to have a woman in charge."

"What if my husband tries to sell off my barony, or mismanages it awfully?" The idea seemed dreadful, even though she'd been thinking about selling it off herself just a few moments ago.

"You see, that's why you mustn't marry Stafford, or any other fortune hunters. It would be best for your title and property to go to your children one day, along with your money. No matter your husband's circumstances, you must manage your holdings with care."

"But how?" she asked, throwing up her hands. "How can I do that when my husband will have all the control? Why can't I just go wherever these Maitland holdings are, and live on my own?"

"Because men can't stand that sort of thing. You can't be setting up on your land, acting independent and capable. The king cannot sleep at night until you've been properly yoked to a more powerful man."

The corners of his mouth turned up as he mouthed this loathsome drivel. He was joking and yet not joking. "I begin to understand why my parents hated England," she said.

"It will not be so bad, as long as you don't marry someone like Stafford. You must try a bit harder to attract a worthy gentleman. You must practice your manners, and wear pretty gowns in cheerful colors, and refrain from hiding behind house plants." He moved toward her. "Lady Maitland, I wish you would not cry."

"I'm not."

But she was afraid she might cry, if he kept painting such a bleak picture. She had cried so very long, and for what? Nothing. She'd felt powerless her entire childhood, powerless as a young woman, and powerless now as an orphaned baroness. Nothing ever changed. It infuriated her. If what he said was true, there was no use going to Chapley anyway. She'd *have* to marry someone, and Lord Warren no longer seemed to want her. That left Lord Stafford, whose smiles never touched his eyes.

No, she couldn't bear it. There had to be some other way.

"Perhaps I am as daft as you say." She gripped her bag to her chest and backed away from him. "I have been very foolish this morning, at any rate. I would be grateful if you'd point me toward the house."

"I will. But first you ought to have something to drink, and more to eat than that bit of bread you've brought." He went to fetch his own satchel, which he'd dropped back on the ground.

"I would rather not," she said. "I would prefer to go back before I'm discovered."

"Hm. Lord Baxter will be angry, won't he? But it's some distance to the house, and I noticed your own water is nearly gone."

He had that look, the steady, obstinate look she remembered from the ballroom. The look that said he had made a decision and must have his way. In fact, since she had glared at him and refused to cry, his manner had changed entirely, from patient irritation to...something else.

It worried her, that she could not identify his mood. He was congenial, only in a very watchful way. He took off his coat and spread it on the ground, then opened his bag and produced biscuits and apples, and fresh red currants, and a skin of water. The food proved too tempting to her empty stomach, and before long she was seated on his coat, biting into a piece of fruit. Josephine found she was powerfully thirsty. Lord Warren urged her to eat and drink all she wanted, even when she took some of his share.

They didn't speak any more about the cottage, or her flight to Chapley, or the fact that she must wed. He asked what she liked to eat, and what sort of foods she had eaten when she lived in India and Africa. She didn't normally like to talk about such things, but he didn't seem disposed to mock. He seemed genuinely interested, so she told him more of her travels, safe memories and observations, until it began to seem too real again and she left off. He began to tell stories of his travels then, and the grand tour he'd taken as a younger man. He and his friends had gone to all the oldest and most cultured cities in Europe, places Josephine would have loved to go. But no, her parents had to choose Bombay, and Marrakesh, and all the little, dirty villages she couldn't remember.

"Well," Lord Warren said, pulling her from her thoughts. "I suppose I had better take you back. And I'm afraid I can't keep this caper of yours a secret. I count Lord Baxter a friend, and I think he'd like to know. I mean, I would want to know if Minette ever wandered alone into the woods, so she could be properly persuaded not to try it again."

Josephine was horrified. "You don't really mean to tell Lord Baxter about my foolishness? Please, you can't."

He shrugged. "He would have figured it out anyway, yes? When the solicitor in Chapley dragged you home by the ear. This isn't India, my dear. Unmarried ladies can't run about the country setting themselves up in cottages."

He was mocking her again, and she didn't like it. "You find my situation comical? I assure you, it isn't funny to me."

"Not comical, no. Rather serious, actually. You know better now, but there must be consequences for this sort of subterfuge. Baxter must know what you've been up to." He looked up at her from beneath his lids. "It's a shame, I agree. I wish I didn't have to tell him. I doubt he'll ever trust you again."

Those words hurt worse than anything he had said before. Kind, protective Lord Baxter, who had treated her as a true member of his family. He would see this as an awful breach of trust. As an act of *subterfuge*, as Lord Warren said. What an ugly word. She had to reason with Lord Warren, bargain if she must. "He cannot know. He will be so disappointed. And I—I can't bear to lose his regard. He and Lady Baxter are the only people on earth who have a care for me."

Lord Warren picked somberly at a bit of grass. "It's because they care for you that they must know."

"But I'll never do such a thing again. As you said, I know better now."

"My sister says the same sorts of things when she's done something wrong. She's still punished, as Baxter will have to punish you."

"Oh, please, I can't bear for him to be angry with me. I beg you not to tell him. I would rather you leave me here in the forest to wander around until I die."

He arched a blond brow. "Minette does that too. Says outrageous and melodramatic things. All the same, he must know what you've been up to."

Josephine put her face in her hands. For a while, Lord Warren had seemed like a friend, but now he'd turned on her in this heartless way. "Please," she begged, not even able to look at him. "I can't bear for him to know."

She heard him shift, and let out a sigh. "All right, Lady Maitland. I won't tell your guardian what you've done, on one condition."

"What condition? Anything."

"You must allow me to punish you instead. There is no other way I could live with myself. If you won't let me tell Baxter, I must take my own steps to discourage you from doing this again."

"W-what kind of steps?"

"We're in England, in the woods," he said, getting to his feet. "A good switching seems appropriate." He held out a hand to. help her up. She stared at it. He wanted to give her *a good switching?*

"I don't believe I want that." She tried to sound firm.

"Then we'll go see Baxter. Come now." He wiggled his fingers. "Before the entire house is awake."

She shook her head. He sighed and put his hands on his hips. "Are you shaking your head about going to see Baxter, or about the switching?"

"Both."

"Well, my dear, you must pick one or the other. We can't dither about here all day."

How had she gotten herself into this dreadful situation? Even if she could escape him, and find her way back alone, he would still tell Lord Baxter what she'd done.

As she considered, Lord Warren lifted her bodily and set her on her feet, and went about packing up his bag. She could barely look at him, but at the same time, something compelled her to look. Perhaps it was his outdoor clothing, the worn leather and open collar that communicated casual athleticism. As he leaned to pick up his coat, she could see that his breeches hugged powerful buttocks and thighs.

Oh, what was she to do? She couldn't bear to be punished by this strong, bracing man, but she so wished to avoid the alternative...

"Let's go then," he said when he'd finished. "As I said, it's a long walk."

She dug in her heels. "No. I will... I will take the other. The switching."

He gazed at her. She searched his eyes, but again, she had that frustrating feeling of not understanding, not comprehending anything in their complex depths.

"Are you sure? It's going to hurt," he said. "Enough to ensure you don't sneak off to Chapley again."

"I know. It can't hurt as much as losing Lord Baxter's affections."

"Eventually he would forgive you."

"Perhaps. But you're right, he'd never trust me again."

He considered another moment, then put down his coat and bag. "All right. Come and stand here." He led her to face a leafy, smooth birch tree. "Draw the back of your skirts up to the tops of your stockings while I go fetch a switch."

How businesslike he was about it. What on earth did he mean, draw up her skirts? A lady didn't show her ankles, much less the entire backs of her legs.

She looked over her shoulder. He was already returning, stripping leaves from a thin, whippy branch. Her whole body trembled.

"Do you need help?" he asked in that kind-yet-unkind way of his. "Unfortunately, one cannot be punished without showing a little skin. Do it like this, so you needn't worry about showing more than you should."

He bunched up her gown and petticoats and pulled them tight to the front, so her legs were nearly bared, but her bottom was covered. "Hold them here," he said, situating the fabric beneath her fists. "And don't let go."

She couldn't believe he was doing this, that this was really happening. He went to stand behind her. Her knees literally knocked together. Air blew up her skirt, brushing parts of her body she usually preferred to forget about.

He paused. "Why are you shaking so violently?"

"Because you're going to hurt me."

"Oh, switchings do hurt. There's nothing to be done about that."

She heard a faint swish, and then a pain so piercingly hot she fell to her knees.

"You can't collapse, my dear," he said with a sigh of frustration. "That was only a single stroke. Stand up and rearrange your skirts as I showed you."

"I can't." She turned to him with a plaintive look. "That hurt terribly."

"You're not telling me anything I don't know. Kindly stand up. You are very hard to discipline, wrapped in a ball like that."

She let him raise her. The backs of her thighs still ached where the switch had whistled across them. She bunched up her skirts on her own, because it alarmed her when he did it. He stood back and let her compose herself.

"Now you know what to expect," he said when she was ready. "You must also know this punishment will continue until it's finished. It can take five minutes or two hours. That is largely your choice. Do you understand?"

Yes, she understood. He meant that no matter how much it smarted, no matter how much she wanted to protect herself, she had to stand still and let the man do his worst. She buried her face in the bundle of black skirts she held before her and braced for more pain. Somehow she managed to keep her feet at the second stroke, although it burned the back of her thighs just as badly as the first. He was landing them just above her stockings and just below her backside, on skin much more sensitive than she had ever realized.

"Oh," she cried at the third stroke. It hurt so awfully. It was *so hard* to stand still. The swish and fire came again, and again, too close in succession. She wailed and let go of her skirts.

"I can't," she sobbed. "It hurts too badly."

He shifted behind her, flicking the tip of the switch against the ground. "Then what are we to do? Five strokes is not an adequate punishment."

"I know. It's only that..." She wiped miserably at her cheeks. "I'm not strong enough to stand and take it."

"Well," he said after a moment. "I could spank you over my lap. It would have to go on a little longer to add up to a proper punishment, but the pain wouldn't be so sharp."

She looked at him over her shoulder. His expression was dark, implacable. Pleas to forget the whole thing, to simply keep her secret, died away in her throat. Very well, she would do what she must to right the wrong of her early morning flight to Chapley—and to escape further switching. She'd been spanked as a child. Hadn't most people? She didn't remember it hurting that badly.

Lord Warren walked a bit further off the path, to a fallen tree trunk. He seated himself upon it and beckoned her. Josephine sighed, mortally embarrassed. She ought to know by now to stay out of forests, she thought as she dragged her feet to his side. When she was close enough, he guided her over his lap, so her stomach was braced upon his thighs.

How big and strange he seemed then, all muscle and force, and masculine-smelling warmth. Her arms and legs hung down awkwardly with nothing to do. He told her to keep them still, and out of the way. She might have braced her palms against the ground, but it was sticky with moss and leaves.

Once he had her positioned the way he liked, he began to draw up her skirts. Josephine jerked and turned on his lap. "What are you doing?"

"Spanking you."

"But—you cannot—"

He stilled her hand as she struggled to pull her skirts back down again. "I'll not molest you in any way. This is punishment, not dalliance. And punishment is best accomplished upon a bare bottom."

He said it so firmly she couldn't find words to argue with him. This was England, she supposed, where women were punished like this every day. The man had pretty much admitted to spanking his own sister. Still, her face flamed hotly as he drew her skirts up to her waist. Her petticoats fell down about her head, and cool morning breezes blew over her skin.

Get it over with, she thought. She couldn't wait to go home and hide in her bed, and stay there forever. Lord Warren paused, taking slow breaths in and out. What was the man waiting for? She felt his fingers trace gently over the sore spots from the switch.

"Are you going to spank me?" she finally asked.

"Yes," he said. He placed a hand upon her naked backside, as if to measure the area he must punish, and then he drew back and brought it down upon her exposed skin.

Owww, she thought. And *Oh no*. Because this was not like her childhood spankings at all.

Chapter Four: Consequences

Warren hadn't any misconceptions about himself. He knew he was the most reprehensible villain in the entire world. He had seen an opportunity, and he'd taken it. He'd capitalized on Lady Maitland's petty crime—and her love for her guardian—to punish her for his personal titillation. This was so very wrong of him.

But so marvelously right.

Now Lady Maitland was over his lap, her luscious derriere exposed, her skin smooth and round and golden as a peach. He nearly groaned aloud every time he spanked her, for she tensed and squirmed in a maddeningly erotic way.

"I don't like to hurt you, of course," he said, holding onto control by launching into a lecture. "But poor behavior has consequences. It will please me if you have trouble sitting down for a few days, because it will remind you to think long and hard before running away again."

"I was not running away," came her muffled voice from beneath her skirts.

He paused. "What were you doing then?"

"Trying to find help."

He rolled his eyes, and resumed the spanking. "We've been over that already."

She made little cries as he picked up the pace, smacking both cheeks in alternation until they were equally pink.

"I hate that no one will listen to me," she said, kicking in time to the blows. "Lord Baxter won't respect my wishes. No one will help me!"

"I'm going to help you." He took her elbow hard when she tried to wiggle off his lap. "I'm going to help you understand that you're fighting a battle you've already lost. You're going to marry, Lady Maitland. Not Stafford, I promise, but someone better."

Someone better than him. He'd lounged beside her and fed her biscuits and currants while he daydreamed about carrying her deeper into the woods, and biting and licking her, and making her cry. All he could think was that her body was lithe and voluptuous, and that he wanted to ravage her. She'd be so easy to claim out here in the woods, with no one to stop him.

But he couldn't ravage her. He did not ruin innocents. He might be evil and selfish and perverse, but he did not avail himself of virginal bodies or tormented souls. He didn't normally spank them either. He didn't know why he had succumbed in this case. Because of her lips as she shared his water? The aphrodisiac of her stormy feline eyes? The quiet wildness of Baxter's woods? Did it matter now? He increased the sting of the blows, holding her wrists when she attempted to shield herself.

"Oh, please, I'm sorry," she said. "I'm so sorry for what I've done. Won't you please stop?"

"I'll stop when I feel you've been punished enough," he replied.

They were quickly nearing that peak. He knew he must be careful not to overdo things, lest he bypass punishment and move into the area of harm. She wasn't some whore at a spanking parlor, with tough skin and a long-developed pain tolerance. She was a goddamned innocent...and he was a lustful bastard for taking advantage of her this way.

He stopped and rested his palm on her heated, heart-shaped bottom. It took herculean control not to spread his fingers apart and caress her. He wanted to stroke her quim so badly. He wanted to taste her, drown in her. *No. Not her. Not unless you want her for your wife.*

"Do you think you have had enough?" he asked. "Do you regret this morning's behavior?"

"Oh, yes. Oh, please, no more."

He let out a breath and righted her, and settled her in his lap. She looked tearful and flushed as she tried to arrange her skirts to some order.

"Leave that," he said gruffly.

"I can't! I feel very ashamed."

It disturbed him, how she plucked and fussed at the material. He grasped her face between his fingers, and stared into her jungle dark, gray-green-amber eyes. She gazed back with an expression of torment. He had done that to her, hurt her and confused her. He had taken advantage of a conflicted young woman.

"I want to kiss you." The awful, inappropriate words escaped from between his clenched teeth. It wasn't even that he wanted to kiss her. He *had* to kiss her, or die of unsatisfied craving. He didn't give her the chance to answer yes or no, only lowered his head to hers and took what he wanted. Myriad sensations assailed him—her small, yielding body against his front, the damp of her tears, the softness of her hair, her light intake of breath. Lady Maitland smelled of flowers and morning breezes. He kissed her at first with the faintest pressure. It was a whisper really, a caress of the most gentle sort. When had he last kissed a woman like this, with such caution and tenderness? Never.

He nibbled her lower lip, catching the sigh that escaped. So beautiful. So sweet. He tilted his head and kissed her again in the same tentative way. He felt her fingers uncurl against his open shirt collar. He thrilled at the light warmth of her touch…and then she kissed him back with all the ardent sweetness in the world.

Oh God. This was his punishment, this devastating kiss. He'd gone too far now, too far to save himself. He deserved it, this annihilation. He basked in it, tightening his arms around her and drawing her as close as her blasted skirts would allow.

As their kiss intensified, he set about teaching her to respond to him with greater skill, encouraging her, rewarding her with little hums when her movements mimicked his. He coaxed her mouth open and pressed his tongue between her lips, and died a little when she responded to him in kind. His hands roved over her back, tracing the elegant shape of her hips and spine, and then they wandered downward. She jumped as he gripped her bottom, but she didn't protest or pull away.

Ah, her kisses were so innocent and raw, and so savage. He couldn't bear to let her go, but there would be trouble if he didn't. As her fingers crept up to his hair and curled about his nape, his cock filled to bursting. He was so rigidly hard that he ached. He could take her now if he wanted. Physically, he could do it. He had only to lay her back on the ground and flip up her skirts, and spread her legs. He could undo his breeches and drive right inside the tight, hot part of her he longed to possess. She wouldn't resist him, he knew. Dreams of sensation filled his mind. His muscles prepared to do what he imagined, to push her back and overcome her.

"Mother of God." He broke away and lifted her off his lap so quickly she nearly stumbled. He caught her around the waist before she fell and brought her to his side, and pressed his face against her neck. "I'm sorry," he said when he had his voice again. "I shouldn't have mauled you like that."

He felt her fingers go still upon his back. "What does that mean? To maul me?"

"It's what I did to you just now."

"Oh. I thought that was a kiss."

Annihilation. Not before, no. Right now. He forced himself to raise his eyes and look at her. "Was that your first kiss, then?"

"My first kiss, and my first spanking...like that."

He closed his eyes and sighed. "You should know: it is very improper for a gentleman to kiss a lady in such an abandoned fashion, unless they are at least engaged to be wed. Even then..."

She shifted, so he had to loosen his grip. "Then you have done something you should not have," she said in a quiet voice. "And I have too, for I kissed you also."

He gave a defeated little laugh. "I fear it was my sin, on the whole. But there are worse things we could have done, and we didn't do them, so we must be thankful for that." He stood and stepped away from her, steeling himself against the feeling of loss. "And now, Lady Maitland, I think it best that we make our way back to the house."

He picked up his coat and put it on, and picked up his satchel and hers. He wanted to comfort her, and yell, and kiss her again, and do all sorts of ridiculous things in that moment, but instead he turned in a north-westerly direction and guided her onto the proper path.

* * * * *

Lord Warren walked ahead of her, helping her over roots and holding branches out of the way. How gentlemanly he could be when he wished it. She did not believe the other things he'd done were gentlemanly. This belief was supported by the fact that he could not seem to meet her eyes.

As for her, her bottom still hurt, along with the backs of her thighs. Her eyes felt achy from crying and her lips felt tender and bruised from the way he'd kissed her. She was afraid anyone who saw them would know at once the things they'd been doing.

What had they been doing?

Why had he kissed her in that intense and singular way, just after he'd spanked her so sternly? He had apologized and said that he'd "mauled" her. The choice of words set her teeth on edge, especially after her tiger dreams.

But it hadn't felt like a mauling at all, even though he'd made tiger-like noises in his throat sometimes when he kissed her. No, it felt like something else. Something violent and exciting and tender at the same time.

"We're almost there," he said over his shoulder. "Are you doing all right?"

"Yes, I'm fine." *Mostly.*

Josephine could see the rooftop of the house now, through some of the trees. He had said they had a far way to walk, but she knew she had walked farther this morning. She must have walked in circles several times. How lowering. What an absolute failure this day had been.

Lord Warren held out his hand. "Stop."

She waited and listened, scratching her arm where a branch had scraped it. Oh, for a bath and her bed. She heard rustling along another path, and a low, muttered oath. Lord Warren turned toward the sound and she turned too, and then both of them gave a start. Lord Baxter stood not twenty feet away, looking distressed and disheveled. As soon as he saw her, his face registered relief. He crashed through the brush to join them.

"My dear girl, where have you been? I sent to speak with you this morning, and the servants informed me you were nowhere to be found."

At some point in this speech, Lord Warren had moved closer, and in front of her. Lord Baxter seemed to notice him for the first time, taking in his entire appearance, including the satchels he carried in his hand. Her guardian's expression changed.

"What, running away together?" He looked specifically at Lord Warren. "I thought you were not of a mind to wed." He turned and gave her the same sharp scrutiny. His eyes narrowed. "Have you been crying?"

Her guardian believed she had been compromised out here in the woods. She could see it in his bearing, his expression. Lord Warren said nothing. But then, he had promised not to, if she agreed to be spanked. But she had to confess her folly now, or Lord Baxter would misunderstand everything. "Please," she said. "Let me explain. This is all because of my great foolishness."

"What has happened?"

"I had meant to walk to Chapley this morning. I can't say why. It was the silliest idea ever, and I got lost, and Lord Warren happened to be walking here too, which was a great bit of fortune, because without him I'd still be wandering around trying to find my way back to the house."

She babbled all this out, and feared she sounded terribly guilty. He wasn't even looking at her as she related this tale. His eyes were fixed squarely on Lord Warren's. "Have you anything to say?" he asked the younger man.

Lord Warren didn't, not for a very long time. The men only stood on the path, in the hazy light, staring at one another in a very serious way. At last, Lord Warren spoke in an uncharacteristically formal voice. "I respectfully request the honor of Lady Maitland's hand in marriage."

"What?" she whispered. "No!"

He reached and caught her hand, and squeezed it. "Hush."

She probably wouldn't have hushed if he hadn't just spanked her, but something in his tone and his glance warned her to obey.

Lord Baxter tilted his head, studying the two of them. Again, he addressed his question—and his regard—to Lord Warren alone. "Would you have requested her hand if I had not caught the both of you out here together?"

"No," Lord Warren said. A muscle ticked in his jaw as he clenched his teeth. "Yes. Eventually. If there was no other way."

"No other way for what?" she asked. He squeezed her hand again and she fell silent.

"What will you do now?" Lord Baxter asked him. "What is the plan?" He glanced at her. "I think the quicker, the better."

"I'll get a license this afternoon, if you think that's soon enough," he replied with a touch of acid. "We can honeymoon in Oxfordshire for a little while."

"Yes, that would be best," said Lord Baxter. "Then you must return to London and behave like a couple swept away by love."

"Of course. That's how it generally goes."

Lord Warren's chilly manner unsettled her. And Baxter's frown... Her guardian had never been anything but kind. She didn't wish him to imagine things about her that weren't true.

"Lord Baxter, you must believe that nothing untoward has happened, nothing at all to require a marriage," she pleaded. "This really isn't necessary."

"I have been patient with you, my dear, but this is not a negotiable thing."

"But I would not have you think badly of me." Her voice cracked on the last words. Not only because she had taken the horrid spanking for nothing, but because she'd die if Lord Baxter despised her. "Nothing happened." She turned to Lord Warren. "Won't you tell him? Won't you explain?"

Something glinted in his deep blue eyes. "Do you really wish me to explain? To tell him all? I said I wouldn't, but I will, if you wish it." He said these words very slowly and deliberately, so she understood exactly what he meant.

She scowled at him and turned back to Lord Baxter. Perhaps she ought to be perfectly honest. Perhaps it was pointless. Lord Warren seemed to think so. He had already given up, given in. He hadn't protested any of this in the slightest.

Lord Baxter came to her and touched her cheek, and gave her a tired smile. "I love you, my dear, and I always will, no matter your mistakes and your stubborn reluctance to marry. In time, you'll see it's not such a bad thing. I only wish you to be protected and taken care of. You'll be a countess now, as well as a baroness by right."

"But…" Her voice trembled as her fate closed around her like a vise. "I don't care about being a countess. I do not wish to marry Lord Warren or anyone else."

The man in question let go of her hand and looked down at her with a daunting expression. His lips were pursed in a very tight line.

* * * * *

Warren married the Baroness Maitland the next day at the small church in Chapley, with only Minette and the Baxters in attendance. His bride wore her second best black gown because she had no other color gown to put on, and because her first best black gown had got hopelessly wrinkled and dusty in the woods the day before.

He brooded over the black, and thought that she deserved a grander wedding, but Baxter had wanted it done quickly, before the lady could launch some further revolt. Thanks to the gossip going around the parlors of Lord Baxter's manor, no one was very surprised at the sudden nuptials. Well, Warren was a bit surprised. By some bizarre cycle of events, the strange woman he'd seen peeking out from a wall of house plants a few days ago was now his wife. In some backward and iniquitous way, he had played the hero after all and rescued her from Stafford.

He wasn't sure whether he ought to be proud.

After the wedding ceremony, Josephine asked for a moment alone in the church, "to pray," she said, but Warren knew she was crying. He sat on a churchyard bench outside with Minette, and looked up at an overcast sky.

"I believe it was a very charming wedding," his sister said in her bright and brisk way. He thought he might hug her for it, or go into the church and start crying along with Josephine. "I mean, some people might think it hurried, or inelegant, or some such thing," she went on, "but all that matters is that the two of you are joined together in affection and love. Stafford put about the worst rumors as soon as he heard the news, but no one thinks him of any account, anyway. They knew he felt jealous that you won her instead of him, and so what else would he say, but that the two of you behaved badly? But I told everyone that was absolutely untrue."

"Thank you, Minette."

"Josephine did want to marry you, didn't she?" Her lips turned down in a frown. "I can't imagine why she wouldn't want to. I think it's ridiculous when people say weddings are forced. She stood up there and said her vows as clear as day."

Minette had not been able to see the tears in Josephine's eyes. Or perhaps she had, and preferred not to let that fact sully her happy view of the world. "Josephine is a little upset," he admitted to his sister. "But I had to marry her. You must trust me when I tell you there was a very good reason to do it. A marriage to Lord Stafford would not have suited her at all." He smiled at her. "And you dreamed of having Lady Maitland for a sister-in-law."

"She'll come to love you, even if she doesn't yet," Minette said staunchly. "I'll tell her you're ever so sweet and kind, and that you're a crack of a horseman, and jolly fun to be around, and that the both of you will have a wonderful marriage."

"How kind of you to try to comfort her, and to speak so highly of me. And you're perfectly right. When she knows me better, everything will be well. Will you do something for me in the meantime, sis? It's very important."

"Of course," she said, nodding. "I'll do anything you need."

"You must stay here with the Baxters while I take Lady Warren away to Oxfordshire for a while."

"For your honeymoon?" she asked, blushing.

"Yes, exactly. And while we're away, you must whisper a very romantic tale in all your friends' ears. You must say how Josephine and I fell madly in love at our first acquaintance. You must speak to them of passion and desire and other such scandalous, silly things, and tell them we simply couldn't wait to wed one another and be joined for life. Perhaps you can allude to the lady's exotic upbringing to explain the impetuousness of this whole affair. Can you do that, Minette? If we're to come back to London and face everyone afterward, we desperately need your help."

"I'll do my best. But, oh, will people say mean things? You won her from Stafford fair and square."

"Stafford will spread the worst gossip of all, because he's a heartless, petty man. But you must tell everyone the truth, that Josephine and I fell in love."

God forgive him for telling such tales. Minette smiled at him with so much trust. She either truly believed, or wanted to believe.

"Felicitations on your marriage," she said, grasping his hand tight. "I'm sure mama and papa are looking down from heaven, and feeling ever so proud of you, and thinking this the most lovely and magical day."

He glanced up at the gray sky. "Yes, probably."

This was not the way he'd pictured his eventual wedding day, but he supposed that could not be helped.

Chapter Five: Complexities

Josephine startled awake. She had dreamed of her tiger again, lithe and snarling in the humid night. She tensed as someone shifted beside her. "Are you all right?" a deep voice asked. "Did you have a nightmare?"

It took a moment to remember where she was, and who she was with. She couldn't see Lord Warren's eyes in the dark carriage, only the tall, broad shape of him silhouetted against the silk paneling. "Go back to sleep," he said after a moment. "I'll wake you when we get to the inn."

She wasn't sure she could go back to sleep now. "It's so dark in here."

"Yes, and quiet."

Lord Warren had been exceptionally quiet on the trip. He only looked at her every so often, as if surprised to find her there. She wondered if he was sad to be married to her. She didn't know how she felt anymore. Sad? Not exactly. Angry, frustrated? Yes. And fearful. She hardly knew this man she was married to.

"You should have allowed Minette to come," she said as the silence stretched out. "Then it wouldn't have been so quiet."

He laughed at that. "I love my sister, but she's not the sort of person you want along on your honeymoon."

He stretched his legs to the opposite bench, stretched his whole body in fact, reaching his arms up and puffing out his chest. It alarmed her, this display of masculine physicality. While he flexed and sighed, Josephine sat very still and thought about a *honeymoon*. The word always made people smile, and sometimes blush. She knew a honeymoon was something newly married people did, that was appropriately private, but she wasn't sure about the finer details or why they had to travel all the way to Oxfordshire to accomplish the thing.

She was not a complete idiot. She knew honeymoons involved intimate behavior. The man beside her would embrace her again, and probably kiss her as he had in the forest. But she'd heard other things that gave her pause. She knew for certain she must not allow him in her bed. She hoped the inn tonight had plenty of beds, so she needn't worry about it.

When Lord Warren finished stretching, he sat forward on the seat. "Would you like me to light the lamp?"

Josephine agreed that she would like that, for she still felt leftover anxiety from her dream. She knew there were no tigers here, and no danger. Well, not the sort of danger she was used to. She stared at Lord Warren's thighs as he reached to light the candle in the glass lamp and hang it overhead. *You've been spanked over those thighs*, she thought. She couldn't stop thinking about that whole affair, or the kiss that had come afterward.

The candle filled the traveling compartment with a soft, warm glow, illuminating velvet pillows and gilt trim. It illuminated him too, so she could see his features and the fine gold embroidery on his coat. He touched her hand, just for a moment, and she remembered the way he'd clasped her in the woods. She remembered the leashed strength in his body, and the way they'd kissed. What did that touch mean? Had the honeymoon begun yet?

"I am curious about Warren Manor," she said.

He seemed pleased at that. "What are you curious about? Would you like me to describe it?"

"Yes, that would be wonderful."

He settled back on the seat. "Let's see. Warren Manor is south of Oxford and west of Cowley. It lies on four hundred or so acres of land, and has been in my family for nine generations. Which means it's rather old, but it's been updated at various times. The home itself has four wings around a central courtyard, and two towers on the south side, along with stables and a servants' residence which was added during the latter part of the previous century."

"I imagine a house of that size has a great many beds."

He gave her a quizzical look. "Yes, it does. Warren Manor is full to the brim with beds. Of course you shall have your own suite of rooms there, to decorate and furnish as you wish. You'll have a dressing room and a sitting room, and a bedroom of your own."

She felt a wave of relief. "Oh. That sounds wonderful."

"Yes. This marriage thing won't be such a trial. You'll see."

He spoke a bit more about Warren Manor, and his parents who had died in that tragic carriage accident. She prayed he wouldn't inquire about her parents, and he didn't, only talked about furnishings, and architectural styles, and refurbishments, and household staff, and a lot of other things that Josephine had trouble following after a while.

"What is a honeymoon anyway?" she interrupted, when it appeared he would not finish talking about his house anytime soon.

He raised a brow. "Do you mean, what happens on a honeymoon?"

"Well, I understand that in a general sense."

"I'm glad to hear it. Otherwise we shall have to have a rather lengthy conversation before we reach Warren Manor."

Josephine picked at a fold in her skirt, then looked back at him. "So, the honeymoon will not begin until we arrive at Warren Manor? It will not commence tonight?"

He gave her a long look. "Are you afraid? Because there's nothing to be afraid of."

What a ludicrous statement. There was everything to be afraid of.

"Are you afraid of me?" he pressed. "Are you afraid to be intimate with me? Is that what all this marital reluctance is about?"

"No. It's not about that at all."

"Then why? Why were you so unwilling to be married?"

"I told you why. Because I wished to live alone."

"Why did you wish to live alone?" he asked, in a great show of patience. "It's not as if we'll be in one another's pockets. You'll have plenty of private time to do anything you want."

Josephine thought a moment, watching the candle's flickering shadows on the walls. "But you'll expect me to do public things too, like go to dinner parties, and attend balls, and go about in society."

"Well, yes, but you've been doing those things already, haven't you?"

"Only because Lord and Lady Baxter thought I should. But I'm bad at them. I don't like to be among people."

"We can't live as hermits," Lord Warren said with his crooked smile. "I'll ask you to do those things sometimes, those dinners and balls, but I also understand you're not at ease in society. I don't expect you to be a glittering pillar of the *ton* from the start."

"I don't even know what that means. I would rather have had my cottage." Her throat felt tight and hot. She stared out the window and thought of her private, peaceful abode, the dream she would never now have. "I don't know anything about anything, which you will discover shortly. You'll come to wish you'd left me in those woods."

She knew she sounded whiny and overdramatic. She couldn't bear to look at him, though she could sense his steady regard.

"I would never have left you in the woods," he said after a moment. "And lonely cottages aren't the paradise you envision."

"How do you know? Have you ever lived in one?"

"Don't snap at me, if you please."

"I'm not snapping. I'm only explaining my side of things. Not that it matters, since no one of the male persuasion will listen to me, or the female persuasion either. No one listens to my plans or opinions. I don't know why I even bother to talk."

He tilted her face to his with a frown. "You sound as if you're feeling very cross and sorry for yourself because you've been made to do something you didn't want to. Do you know what's good for fixing surly dispositions?"

"No," she said in an extremely surly fashion. "I'm sure I don't."

Before she knew what he was about, he had lifted her and tossed her across his lap. She tried in vain to hold down her skirts; they were soon bunched up about her waist, along with her petticoats. He gave her two sharp, stinging spanks on either side of her bottom. The sound echoed off the walls as she threw an arm back to shield herself.

"Please don't spank me again," she cried.

"Are you finished being peevish?"

"Yes!"

"Answer *Yes, my lord* when you're being scolded. It sounds much prettier. Look up at me and say it."

She couldn't meet his eyes, not while she was in this ignominious position. Her shoulders trembled, and she tensed, fearing he would hit her again.

"Look at me, Josephine," he said.

She twisted to look up at him, and finally managed to meet his cool, blue gaze.

"Good. Now say it like you mean it. *Yes, my lord.*"

She forced out the words he demanded. "Yes, my lord."

"Because if you don't mean it, then you'll require more spanking, which I'm only too happy to provide."

"I don't want to be spanked anymore," she said in as apologetic a voice as she could muster. *Just as I don't want to be married to you.* How many spankings were in her future, considering all the things that were wrong with her? She couldn't bear to think about it. His palm still rested on her backside like a threat. His other arm held her fast across his lap so she couldn't move. "Will you let me up please? My lord?"

"In a moment." His voice sounded rough. Josephine tried to stop shivering, and stayed as still as she could while dangling over his thighs. She didn't want to anger him when she was trapped in this position—for whenever he was angry, her posterior seemed to pay the price.

Warren knew he ought to release her. She was scared. She trembled beneath his hands, but he wasn't finished with her yet. He traced a fingertip across the fading switch marks on the backs of her thighs. Her trembling turned into a shudder.

"Be still," he said. "I am...checking the marks."

Yes, he'd put marks on his wife before she was even his wife. He had her over his lap now, her bottom bared for his own desirous enjoyment. He moved his fingers up the back of her leg, to the alluring curves of her rounded cheeks. He ran his thumb up over one of them, marveling at her smooth skin, stained pink by two solid spanks. He could feel her breathing change when he did it. Ah, God, she was so sensitive.

The things he could do with that sensitivity... He couldn't wait to exploit it, expand it. Revel in it. He ached to slide his palm down between her legs, and thrust fingers into her tight, virginal opening. He wondered if she was wet. He was dying to know, but he wouldn't allow himself to touch her right this moment, because if he found her ready, he'd take her to the floor of the coach and show her the world was an even scarier place than she already believed.

And he didn't want to do that yet.

Soon, but not yet, because she was afraid. Not only afraid of being married, which she admitted, but afraid of him. He could see it in her eyes, in the way she held her body, that he frightened her. Of course, this both dismayed and excited him, because he was both a civilized man and a beast. Sometimes he would let the beast out to play with her, and she would enjoy it for all that. But tonight, their wedding night, in this carriage with her shaking in terror, he would be the civilized man no matter the beastly thoughts crowding his head.

He gave her tantalizing backside one last caress, and pulled her skirts down. "Sit up now, and behave. No more grousing about being a married lady. We've a nice, relaxing honeymoon to enjoy, and you'll be pleased to know it won't involve anyone else in society. Only you, and me."

"Oh," she said, smoothing down her skirts with palpable relief. "That's good to know. And as you've said, there are plenty of beds."

Lord save him from innocents. He stifled a sigh. Lady Baxter apparently hadn't offered his bride any parting words of marital advice. "I perceive you are not very knowledgeable in the affairs of men and women," he said.

If she smoothed her gown anymore, she would wear a hole in it. "I only know they should not be in bed together."

He raised a brow. "Ever?"

"It's best that way, yes. I understand that gentlemen sometimes entertain...wild humors."

"Wild humors? My goodness." He nearly laughed at this revelation, but she looked so serious he composed his expression. "Tell me about these wild humors. Do all gentlemen have them, or only certain types?"

She looked at him warily, as if he mocked, but he was taking this conversation very seriously. "I don't know," she said, biting her lip. "I only know that women and men are not supposed to go to bed together because…"

"Because why?" He was almost afraid to ask. "Because a man might be seized by wild humors?"

She swallowed hard. "I don't wish to speak of it."

"Because you're afraid, which I find very vexing."

"I'm not afraid. It's only that… My mother always told me men were not to be trusted. That they could be aggressive, and harm you."

His eyes narrowed. "Some can, I suppose. But it's hardly an intrinsic male trait. Have I harmed you yet?"

"You spanked me just now," she pointed out. "And before, in the woods, you used a switch on me, and that really hurt."

"Yes, and I stopped after five middling strokes, because you were teetering on the edge of utter disintegration. At any rate, you needed to be punished because you'd done a bad thing, and you felt terrible about it. There are logical, practical reasons behind the act of corporal punishment. Sometimes a man's got to dole out a spanking or switching to make a fussing woman come around."

"A fussing woman?" She ruffled up like an angry cat.

"Do not become peevish again, Josephine. You remember what happened, oh, five minutes ago." The wretched thing went back to smoothing her skirts again, while he thought what a puzzle she was. "My dear, you must admit that you felt better after I spanked you. Expiated and all that. It would have been the end of the whole matter, if Baxter hadn't found us on the way back."

"But he did find us."

"Yes, and I married you, which he wanted from the beginning. It has happened and we must resign ourselves to it. Come here, would you? Stop picking at your skirts." He hauled her onto his lap and clasped her restless fingers in his. "Listen to me. There are men with whom you can feel safe, and men with whom you decidedly cannot. I promise you will always be safe with me, no matter how aggressive and wild you imagine men are. That's not to say I won't demand my marital rights."

She stiffened in his arms. "What does that mean? That you'll spank me whenever you like?"

He laughed, then sobered when he saw her expression. "Oh, my sweet, confused girl. Do you think we've been talking this entire time about spanking?"

He watched the flush spread across her cheeks. "I don't know. I'm sure I don't know what we've been talking about." She tried to escape his lap, but he pulled her back and circled her in his arms, and made her face him.

"Do you even know what marital rights are?"

"I don't want to know," she said, shrinking back from him.

"I suppose you believe they involve wild humors. Whatever the hell those are." He shouldn't curse. He should look at her innocence as an opportunity. Above all, he mustn't frighten her any more than she already was. "Marital rights are best explained in the moment," he said. "I'll tell you more about them tomorrow, once we've settled in at Warren Manor. Unless you'd like to start our honeymoon tonight?"

"Oh. Well. No, I would rather..." She stared past him at the wall, then turned toward the window as the carriage slowed. He could see the lights of the inn blazing in darkness. "I suppose Warren Manor will be soon enough."

It wouldn't be soon enough for him, not by any stretch, but he'd give her one night of respite. He hoped she would come around, not just in the bedroom but in her other misgivings. His friend Townsend had fought tooth and nail against the constraints of marriage, and was now blissfully wed, so Warren felt a calmness about the whole thing. Eventually they would grow comfortable with one another and figure out how to go on, and if he must be married, he preferred the interesting, complex Baroness Maitland to some simpering milksop.

If only she were not *quite* so complex.

Chapter Six:
Marital Rights

They arrived the following afternoon at Lord Warren's grand ancestral seat, comprised of acres of fields and forests, and a pretty, tree-lined drive that swooped about to the front of the house. No, it wasn't a house. More like a mansion, or a palace, with rows of gleaming windows and a crenellated roofline, and yes, two round, pointed towers. When Josephine stepped out of the coach to gawp at the towering stone edifice, she came to understand how rich and esteemed a person her new husband was.

Inside, painted ceilings soared overhead, with ornately wrought chandeliers, and every kind of molded trim. The floors were of waxed and inlaid wood, and they echoed when you walked on them. Hallways led off in every direction from the grand set of stairs. Footmen stood about in bronze livery trimmed in blue, bowing and assisting, and opening doors before one could touch them.

From the gleaming state of the fixtures and furniture, and the size of the staff, it seemed clear that servants maintained the home even when no one was in residence. Each person, from the head housekeeper to the lowliest stable boy, afforded Lord Warren a respectful deference, and of course, showed her the same deference as his new wife. It all seemed intimidatingly fine, especially when she thought of the ramshackle shelters she'd grown up in.

But there were no more steaming jungles or parched savannas, or wild animals, or snakes, or spiders the size of her head. There were no more leaking abodes or foreign faces giving one inscrutable and terrifying looks. There was no more danger, which she knew in her mind, but could not quite fathom in her heart.

Lord Warren's face was not foreign as they dined together in his elegantly appointed dining room. No, she'd come to know it well over the many hours in the carriage, although his expressions were still difficult for her to figure out. She worried about his propensity for wild humors, and whether and when he might kiss her again, and what she would do when he did. She wondered why he kept looking at her in that assessing way.

"Do you like your new home?" he asked as the footmen shuttled dishes in and out.

"Yes, it's beautiful," she replied. "It's very grand."

When she was young, her father used to tell her about the time he'd visited a pasha's kingdom. He said there had been dancing horses and graceful, veiled women, and everything had glittered golden. Josephine always wished they might see something like that again but they never had, and she had started to wonder if her father's stories were true.

Perhaps Lord Warren had dancing horses in his stables.

"If you don't like the food, I can have the cook prepare something more to your tastes," he said, interrupting her memories.

"The meal is fine. It's delicious," she lied, for she couldn't taste a thing.

He put down his fork and knife, tracing the silver with a light fingertip. "I wish you would not be frightened." The fingertip stopped its motion and he stood, and put down her knife and fork by taking them from her fingers. Then he leaned down and swept her into his arms.

She grabbed at him, rendered mute by shock as he carried her past footmen whose faces reflected no alarm at all. "Oh, you must put me down," she finally managed to cry.

"Fears should be faced, don't you think? We're going upstairs, where I shall assert those dreaded marital rights. You'll survive it. I daresay you'll even enjoy it."

"Oh, but— Must we? Right now?"

"Yes."

He carried her up the curving staircase and down the hall, past more stone-faced footmen. When they reached his bedroom, she took in the surroundings with a wary glance: tall windows, stately wainscoting and furniture, and a massive canopied bed against the far wall.

"I think—perhaps—I would rather go back and eat," she said.

The door shut behind him as he crossed to deposit her on his bed. "I'll have them send up a tray later if you're still hungry."

As soon as he let her go, she scrambled off the bed and nearer the window. Faint light still shone from outside, but he lit more candles, and she was glad because she was sometimes afraid of the dark. Tonight she was afraid of so many things.

He began to undress, taking off his coat, his high collar and cravat, his waistcoat and shirt, and his shoes and stockings. He stripped with a focused intent that alarmed her, as he revealed shoulders, arms, chest, waist, broad and masculine parts comprising a startling whole. She had seen scantily clad natives, even fully naked natives in her travels, but this was different. She was used to seeing Lord Warren covered in layers of clothing, looking a civilized gentleman, and he looked less and less civilized the more he took off. When he wore only his breeches, he appeared positively primitive and more than a little dangerous as he turned to her in the oppressive silence.

She clamped her lips together as she stared at the physical reality of him. His shoulders were smooth and round and wide. A ladder of muscles defined his torso, two of them trailing to disappear below his waistband at either side of his hips, along with a trail of glinting hair. He looked tall and powerful, and even with his breeches on, she could discern the sculpted strength of his upper thighs. When he shifted, the muscles flexed, and when he moved toward her, she saw the same fascinating flexion in his arms and chest. She didn't remember such showy musculature in the natives. Perhaps in the wild animals in the wood...

She was not yet ready to see him in the altogether. She simply wasn't. When he approached, she backed away with a shake of her head. He dropped his hands, his expression softening. "Josephine. Come here."

She didn't want to go to him, but she had nowhere else to go. She had backed herself to the wall. She stared at him wide-eyed, wondering what he would do if she didn't comply with his request. Would he lose his temper? Grasp her and drag her forcefully to the bed? She thought, *wild humors*. The idea frightened her so much she moved toward him as he asked, feeling leaden and scared.

She only made it halfway. He came the rest of the way and cupped her face in his hands. "How brave you're being," he said, even though they both knew it wasn't true. She felt like her insides were about to melt out through her navel, like her face was about to catch fire. "Shall I help you undress?"

She understood it was a rhetorical question, as he turned her around and started on the laces of her second-best black gown. Her wedding gown. It wasn't at all the thing to be married in black, but she couldn't be bright and pastel when none of this was what she wanted, and when she had no control of her life and her future.

Marital rights... She didn't know why he should have the privilege of them, or anyone else.

"Please," she whispered when he had loosened her dress enough to draw it down off her shoulders. "Please, I would rather wait a bit longer for the honeymoon to begin. A few more days."

"This is going to happen now," he said. "But don't worry. It's not a frightening thing."

She crossed her arms over her chest. "It's only... Well, if I knew you a little better..."

"Fortunately, you needn't know someone extremely well to accomplish this task." His fingers worked at her stays, giving gentle tugs. "You're afraid because you're not well informed, but I intend to change that." His breath whispered against her nape. "My darling, there's so much I'm going to teach you. Eventually, we'll know each other very well."

She could feel his heat against her back. She clutched at her stays as he unhooked the front and drew it from her waist. Next, he knelt and removed her shoes, as if she were helpless as an infant. At last she stood shivering in only her shift and stockings, feeling so vulnerable, so cold, that when he took her in his arms she went willingly, hiding herself against the expanse of his chest. He made a soft sound and then began to pluck out her hair pins, finding them with an oddly attuned facility, as if he knew where every pin was. She heard a faint clink as he put each one down on a nearby table.

When all of them were gone he ran his fingers through her hair, spreading it out upon her shoulders. "You're every bit as beautiful as I imagined. You are beautiful, Josephine."

"I'm afraid," she said in reply. "I don't want to do this."

He gave her a long, silent, rather unnerving look. "You don't even know what we are to do. Shall I show you?"

"Must you? I have no choice, do I?" Her voice sounded petulant as he dragged her toward the bed. "I have no choice in anything, whether I am rich or a baroness, or whatever."

He lifted her up onto the mattress as if she weighed nothing. "You're a countess now. *My* countess," he emphasized with the arch of one brow. He came over her, a great, heavy shape that seemed to trap her. "You did consent before a priest, and signed the marriage lines. You signed a binding contract."

"Because I had to," she said, bracing her palms against his chest. "Because no one would let me live in my cottage."

He gathered both her hands in his. "If you don't leave off about your cottage, Lady Warren, I'll spank you again."

She hadn't realized how close she was to tears until they burst out of her in a rough, broken wail. She couldn't muffle the harsh sound for he still held her hands. Wetness flooded her cheeks as her body shook with tremors she couldn't control. He frightened her so, with his power and his will. "Please," she whispered. "Please, please, please, *please*." She couldn't think of anything else to say, only that one word over and over in a hysterical repetition.

She heard him curse through the maelstrom of her terror. He let go of her hands and pulled her against him. She could feel the smooth fabric of his breeches between her thighs, where her shift had ridden up. She wanted to fight but was afraid of how he would subdue her. "Please," she begged again.

"Please stop saying please," he whispered. "I'm not going to hurt you. My God, this is more than a virgin's fear." He brushed her hair back and wiped away her leaking tears. "Did someone previously abuse you?"

If she lied and said yes, would he release her from this duty? But she felt too scared and raw to lie. "It's just t—that— I'm— I'm a—afraid you will h—hurt me." Her voice guttered out in fits and starts that humiliated her on top of the panic. "I d—don't know what you int—intend to do."

"You're behaving as if you expect me to lop off your arms and legs. It's nothing like that. Will you listen to me? Stop crying for a moment and listen. Take some deep breaths." He paused and made her breathe, in and out, in and out, along with the rise and fall of his chest. He wiped away more tears and left his thumb there on her cheek, stroking back and forth. "Whatever you imagine is about to happen, you have been misinformed. I'm not going to hurt you. I'm going to try very, very hard to make you feel good. Although you are making it damnably difficult for me to maintain my confidence. Keep breathing, my dear. Would it upset you terribly if I kissed you?"

"Kissed me?" She lay stiff as a board, her palms open against the bed.

"Yes, kissed you. It's this thing where we press our lips together and move our heads back and forth. We did it once before, you remember. Shall I demonstrate?"

Before she could reply, he lowered his lips to hers. She did remember this, of course, in a vague sort of way, although now, in a bed with him looming over her, it felt different. The first contact was carefully gentle, a solemn press of warmth underlain by control. "And now I shall tilt my head that way," he said, and she knew he was making a joke. She couldn't laugh. She was too tense, too nervous about what this might develop into.

Once he tilted his head, his tongue came out to tickle at the edges of her lower lip. "Open for me. Ah, yes, you remember now." When she parted her lips, he parted his too and gave her open mouthed kisses that felt even more intimate than the previous ones. Now and again he licked her lips, or the tips of her teeth, in a way that made her think he was very practiced at this kissing thing. In fact, as time went by, her limbs relaxed and her body began to react quite outside the agitation of her mind. Her stomach muscles fluttered. Her back arched and her hips snuggled closer to his.

"That's a brave, good girl," he said in a hushed voice against her mouth. "It doesn't hurt, does it?"

She shook her head, and he drew back. "You taste as beautiful as you look," he said, rising a bit above her on his elbows. "May I...?"

His voice trailed off. He never actually asked a question, only set about untying the ribbon at the neckline of her ivory shift. Like the black gown, it was only an everyday thing, not fine or suited for a wedding night. He didn't seem to care as he traced along the gathers and parted the placket with roughly masculine effort. His hand seemed as big as her whole chest.

Don't think of that. Don't think of how big he is! She had only just emerged from her heart-racing terror and had no wish to plunge back into it again. No, this felt too pleasant, his stroking and caresses. He peered down at her, studying her face. Did he see the effort she made to keep the hysteria at bay?

"I would like to see your whole body, and admire it, and shape it with my palms, darling. May I?" His words sounded so pretty, so like poetry, that she couldn't bring herself to say no. She leaned forward so he might gather her cotton shift and draw it up over her head. He laid it beside her as if to say, *there, it's right there if you need it.*

"Lie down now," he said, pressing her back by the shoulders. "Yes, just like that. Let me play with you a while."

Play with her? Oh goodness. He dropped kisses down the line of her throat, wet, wicked kisses that lingered and heated her skin. He caressed her breasts, even though she shrank back and tried to push his hands away. He merely used his mouth instead, licking across the tip and laughing softly when she made a shocked sound at the sensation. The teasing touch made her hips move again, made her whole body arch to him. He licked the other nipple in a slow, lazy swirl that caused unsettling amounts of sensitivity. Then he closed his teeth and bit down upon the tip.

"Oh!" She tried to squirm away but he trapped her with his legs. "Oh, did you mean to do that?"

"Yes, I did mean to. I adore those lovely, frantic noises you make." When she scowled, he grinned at her and went back to the languid teasing. And my, it felt very fine, though her one nipple ached with extra intensity. Then he held her down and bit the other, in a blooming eruption of pain. "I had to make them match," he said when she protested. "I can't nip one and not the other."

"I wish you would stop nipping altogether." Were these the wild humors her mother had warned her about? Gentlemen shouldn't bite ladies. She was about to tell him so when he distracted her by kissing lower, along her torso to her trembling waist. He blew against the curving flare of her hip in the most tantalizing way and peeked up at her through his lashes. "The first time I saw you, I wanted to touch you here. I wanted to hold you and…" He smiled. "Well, I'll show you in a bit. Is anything hurting yet?"

"No," she said, having forgotten about wild humors for the moment. "It feels rather…nice."

"It gets better. Let me show you." As he said it, he pressed her legs open, persisting when she would have closed them. "There's a secret, lovely part of you here." He delved his fingers through her nether curls while she shuddered at the intimate touch.

"You shouldn't do that," she said.

"Oh, but I should. You'll see." He moved his fingers to a particular spot, a spot she'd become more aware of as he kissed her and licked her nipples. He teased at it now, a soft touch that set off an explosion of heated, enervating…warmth. No, warmth was not the word for it. It was rather more exotic and tingling than that.

"What are you doing?" she asked.

"Making you feel good, I hope. Are you still breathing? Keep your legs still."

She did as he asked, only because he seemed to know all about this marital rights thing. He knew exactly what he ought to do and really what she ought to do too, which seemed a formidable talent indeed. She watched him, waiting for further instructions, but he'd moved his head lower, to nestle his lips against the place where his fingers had caused such an uproar. He parted her and kissed her there, and Josephine lost all power to speak.

Why, he was marvelous. The things he could do, with such deftness and confidence. He licked her center, massaging the tiny bud that ached between her legs. She tossed her head from side to side, wondering how on earth he had learned to do this thing that rendered her speechless and powerless to resist. She had never felt such intense sensation, such thick and heady pleasure. She thought to herself, *My mother was so wrong. This isn't the kind of hurt that causes pain and agony. This hurt is something else altogether.* It was longing and agitation, and tactility, and nagging, spiraling need.

"Oh, please," she sighed, grabbing handfuls of his light blond hair, and this time she wasn't pleading for him to stop. She was pleading for him to keep going. His lips and tongue curled around that tender, needful place, driving the pleasure higher. To her shock, he pushed a finger inside her, stretching and working her quim's opening until her hips bucked.

"Please," she begged. "Please!" She had no idea what she was begging for, but he must have, for his fingers pressed inside her harder, deeper.

"Let it come," he said, in between stroking and kissing her there. "You needn't wait."

Oh, she had no ability to wait, or regain any semblance of control. She felt so curiously frantic and full where he caressed her, and hot and wet and wild with urges she'd never felt before. She threw back her head as his fingers and mouth caressed her, and then the fullness peaked and seemed to overflow. The lower half of her body tensed inward and contracted in an undulating sort of wave. She knew that word, *ecstasy*, but until now she had never really felt it. Her body squeezed and shivered, the warmth of his tongue soothing at first and then so sensitive she pushed him away. He laughed and drew back, kissing her body, part by part, region by region, all the way back up to her lips. She tasted her scent on him, wondering at the piquant flavor. So many mysteries she'd never known. The biggest mystery of all was that a man's touch could make her feel this way.

"It didn't hurt at all," she said when she got her voice back.

His fingertips played against the top of her stockings, tracing the garters. "There's more."

"Oh."

"Don't be alarmed." He kissed her again, as if to give her strength. "It doesn't hurt any more than the first part, which you seemed to enjoy very much. Well, perhaps it will hurt just a bit the first time, but nothing like having your arms and legs lopped off. And it only smarts at the very beginning of the first time, or so I'm told."

She froze, her contentment ebbing away. "You've never done this part before?"

"No, I have," he said, working at the front of his breeches. "But never with a virgin. So, you and I must make our best attempt to muddle through. Do you know how men are made, Josephine?"

He pushed his breeches down and off and knelt back, so she could see the entirety of him. She tried not to look shocked. He was huge in front, and stiff, and thick.

"You remember when I slipped my fingers inside you? Inside your pussy?"

She flinched at the bizarre word. "My...*pussy?*"

"Inside you, where you were hot and wet? Well..."

She worked the rest out herself, and shook her head. "I can't imagine that will work."

"It will work just fine, aside from the initial pain I mentioned, which is possibly just a myth."

She continued to stare at his swollen organ. If he were to lessen in size, all of this would make more sense. A finger was one thing, but that rod of his was the size of five fingers. Perhaps six. Seven? The more she gazed at it, the greater and harder it seemed to grow. "Is it necessary to do this part?" she asked, swallowing hard.

He made a fist of his hand and stroked it down the length of his swollen shaft. "It most certainly is. Would you like to touch me? I don't want you to be afraid."

It's a bit late for that. Panic sheared along her nerves. This was the hurt she had heard whispers about. This was the hurt her mother warned her against. *Men are brutes. They can't help it. You must protect yourself from them at all cost.*

"Do you trust me?" he said. He took her hand and placed it upon his upthrust organ. It was warm and velvety in texture, but so hard beneath. He stroked her hand up and down it, which only made her more aware of its outrageous size.

"Oh, well," she whispered. "I'm sure it won't fit."

"Will you let me try?"

He came down over her again, his legs and hips warm against hers, no longer encased in his breeches. The muscles she had noticed and admired were now pressed right against her. He dug his knees into the bed and she braced, but he only smoothed the length of his shaft along the hot, wet crevice between her legs.

"It will feel strange at first to have me inside you," he said against her ear. "But it will feel less strange when you give it some time."

"How long will it hurt?" she whispered.

"Only a very, very short time."

* * * * *

Warren sometimes liked to hurt women. In fact, he'd developed an extensive repertoire of techniques to make women writhe in erotic torment, but he didn't want to hurt Josephine tonight. Not now, not her first time. He held himself carefully above her as he nestled the head of his cock against her virginity. "Look at me," he said, thinking to distract her with a kiss. He touched his lips to hers, catching her breathless pants of terror in his mouth. Now that she'd seen his prodigious size and knew exactly where he intended to put it, it was probably best to get the deed done rather than make her wait.

He pressed tentatively against her, grasping for control. Her heat and tightness, her very virginity fired his blood so much that he wished to thrust inside her to the hilt, but she wasn't a courtesan, or a whore. She was an innocent, and she was afraid.

He spread her legs wider with his knees. She trembled as he kissed her again, and then he began to ease himself into her tight sheath. Even with the moisture of her arousal, it was a challenging task. She dug her fingernails into his skin and went rigidly tense. He held her close, kissing her jawline, nuzzling her cheekbone and temple when she turned her face away.

"It hurts," she said in a soft whine. "It hurts a great deal."

"Just for now, I promise. Give it a moment. You'll grow accustomed to me."

He had no doubt she felt very uncomfortably impaled, but he was uncomfortable too, for very different reasons. Namely, his balls and cock felt about to explode.

"It's so tight," she said, tilting her hips in tiny increments.

"Oh, yes. I know," he replied through gritted teeth. "It's very tight, and very hot. And very..." He moved in the same small, controlled way she did, feeling her pussy's caress in every screaming nerve. "Is it getting any better?"

"A little."

He slid deeper, then out again, more a movement of his hips than a genuine thrust. But oh, how he wished to pound inside her, all the way out and all the way in, so powerfully and roughly that he lifted her from the bed. "You're mine now," he said, touching his forehead to hers. "I'm inside you."

Her hands had begun to relax on his shoulders. Now they tightened again. "Is there more?"

He muttered something like "*Oh God*" or "*Bloody hell*" or something else quite graceless and inappropriate. He couldn't remember the words past the time they left his lips. He could only think about the movement of her hips, the welcoming ease in the tension of her thighs. He slid halfway out, shuddering. "Are you ready for more?" he asked when his sanity returned. "I want to move inside you. It feels so good to move inside you."

She said nothing, only drew him forward with her hands. He wished to be slow, to be dignified and controlled, but her beautiful sighs made it difficult. Her hair spread beneath him, over the pillow, and her legs opened wider to accommodate his thickness.

"How does it feel now?" he asked.

Her answering moan was the most beautiful music he'd ever heard. He caressed her breasts and rolled her nipples between his fingertips, thrilling at every abandoned reaction. How was he to survive this? How was he to survive *her*? What began as slow, controlled lovemaking quickly devolved into something baser and more intense. He dug his knees into the mattress and surged into her, driving deep and wreaking every last bit of sensation from his steady thrusts.

It was not only him losing control. Josephine proved to be as uninhibited and sensitive as he'd hoped. Now that he was inside her, she urged him on, arching and grasping at him. He kissed her everywhere, feasting on her eager responses. He nipped at her earlobes and licked her neck, and tugged her nipples into his mouth, suckling until she cried out and squeezed around him again.

"Yes," he gasped. "Do what feels good. Surrender to your body's needs."

"Oh, please, help me." She held his shoulders and pressed against him, seeking a release she'd only just come to know. He postponed his own needs and worked with the signals of her body to give her the help for which she begged. She was almost there. He could tell by her trembling limbs and her gasping breaths.

"Oh, my. It's— It's so close."

"I know."

"Don't stop."

"Never. I won't stop, kitten. Take whatever you need."

Her nails raked over his skin, and for a moment she held her breath. Then she let it out and gripped him harder, panting against his neck. The rhythmic pulses of her crisis undid the very last tethers of his control. He pounded into her the way he'd wished to from the beginning. She clung to him, so they were pressed together in shared rhapsody. He felt wrung out by the force of his release, so when the tremors finally left him, he collapsed atop her. Intermittent ripples of pleasure still teased along his cock.

When he could think again, he smiled at her dazed expression and stroked his thumb across her cheek. "You see? It worked after all."

She gazed back very soberly, as if her world still didn't make sense. It must be strange to go from dreading an act to enjoying it so thoroughly— more thoroughly than any typical English miss. "How courageous you were, even when it hurt," he praised.

"You were right. It didn't hurt very long. It only felt a bit...astonishing." She squeezed around his cock, so his thoughts went hazy and unfocused.

"Dear Josephine. Be merciful, would you?" He eased from her before he was tempted to begin all over again. As much as he wanted to, he imagined she was tender.

"Oh," she sighed. "I feel empty now. How peculiar all of that was. I never knew..." Her voice trailed off, her cheeks reddening to a blush beneath his gaze.

Yes, she hadn't known a thing, but he hoped that would serve them well in this marriage. Her lack of knowledge had been matched by an equal lack of reservation once things were underway.

"Was it as pleasing for you as it was for me?" she asked shyly.

He wanted to eat her alive, devour her, chain her to his bed and never stop fucking her, although to say so might alarm her at this particular moment. "You pleased me immensely," he said instead, kissing her brow and each of her eyes, and the tip of her nose. He nuzzled her cheek, breathing in her fresh, drowsy scent. "Will you have that dinner tray now?"

"I think..." Her breath caught as he moved lower to nibble her jaw. "I think I would rather stay here...with you...a bit longer."

He smiled against the delicate velvet of her throat. Thus was heroism rewarded.

"Just a moment, darling. Let me snuff the candles first."

Chapter Seven:
Wonderful

Josephine floated in weightless and billowing pleasure. She arched her hips so he would touch her there, in that lovely place he had helped her discover. *So warm, so wet...* She tossed her head from side to side. So intense. The sensation was so intense she almost couldn't bear it. She tried to close her legs but they were pressed open again.

I want you, he said. His voice sounded low and rough, and far away.

She blinked her eyes, slowly coming awake. Lord Warren was with her in bed, naked. His head was down between her thighs. Oh. *Ohh.* The tingling pleasure was coming from him; the warm wetness was his mouth and tongue. It felt so good it hurt her. It was too much!

She tried to reach down to him, to tell him that he was making her feel too good, but her hands wouldn't work. *She couldn't move her arms!*

"It's all right, darling. I've got you." He leaned up over her, so she could see his great, thick shaft and all of his muscular body. It was broad daylight, and both of them utterly naked.

"My arms won't work," she said.

"That's because I've tied them to the bed frame with one of your stockings."

"Oh." As she looked up, he moved back down and lowered his head to her...what was that scandalous word he had used? Her *pussy*. He really mustn't kiss her there, not now in the brightness of day. She tried to close her legs.

His only answer was to place his palms on the insides of her thighs and push them open wider. Really, frighteningly wide.

"I'm not sure you ought to... Oh, my goodness."

He touched his tongue to her center, right at the place that ached the most. She bucked her hips up, straining at her bonds. His tongue teased down, down, down, until she was absolutely certain he was licking an indecent part of her body.

"Please, you must stop that," she begged.

"I'll stop when you come."

"W-what does that mean?"

He paused in his licentious efforts and gazed up at her. "You remember."

Oh, yes. She did remember. "But how am I to manage that?" She tugged at her bound wrists. "You've tied me up."

He grinned. "Isn't it exciting? Now you can't stop me from doing whatever I want to your body. These honeymoons are a fine thing."

She watched in helpless captivity as he lowered his head and resumed licking her in a voracious way. Each touch, each heated gust of breath built on the one before it. She began to feel so full down there she thought she must explode.

"Please, untie me." She wanted to touch him, to guide his head to the exact places it was already going. He ignored her pleas and used his fingers to part secret flesh, manipulating the folds. She could feel how wet she was. "Please, let me go." It alarmed her to feel so powerless.

He stopped and reached to put his hands over hers. "Don't pull like that. You'll get abrasions on your wrists. Just accept that you're at my mercy for the moment." He leaned to kiss her, brushing her scent and heat across her lips. "I love to touch and taste you everywhere. You're mine now, Josephine. Let me do what I will."

"But it's light outside. I think—" He cut off her words with another deep kiss. She could barely hold on to coherent thought. "Perhaps we ought to rise for the day, and dress."

"You don't wear clothes on a honeymoon, silly."

78

She opened her mouth in surprise, and he stuck his tongue right inside it. She moaned as he pinched one of her nipples. His knee was between her legs, pressed right against her pulsing center.

"I can't go about naked," she insisted when she was able. "One must wear clothing every day."

"Not on a honeymoon," he insisted in an equally firm voice. "Your things were taken downstairs for cleaning and that's where they shall stay until it becomes absolutely necessary to put them back on again."

Josephine thought it was absolutely necessary to put them on *now*, for the liberties he took with her body shocked her. He moved his knee and gave a sharp, firm slap to the tingling part of her he'd just been caressing with his tongue.

"Don't hit me," she pleaded against his lips.

"Not hitting. Love taps. Arch your hips for me. Keep your legs open."

She didn't want to, but some edge in his voice compelled her to obey. He slapped her there again, not terribly hard, but hard enough that her entire middle gave a great throbbing pulse of excitement. *Wild humors*, she thought in dismay. *I am having them now too.* He palmed her center and slid his fingers inside. It felt good but still a little tender. There had been blood last night at the beginning, and after the third time he took her, he said he wouldn't again.

But this felt nearly as intense as when his male part entered her. He gave another slap that made her cry out against his mouth, and then he found the spot that pulsed and closed his fingers upon it, and pinched it. She began to pant. As the pinch sharpened, her pants rose to an alarmed whine. "That hurts. Oh, please, my lord."

"Warren," he corrected her. "*My lord* is for when you're being scolded. Warren is for times like these. Does it hurt very badly, my darling?"

She tried to wiggle away from him as the pinch sharpened. "It hurts awfully."

"But you're getting wetter." His pinching fingers let go, only to slide inside her again. Yes, she was even wetter. She felt so ashamed about it, but there was nothing she could do but lie there with her arms held over her head. When she tried to clasp her thighs together, he told her no, and pressed them open. He went back to licking her in his ardent way, and now it felt impossibly complex, because it both hurt and felt wonderful.

"I would really rather get dressed," she murmured, trembling. "You ought to put on clothes also. Honeymoon or no."

"Tell me when it starts to feel better again," he said, ignoring her suggestions.

"When it feels better again, what will you do?"

"See if I can make you come. This is called oral pleasuring, by the way, and ladies can do it to gentlemen too. After this, I'll let you take your turn."

She gazed down at his industrious blond head and thought he must be the daft one. How on earth was she to do this to him, with that great big organ of his jutting up between his legs? "Are you thinking about coming?" he prompted when she tried to close her legs again.

She didn't want to think about coming. It would be too frightening to lose control like that now, while she was tied up. "I don't know if I'll be able to do it."

He slapped her again, right between the legs. "I want you to try."

Each time he slapped her, she felt hot and aroused all over, especially in that brimming, sensitive spot he kept licking. The next time he slapped her, a groan escaped her, a begging sort of exhalation. She flushed hot that she would even make such a sound. He knelt over her and kissed her mouth, so her scent was all over her again. She licked it from her lips, and from his too. "Am I hurting you, kitten?" he said in a voice that was not so much concerned as pleased.

"Yes, you are hurting me," she said, making her hands into fists.

"Open your legs. I want you to keep them open, do you understand?" He pressed them apart until she was most obscenely on display, then leaned down and brushed his tongue over all her most private parts. "Arch for me," he said. "Offer yourself to me."

She bit back the most improper noises as he teased her overstimulated flesh. "Oh, I can't…"

He left off licking her and kissed up her hips to her waist, and then up to her breasts. "Look how hard you are," he said with a piratical smile. She didn't know what he meant until he tapped the peak of one of her nipples, which had indeed drawn up into a tight point. Somehow, she felt that tap more between her legs than in her breasts. He closed his fingers on the nipple and pinched it even harder than he'd pinched her pussy.

"*Oww*," she whined, flailing about.

"Open your legs!"

"I can't."

"Open them." He gave her pussy several slaps in succession, until she felt she must open her legs wide the way he wanted. Her center pulsed with excruciating need.

"What are you doing to me?" she cried. He was pinching both nipples now with increasing severity.

"I'm teaching you about your body," he said. "About pleasure and pain, and how they sometimes work together. Do you want me to hurt your pussy again?"

"No!" she said. But in her mind she thought *yes*. She turned her face away, burying it against her arm. She felt so ashamed and wild and hungry for more of what he was doing. "Please release me. It hurts."

"I want you to come for me."

More slapping, more pinching down there, while he scolded her to keep her legs open. He gave her no relief, no protection, no way to retreat from her own lustful urges.

"Yes, my good girl," he whispered when she moved her hips and pressed herself against his palm. "Open wider. Give me all of you." He ducked down to caress her again with his tongue, teasing that magic spot, the spot that made need surge and tangle inside her.

"Please let me— Please," she gasped.

"Come on, I'm waiting," he said against her skin. "I want to see it. I love you like this. Come for me, now."

His urgent orders finally overcame her resistance. She let go of self-consciousness and shyness and let the pulses within her expand into full fruition. Her legs strained as she tried to keep them open, even now. He pressed her apart with his palms and sucked at her as she clenched and squirmed and arched into his mouth in the throes of overwhelming pleasure. It felt so lovely, but different from last night when he'd been within her. Her crisis felt a bit empty, as if she were not quite full enough or close enough to him.

But she didn't dare say so. She had no doubt he'd start tormenting her all over again, and this time he'd be inside her, driving deep within her, and she wasn't sure she had the energy for that just yet.

He was gentle to her now as she rested. No more pinching and slapping. He caressed her all over with his fingertips, slow, meandering trails that made her shivery and sated at once. Her hands and arms finally relaxed in their bondage. She felt...replete.

"What was that called again?" she asked when she had recuperated. "Oral pressures?"

"Oral pleasures. That's one word for it anyway. It's called other things." He lay beside her and rested his head against her shoulder.

"It's quite a singular activity," she said. "Is it only for honeymoons?"

He laughed. "No. It's for anytime. I've done it in carriages, haylofts, drawing rooms, garden follies. I even tried to do it on the back of a horse once. I can't recommend that."

My goodness, Lord Warren had done this so many times. No wonder he was so good at it. But part of her felt jealous of all the women he'd kissed and caressed before her. "Were they nice? The women you did that with?"

"Nice?" His expression went strangely cloaked. "They were just women. Men visit certain establishments in their younger years, to learn how to go about things. To learn proper lovemaking for when they get wives, that sort of thing. It's nothing you want to know about, I'm sure."

"You mean, they're like teachers?"

He hesitated a moment. "Yes, that's exactly what they are."

"You must have had some very good ones," she said shyly.

By now, he had flushed a deep shade of red. "I suppose I did. I hope I can pass some of that teaching along to you. You remember I said that women can give men oral pleasures?"

Josephine glanced down at Lord Warren's organ, which was even more red than his face. She licked her lips, her satisfaction of moments before giving way to a bit of nervousness. "Yes, I remember."

"Would you like to try?" He reached to untie her wrists. "It's not something you master in a day, but you might begin learning the rudiments."

"Are there...a great many rudiments to learn?"

He glanced down at her with another soft laugh. "Not so many, at the end of it. And it doesn't take much skill when a man's in a condition like this." He indicated his engorged staff. "I'm very aroused, as you see."

Josephine thought she must at least try to learn some of these rudiments, since he seemed in a dire state.

"And do I tie you to the bedstead too?" she asked.

She could not understand his expression at all then. He blinked at her and shrugged, and chuckled once, and gave a dashing grin.

"Of course you tie me to the bedstead, darling. Whyever not?"

Warren loved a good lark. All his friends knew that about him, and being bound to a bed by his mostly-innocent-but-also-somewhat-debauched wife certainly qualified as a lark.

"Tie it tight enough that I can't get away," he suggested, as she carefully fastened the stocking about his wrists.

"Will you try to get away?" she asked.

He licked one of her full, lush breasts when it came close enough to his mouth. "*You* wanted to get away, didn't you?"

She sat back on her knees, her knot completed, and smiled. "That's because I had no idea what you were up to. But I imagine you've done this before."

Not like this, he wanted to say. *Never like this.*

She had not tied him tight enough. He could escape his bonds if he tried, but he didn't want to try. As much as he liked to be the one doing the tying and tormenting, there was something deliciously depraved about lying here under her power. She knelt beside him, gazing with wary attention at his swollen manhood. Even that aroused him. His cock gave a bouncing jump.

Her eyes went wide. "You can move it?"

"It's part of my body, kitten, not some inanimate thing. Of course I can move it. You can too. Touch it. Stroke it gently. That's a good way to begin."

She bit her lip, an enticing sign of concentration as she reached to caress a finger up his length. He'd taken her three times last night—more times than he should have—but there had been none of this, no playful teasing and exploration, especially from her side. He noticed now how small and delicate her fingers were. He wanted to guide her hand, to show her the proper pace and pressure to please him, but he couldn't. He tensed and untensed his arms.

"You won't hurt me," he said. "Don't be afraid."

"I'm not afraid."

The little liar. He would spank her for plenty of made-up things over the course of their marriage, but some time he'd have to spank her for all the times she claimed she wasn't afraid when she so obviously was.

"Sit between my legs," he said. "Find a comfortable position and pleasure me from there."

She did, staring at his cock and balls as if she expected them to rise up and attack her. This was the time he ought to have begun wishing for one of Pearl's whores to be here, to fall on him and worship him, and mouth him sloppily, and suck him to a paralyzing peak. But he didn't. He only tensed his arms again and moved his hips in a gesture of need.

"You must tell me precisely what to do," she said. "I haven't the slightest idea how to go about this. I wasn't paying attention to specifics while you were doing it to me."

He gritted his teeth against laughter and comical frustration. "It's all right, I'll tell you everything to do."

"Yes, that would be lovely."

My God, it would be lovely to shove his cock into her pretty little mouth and lodge it in the back of her throat. That would be magnificent indeed. "First get your mouth nice and wet," he said. "The wetter, the better. That's the first rudiment, I'd say, to use plenty of moisture. Once your mouth is nice and wet I want you to kiss and suck the tip."

He had to wait in his bonds while she went to fetch a sip of water from the pitcher on the nightstand. He deserved this, probably. "Teachers," indeed. A hardened, sadistic lecher like him didn't deserve to bask in her innocence. She returned to her place between his legs and leaned down, her thick auburn hair tickling his stomach and thighs.

"If I do something wrong, let me know," she said.

"I will. Just think of it as a sweet you're sucking on."

She wet her lips once more—ah, so luscious—and then she licked very slowly and delicately around the head of his cock. Pleasure shot down his shaft, mixing with the heat of her closeness. "Yes," he said in a rasp. "Continue like that for a bit."

She had no idea what she was doing to him, he was certain. No idea of the teasing torment. Otherwise, she would not be so blithely cruel. He clenched his hands with the effort to keep them in her loose bonds. He wanted to grasp her head in his palms and drive between her hot, wet lips. She opened her mouth and sucked him in sweet little pulls. "No teeth," he managed to say past the haze of hot sensation. "Rudiment number two."

She obediently used only her lips and tongue. She had less than a quarter of his length in her mouth, but it felt like heaven.

"If you can take more of me…" he suggested. "Don't be shy."

She took a little more, but not much. Even so, it pushed him to the limits of his control. If she continued with these hapless, innocent ministrations, this would be over in less than a minute. "You don't only have to lick my cock," he said. "You can caress me other places as well, to draw out the pleasure. You remember, the way I did to you?"

She leaned back and looked up at him with a shy smile. Damn, if his cock didn't jump again. She spread her hands open on either side of his navel. Her fingertips traced over the tensing ridges of his muscles. "You look so…interesting here. And you feel so strong. Mmm."

It took all his strength to lie still and let her handle him. What in God's name had ever possessed him to let a woman tie him up? He was going to shame himself in a moment and spurt all over her face. She bent and kissed him on the stomach, and then he felt her tongue run along the furrow of a muscle. He gripped the headboard so hard the bed shook. *Please.* It was on the tip of his tongue. When had he ever begged for sex, begged for pleasure without just taking it?

Once she'd taken her time teasing him to madness by licking his torso, she sat up again, looking pleased and lusciously rumpled. As he gazed at her, lights exploded in his brain. *Oh, no. Pain. Excruciating pain.* She'd just given his balls a hell of a whack. "Oh, God. No," he gasped. "No slapping in this, Josephine. Rudiment number three. Never slap a man's balls."

She looked at him indignantly. "You slapped me between the legs. *Several* times."

"It's different with men." He took deep breaths, processing the throbbing pain. "You must trust me on this. Men do not respond the same way women do. No more hitting that area of my body. Ever." Deep breaths. Eventually it would stop hurting. At least now he could hold off a bit longer.

"Are you all right?" she asked guiltily.

"I'm fine." He closed his eyes and laid his head back. "Make it feel better, darling. Stroke me and kiss me in your sweet way." She did, reaching up now and again to massage his clenching muscles. After a while, she kissed up his torso and opened her teeth against his nipples. She didn't bite him very hard, the way he'd done to her, but he made appreciative sounds while trying to hump her leg.

"Do all married couples do this on their honeymoon?" she asked.

"Oh yes, everyone," he lied.

As much as he would have liked this decadent misery to go on forever, he was fast reaching the limits of his control. He sucked in a breath as she teased the head of his cock with her tongue.

"Stop. Untie me. Quickly, love." She obeyed him with a worried look. "No, you haven't done anything wrong. I only want to finish things in a more traditional way."

As soon as his hands were free, he tumbled her beneath him. How sweet and brave she was, and how utterly game for anything. He would have to be careful not to push her too far. She flinched when he pressed his cock to her opening.

"Does it still hurt?"

"It's only a little tender," she said. "It's all right."

"I'm going to try something." He rolled off the bed and crossed to a chest, and rummaged in the topmost drawer for what he wanted. He used this slick, aromatic oil for all sorts of purposes, most often the introduction of his large organ into very tight female spaces. He applied it to his cock, then carried it to the bed and drizzled a good bit of it between Josephine's legs. "This will soothe you and make it easier," he said. "But if it still hurts, you must tell me so."

She gazed up at him, half kittenish, half afraid. "What if it only hurts a little?"

Good lord, he wanted to fuck her to pieces. He wanted to fuck her inside out, and then all over again. "Then you must decide what to do, if you wish to stop me."

He was bursting to be inside her. He ached beyond any ache he'd ever felt. It took an excruciating amount of control to hold himself over her, and press his cock inside her inch by meager inch while watching to be certain he didn't hurt her more than "a little bit." But the oil seemed to ease her sufficiently. She spread her legs and opened her arms and held onto him.

"Oh," she said. "That feels very warm and fine."

He could say nothing for long moments. The feeling of being inside her after the wait, and the teasing, and the bondage—he could barely catch his breath as sensation rocked up to his chest and down to his thighs. Heavy need weighed in his balls. He tried to be slow, to bring her along with him, but her wildness sapped his control.

"You're full of me, aren't you?" he growled. "You like me inside you, filling you up."

"Yes. Oh, how lovely it feels."

She clung to him tighter, so her breasts were crushed against his chest. His hands were slippery from the oil. He massaged her back and her bottom, and squeezed her tensing cheeks. Then he dipped his fingers between them and massaged her bottom hole, slipping the tip of his finger inside.

"Goodness. Did you mean to do that?" she asked.

"Yes."

"I thought maybe the oil—"

"I meant to put my finger in your bottom." As if to emphasize his words, he pressed it deeper. The oil eased the way inside her tight passage. "You're mine, little kitten. I like to be inside you everywhere."

"Do all married couples—"

"Yes, hush. Everything I do to you is perfectly all right."

She gave a little gasp as he moved his finger in and out of her arse. Her hips arched in a sinuous way that drove him mad. "I can't believe these honeymoon activities," she said in a hushed voice. "They are so…"

She never finished her sentence, but he knew what she meant. They were so intense and risky, and so abandoned, and so magnificent. He came before she did, exploding into an oblivion he couldn't hold back anymore, but she came too as he bucked through the aftershocks. He felt her clench around his cock and the finger buried in her bottom, and he thought how lucky a man he was, to have ended up shackled to this woman who had no understanding of propriety, or honeymoons, or what was normal between men and women.

Lord knew he himself had never really cared.

* * * * *

Josephine ate dinner in bed with her husband on the third day—or was it the fourth? She had rather lost track of the days in their unclothed and libidinous existence.

Lord Warren had been correct on the subject of honeymoons. They were nice and relaxing, and even better, they did not involve anyone but the two of them. No eyes to judge, no gossip to worry about. Even the servants made themselves scarce, only appearing when she and Lord Warren needed to eat or bathe.

Her husband made love to her in a surprising variety of ways, and then they slept, and then they woke and talked together, and had wonderful meals like this. Fresh bread, meat and fish, cheese, wine, and fruit that he fed her in little bits. There were cakes and tea twice a day, and more cakes at night if he rang the bell for it. Sometimes they stayed too busy doing other things.

Josephine felt perpetually shocked at the things she hadn't known about her body, that her new husband taught her with his hands and his mouth, and his own body, which was perpetually shocking as well. She had been walking around for nineteen years, the entire time capable of enormous pleasure. If only she'd realized it.

"Not everyone appreciates these things," he said, pouring her more wine. "You see, some people, especially English people, are frightened of sex. You were frightened by things your mother had told you."

"But those things weren't true."

"Your mother probably said such things so you would keep yourself decent until you were married. Older ladies will spread stories to frighten young girls for the same reason. Unfortunately, the stories are told with such regularity that women come to believe them."

"I believed," she said, feeling rather disgruntled about it. "I shall tell every young woman I know the truth about things, and all the ways men and women might touch each other and make one another feel glorious."

She thought he'd be the first to agree with this plan, but instead he gave a little frown. "My dear, that would not be advisable. Only because the things we do to one another are private. They're too intimate to share

88

with others. Some might even find them improper, the people I told you about, who feel threatened by sex. It's best to let each husband teach his wife what he would like her to know."

Something in his tone made her suspicious. Had he taught her improper things? "You told me that everyone does the things we've done. Is that not true?"

He pushed the tray away and pulled her close, fastening fingertips about one nipple and pinching it to an exquisite peak of pleasure and pain. He had explained about that too, about intensity and sensation. "Do you enjoy the things I've taught you?"

She squirmed at the pressure of his pinching fingers. "Yes, of course I do. But if they're improper..."

"That depends on whom you ask." He released her nipple and bent to tease it with gentle strokes of his tongue. Her hips tensed, the lower part of her body coming to life as she arched against him. "But if you think they're improper," he said, "I won't do them to you anymore."

"I think...oh..." She let out a gasping breath as his fingers found the secret part of her that ached so shamelessly for his caress. "I think you had better continue to do them. If you like."

"Do you like?" he murmured, tracing a path over and around her center. "Shall I touch you, then, wherever I please, whether it's proper or not?"

"Oh, I don't know..." He had a way of taking over her with pleasure and sensation until she couldn't string two thoughts together. "You must do as you wish. I—I do enjoy it."

"That's what I like to hear. You must let me have my way with your body, hmm? Because I know how to make you feel wonderful."

Yes, he certainly did. In some part of her brain, she realized he'd never answered her question about the decency of their activities. But since he was so skilled at those activities, she soon forgot to care.

Chapter Eight: Rubble

Josephine turned as Lord Warren leaned over the bed. Fingers twined in her hair, and gentle teeth nipped at her lips. "It's you," she said drowsily, reaching to touch his cheek.

"Did you think it might be someone else?" He arched his brow in that way that always made her laugh. Then she noticed something quite strange about him. He was dressed. Not just dressed to loiter about the house or wander in the woods as he had that day, but dressed quite formally, in a deep blue ensemble with an intricately tied cravat.

She sat up, clutching the sheets to her chest, for she was still quite naked. "Is the honeymoon over?" she asked.

"Almost. But not quite. We're going somewhere today. It's a surprise, and I've another surprise for you too. Get out of bed, darling."

She gazed at the whole of him. "You look very handsome."

Now his brows drew together in a line. "You're not going to tempt me back to dissolution. We'll never rejoin society at this rate."

All the warm, fuzzy feelings of contentment bled away. "I don't want to rejoin society."

"Yes, I know, but we, in particular, do not have that choice. There will be gossip after our sudden wedding at Baxter's. We've got to get back to London and plan some grand, notable entertainment, and invite hordes of people to our home to see that we adore one another." He bent down to kiss her again. "You do adore me, don't you?"

"What kind of grand, notable entertainment?" she asked, feeling a frisson of fear.

He shrugged. "I don't know. A ball, I suppose, with music and food. We're on Park Street, you know, in a big house with a ballroom twice the size of Warren Manor's. I think it'll be the easiest way to make everything right. I'm a little put out that you haven't answered my question. I've spent this entire honeymoon trying to win your heart."

"What was your question?"

"Do...you...adore...me?" he asked, pausing between each word to kiss her.

"I do adore you." Heat colored her cheeks. "Of course I do, but I don't want to have a ball."

"Don't worry, I'll take care of everything. You only have to be there and gaze at me lovingly, so Stafford can choke on his blasted rings and all the gossip can be put to rest. Now, please, get up. We're riding an hour away."

He said he would take care of everything, but he wasn't the one everyone would be staring at. He wasn't the one everyone thought strange and daft. "I don't know how to ride very well." She knew she sounded sullen, but she couldn't help it. "Maybe you ought to go without me."

"No, you must come because I've a surprise, as I told you. We'll take the curricle." He whipped off the sheets and picked her up, and threw her over his shoulder like a sack of grain. "Come and see what else I've got you, lazy miss."

She clung to his coat, bouncing along through the passageway between their rooms and into her dressing room, which was previously quite empty for honeymoon purposes. He set her down and gestured proudly to a row of lace- and ribbon-trimmed gowns. One was of pale gray, another lavender, and the other two cream and white, embellished with pastel flowers.

She looked about for her mourning wear. "Those are pretty, but where are *my* gowns?"

"These are your gowns, silly. I sent your black ones into town and had the seamstress do up these new ones based on the measurements. Of course, you shall have more once we get to London, in all sorts of colors, but these will do for a start."

"But...where are they? My black gowns?"

His lips tightened a little. "I don't know. I told her to give them to the poor house when she was finished. You don't need them any longer."

She stared at him. "I'm in mourning."

"For whom? For your parents? They died over a year ago, and anyway, you said you hated them."

"I want my black gowns back."

She felt curiously close to tears. It seemed a betrayal, for him to take them away without even asking first. They were the mourning gowns the Baxters had so kindly provided when she first arrived from India, the first proper English gowns she'd had. Perhaps they had grown a bit worn, but they suited her and allowed her to avoid such horrible things as grand entertainments.

"It was very wrong of you to give away my clothes," she said. She couldn't bear to look at the ones he'd gotten her. "You didn't even give me a choice."

"Because you don't have a choice." He sounded as irritated as she. "A countess cannot alternate three plain black gowns interminably, and avoid becoming the subject of gossip."

"I was in mourning!"

"You weren't in mourning, Josephine. You were in hiding, and you can't hide anymore. The gray and lavender might be considered half-mourning, if you must cling to this nonsense."

Nonsense, he said. It wasn't nonsense, and the gray and lavender looked nothing like mourning gowns, with their fine trims and ruffles and lace. She *needed* to hide, or else she'd be studied and scrutinized as she was in India for so many years. She stared at the loathsome, beautiful things until tears blurred her vision.

"I thought you would be happy," he said in a hurt voice. "I thought the dressmaker did very well in the colors, for your eyes and your hair. You're going to wear these gowns, Josephine."

He said it in the same way he had said *poor behavior has consequences* that day in the woods. She put her face in her hands and tried to master her feelings, but the tears overflowed anyway. That tone of his frightened her.

Balls frightened her, and society, and finely dressed husbands, and exquisitely crafted frocks.

"Wear the gray, if you're going to get upset," he said gruffly. "It's the closest to black. There are new stays too, and stockings, and slippers to match."

"Thank you," she choked out.

"I'll send one of Minette's maids to help you dress. I suppose you must have your own lady's maid when we get to London." She heard him turn to go, but then he came back and took her arm. He embraced her, pressing his cheek against hers while she stood there feeling naked and scared. "I'm sorry. I never imagined you'd react this way."

That only made her feel worse. Yes, she was so hopelessly strange. He dug in his pocket for a square of linen and dabbed at her cheeks. "Perhaps you only need some fresh air and sunshine. I'll have them put a team to the curricle, if you'll come down when you're ready."

"Yes, my lord," she said, avoiding his gaze.

He tipped her chin up. "Don't 'my lord' me right now, if you please. I'm not scolding." He bit his lip, staring at her in a disconcerting way. "I'm only trying to understand you."

Josephine wished him the best of luck with that. Most times, she couldn't even understand herself.

* * * * *

Soon afterward, they set out in the curricle on his "surprise" journey. Lord Warren took the ribbons, since there was no room for a groom on the sleek conveyance. He handled the spirited horses with the same nonchalant expertise he displayed in everything else. She sat beside him in her elegant new silver dress. He had called it gray to make her feel better, but it was silver, with iridescent pearl trim. It must have cost a fortune, and she'd sobbed over it like some sort of madwoman.

She still felt unsettled by his words. *You weren't in mourning, Josephine. You were in hiding.* He dissected her so easily, with his blunt, blasé facility. He dug down to her truths and flung them at her, but she had no such ability to understand him.

No, she only knew that he was rich, and skilled at bed play, and good with horses. Now and again he looked down at her and smiled, but most of the time he kept his eyes on the bumpy country roads. It was a pleasant spring day, not too chilly, but not too warm either. It seemed all of England waited to bloom, with unexpected color peeking out here and there.

"We've nearly arrived, I think," he said, after an hour or so had passed.

"Where are we going?"

"Shall I ruin the surprise?"

"I'm curious," she said in a pleading tone.

He smiled. "We're headed to Maitland Glen and the surrounding barony, if I haven't lost my way."

She was too shocked at first to respond. "Maitland Glen? My father's home?"

"Your home now. It's not so distant from my country estate. Close enough to visit, on any account. Don't you wish to see it?"

She blinked at him. "Of course I do. I just didn't know it was so close." Her voice trailed off at the end. How paltry, to not know where her holdings lay, when she had been the baroness for over a year. She only had the vaguest notion to what part of England Lord Warren had brought her when he married her, but now she realized that yes, their properties must be in proximity. She remembered Lord Warren lecturing her about the Maitland title and holdings. She wondered who had been managing the estate while her father was away.

"It's not a vast holding," he said, as if to answer her thoughts. "I could find no record of a steward, nor extended family interest, but perhaps it wasn't warranted. You've ten acres and a manor house, and no tenants I could find."

"You looked?"

"I had someone look into it, yes. The Maitland barony is a modest estate, but it's your own, and I thought it might be pleasant to see it before we head back to London."

The surrounding countryside seemed different now that he'd said where they were headed. She had a house nearby, and no idea what it looked like. She hadn't been back to Maitland Glen since she was a very young child. She was excited to see it, and scared, and nervous that she wouldn't remember anything about it. Wasn't ten acres awfully small for an estate? By the time he slowed and started looking in earnest for the boundaries of her property, her mind was a muddle of hot, anxious thoughts.

He stopped for directions in a village, and was motioned a little ways on, to the rim of the valley beyond the old barrow. It was there they came upon a very decrepit and crumbling manor house on the edge of an overgrown field. It was fenced, with an iron gate and a weather-pocked sign bearing the Maitland family crest.

She had hoped this wasn't it, that there was some mistake. This couldn't possibly be her ancestral home, not this sad little pile of rocks. The walls, where one could see them, were light brick, bleached by decades of sun. The cobbled roof looked overtaken by moss, and only half the small, leaded-pane windows were intact. A dense wooded area stretched behind the manor, having encroached along both sides so that the walls and eaves of the house abounded with vines.

"Shall we have a look inside?" he said in a bright voice, as if the home were not a complete disaster. Part of her loved him for it. Part of her felt cold and ill and sickeningly disappointed. Baroness Maitland indeed.

"I thought the estate house would be bigger. That there would be more land," she said, trying to keep her voice steady.

"I gather it's been sold off in parcels." Warren whacked at weeds and shrubs as they traversed what used to be a courtyard. "But you've plenty of money in the bank. If you like, we can set about buying them back."

She cast a look at the appalling house. "I don't know why we would."

She stopped at the great wood door. They hadn't a key, but Warren gave a smart shove to the lock and the door's frame gave way. Windows threw light onto dusty stone floors and disarranged furnishings. White covers glowed ghostly in the dim interior, draped over tables and sofas. Chairs were stacked in corners, and half burned candles waited in lamps, their wicks obscured with many years' worth of dust. Josephine looked around and tried to remember it, any of it.

Nothing. She had no memories, no connection to this place.

No home.

"Perhaps I'll look upstairs," she said, to escape his concerned regard. What must he think of her, coming from this place? She went up the creaking staircase while Warren called out to her to slow down and take care.

She stopped and peered into the first room at the top of the stairs. It contained the same ghostly, slip-covered furniture, including a shabby looking bed. Her mother's? Her father's? The adjacent dressing room was empty of everything but some wrinkled bits of lace, and a pair of dusty slippers that looked to be Josephine's own size. She followed the dressing room through to the next room and found what must have been the nursery.

She heard Warren's footsteps in the hall, and then his face appeared at the door. They both looked at the cradle in the middle of the room, and the discarded china doll slung over the side of it. She wondered why they had left the doll when they set off with her on their travels. Had she wished for it? Had she missed the comforts of her nursery room?

It was a small space, lit by a high-set window. A cozy room, in a way, with more slipcovered furniture in the corners that might contain baby clothes, or child-sized tables, or toys. A pink and yellow needlework on the wall spelled out *Josephine Victoria*.

She turned to him, the edges of her world turning as black as her lost dresses. "I wish to go."

He looked once more around the room, then nodded and followed her down the stairs. At the bottom she turned, throwing out her hands to indicate the ghastly, crumbling disappointment of the place. "Did you know what a pathetic pile of rubble this was?"

"It's not a pile of rubble, Josephine."

"*Did you know?*"

"No, I didn't know. I hadn't spoken to anyone who'd been here." He gazed at her, his lips tight. "Any house can be fixed up, you realize. This house has good bones. It's mostly intact. After almost twenty years, what did you expect to find?"

She had found exactly what she hoped not to: more shabbiness and more frustration. Now they would ride back to his own glittering place, with its soaring corridors and smartly attired servants, and this shame would roil in her chest, this house and property that gave even more evidence of what she was not.

"I wish my parents had been proper people who kept a nice home, and stayed in England where they belonged." Her voice echoed, shrill and angry, against the high walls. "I wish I had been able to grow up like those other ladies. I don't know why they had to drag me around the world."

"I don't either." He came to her and embraced her. "It's not your fault, the way you were raised. But you're in charge now, remember? If you wish to revive this manor—"

"I don't," she said, pushing away from the comfort he offered. "I wish it to go to the devil." They weren't ladylike words, but in this house, in this moment, she didn't feel ladylike. She felt as if she were falling apart. "Please, may we leave at once?"

"Of course. I'm sorry to have caused you distress. I only brought you because I thought you might wish to see it."

She said nothing, just turned and fled outside to wait by the curricle while Lord Warren wedged shut the sagging front door.

* * * * *

Josephine brooded the rest of the day, lost in private misery. She kept thinking about the gowns, the visit to Maitland Glen, and Warren's careful solicitude afterward. No matter how polite he was about it all, he must consider her property a disaster. She certainly did. She'd never imagined her baronial home might be a ramshackle shell of its former glory—which had never been much glory at all.

At last, Warren took her upstairs, ordering her out of the clothes that had caused her such distress. They bathed together and had dinner in bed, though nothing on the trays tempted her appetite. Warren told silly little jokes, and flirted, and refused to let her cover herself even when she grew chilled.

"It's not that cold," he chided. "It's only that your hair's still wet." He brought over her hair brush to smooth her tangled locks, a ritual she had come to appreciate the past few days. He mussed it up in exertions of the most carnal type, and then fixed it back again, stroke by stroke.

"I would be warmer if you gave me something to wear," she said, drawing her knees to her chest.

"Something black?" he replied acidly. "I want you naked a bit longer. Our honeymoon is not yet over."

She reached beside her to pluck at the soft bedding. Their honeymoon? She could hardly believe he still desired her after today.

"Don't frown so," he said. "Once I've tamed your tangles, I'm going to warm you right up."

"That's not going to help. I feel awful. I feel I'm nothing but rubble, just like my house."

"You said you'd be happy to live in a cottage," he said, working through a snarl. "Now you're upset that you own a manor house, however rough it is."

"My cottage would have been pretty, and kept up in good order. There would have been flowers in beds by the entrance, and clear windows without any cracks."

He put his hand on her cheek to still her head. "Is it your pride that's hurt?" he asked. "I'm trying to understand you."

"I'm just angry. I'm angry at them, I suppose. My parents."

"You have to let go of that. They're gone now. You're holding tight to ghosts who never even cared for you properly. Perhaps that's one of the reasons you're so frustrated with yourself."

She twitched as he pulled at a knot. "I'm not frustrated with myself."

"You said you were nothing but rubble, not even a minute ago," he reminded her.

"Because I am. But that has nothing to do with being frustrated. It has to do with being a complete mess of a person who simply does not measure up. That is a fact. I don't belong with you here. I belong…"

"Where?" he asked. "In a cottage? With flowers? If it will make you stop fussing, I'll have one built on the property. Perhaps then I can have a moment of peace without you whining about how miserable you are." The brush caught in a tangle as he scolded her.

"Ouch!" She shied away and turned to him. "If you're going to pull so, I'd rather you didn't brush it at all."

"Turn back around." He waved the brush at her until she complied. "I wish you wouldn't fret. The condition of your home and property means less than nothing to me, Josephine."

"Because your own is so grand."

"No, because my regard for you is not based on your fortune or the value of your holdings."

"Your regard for me?" Her voice trembled with indignation. "You only wed me because Lord Baxter forced you, so spare me your facile lies."

He stopped mid-stroke and palmed the hair brush. "Come with me, then," he said, guiding her off the bed.

"Come with you where?" she asked. "What are you going to do?"

"I should think that's obvious. I'm going to spank you."

"What! Why?"

When she tried to resist him, he lifted her bodily and hauled her toward a chair before the fire. "Because you've done enough sulking for one day, and you called me a liar just now, to which I take great offense."

He pulled her across his lap, gathering her arms and legs and tucking them into submission. The more she tried to extricate herself, the more she realized his size and power far outstripped hers. Oh, she didn't want to be spanked. This day had been awful enough with everything else that had happened.

"Be still," he said. "When you earn a punishment, you're going to get it, one way or another."

"But I haven't done anything! I'll scream if you don't stop. I'll scream until the servants break down the door."

"They won't break down the door when they hear the sounds coming from inside. They'll assume you're being disciplined and they won't interfere, although they may mill about and listen if you make enough of a fuss. Now, I suggest you lie still and submit to this paddling, or things will go much worse for you."

"I don't know how they could go worse than they are right now," she said, trying to wiggle away.

"Then you don't understand me very well. I'm going to give you to the count of three to stop flailing and kicking. If you don't, I can't be responsible for what happens after that. One." He paused, holding her struggling figure. "Two."

Before he could utter "three," she went still across his lap. "I think you are horrible," she said. "I can't believe you would do this."

"Can't you? That's strange, because I've spanked you twice already before." He gave her some warm up smacks, until her buttocks tingled very uncomfortably. "As I've told you, behavior has consequences. You've been cross and ungrateful. You've snapped at me and named me a liar when I was only trying to be kind. I don't behave that way toward you."

"No, you only spank me as if I were a child."

"When you act like a child, you'll be spanked like one." He corralled one errant leg, pressing it down into position. "Keep your toes on the floor, young lady. The more you resist, the longer this will go on. Now, you shall be paddled with the back of your own hair brush, and don't think I won't do such a thing again if the situation calls for it."

With that warning, he landed the first proper stroke. She screamed and arched off his knees, pulling away from him to cover her bottom. The hard, round back of the brush seemed to leave a brand upon her skin. "That hurts too much! Even worse than the switching! You can't really mean to spank me like this."

"Move your hand."

"Please! Warren, I'm sorry."

"Move your hand or I'll move it for you."

With a plaintive sob, she moved her hand from her bare cheeks and braced it against the floor.

"No," he said, on second thought, "you had better give it to me to hold out of the way." When he had both her hands secured at the small of her back, he commenced with a very firm paddling, smacking first one cheek and then the other in an alternating pattern. Josephine wailed and kicked her legs, even though she didn't mean to. It was impossible to be still with the fiery blows stinging her arse cheeks.

"Ouch. Oww. *Ohhh!*" Whenever her toes came off the floor, he gave a tap to the back of her thighs to tame them down again. She jerked and tugged but he kept her in check, delivering a steady tattoo of cracks until her skin felt like it might explode. Her protests for mercy gave way to apologies and finally to whimpers, when she couldn't find the wherewithal to fight anymore. At that point, he put down the hair brush and smoothed his palm across her red hot cheeks.

"Now," he said, pulling her up to stand before him. "You'll apologize for calling me a liar and whining about everything in a most unladylike way."

She tried to reach behind her to soothe her throbbing cheeks, but he held her hands at her waist so she couldn't do it. "Don't rub your bottom," he said. "Apologize for your poor behavior, or, if you feel you haven't sufficiently learned your lesson, you may bend back over my lap."

She couldn't bear to do that. "I'm sorry," she said. "I'm sorry I whined and called you a liar."

"You know, I only meant to be kind when I took you to Maitland, and when I tried to comfort you afterward. You had no cause to cut up at me, even if you aren't feeling quite happy about everything."

"I know. I'm sorry."

He let go of her hands and drew her against him. "Go ahead and cry a bit, if it will make you feel better."

"I don't want to cry." Even as she said it, tears flooded her cheeks. "You h-hurt me."

"I disciplined you," he corrected her. "There is a difference, which you'll understand in time. If I only meant to hurt you, I could have done a lot worse."

She pressed her fingers against her eyes. "But you did hurt me. Even now, it hurts."

"Corporal discipline is a method of molding behavior. It hurts, but not for the sake of hurting. There's a purpose. You learned something, didn't you, through this spanking?"

"Yes!" She turned her head and sniffled against his shoulder. "I learned that I don't like being paddled with the back of a hair brush."

"Exactly. You've learned to avoid unpleasant consequences by exhibiting better behavior." He held her close and pressed a kiss to her forehead. "I think deep down inside, you want to be made to behave. Deep down inside you want nothing more than to be a proper English lady whom other people respect, and I am going to make you that lady, Josephine."

"You won't be able to," she said miserably.

"Oh goodness, let's not start all over again. Go put away your brush, at least for the moment." She obeyed, reaching behind her to rub her aching bottom a time or two. She couldn't tell if it made things better or worse. Meanwhile, Warren watched her from the bed with his head propped on his hand. She waited across the room, staring at his thickening cock. He beckoned her with a crook of his finger. "Come on, then. Let's not have any more sulking nonsense."

She crossed to him with a tiny bit of sulkiness, but not enough for him to fetch the hair brush again. Did he wish for love play now? She was tired and confused, and in more than a little pain. When she was near enough, he drew her naked form beneath him, settling his hips against hers. He took her hands and pulled them over her head, tracing his fingers along the delicate inner skin of her forearms and stopping at her wrists. "I want you to leave your hands right there. You've been a very naughty girl, and now you must let me do whatever I like, to put me in a better humor."

She stared up at him. "What are you going to do?"

"Nice things." He moved his hips, nestling the head of his shaft between her tightly closed legs. Her hands came down to check him but he pushed them back up. "Are you going to resist me?" he asked softly. "That is probably unwise."

After a moment, she shook her head. "I'm not resisting. It's just that I don't know... I don't know how to feel."

"What do you mean?"

"I mean that you've lectured me and spanked me and made me feel awful. I'm not sure I'm ready to be close to you. Not like this."

He leaned down to whisper a soft breath against one flagrantly hard nipple. "Whether you're ready or not, I plan to have my way with you, darling." As he suckled her breasts, he ran one palm down her thigh and shoved her legs apart. "Leave them open wide for me, or you'll be paddled again. You must allow me to do as I like. Marital rights and all that."

He trapped her beneath him, holding her open with his knees. The more she tried to close her legs, the more he pressed them open, until she desisted with a frustrated sigh. Marital rights! She wished she'd never heard of the concept, especially when her body responded—quite against her will—to his sensual manipulations. He squeezed her breasts and pinched her nipples, and then kissed her as he positioned himself between her legs. She expected him to enter her at once, *wanted* him to enter her at once, but instead he drove shallowly against her, in and out, just the tip caressing her folds and the little pearl she continuously tried to thrust against him. He smiled at her frustrated noises and held her wrists against the headboard.

"When will you come inside?" she asked when she couldn't bear it anymore.

"When I want to, Lady Warren. Not a moment before."

Her breath came in sharp pants as she gazed at him. How humiliating, to be teased and toyed with today of all days. She gritted her teeth and scowled at him, and tried not to respond to his nearness and heat, and his scent, and his caresses, but she was past the point of coldness. She burned for him to fill her up and chase away this nagging want.

"It's all right," he whispered, tracing his thumbs across her brow and then cupping her chin. "It's all right to enjoy this."

"I don't enjoy it," she said with a pout.

"You're a liar. Shall I punish you again?"

But he was already punishing her with this teasing, and his knowing, mocking smiles. "Don't move your hands," he reminded her. "Leave them against the headboard, if you please."

"I don't please. *Oh...*" Her whining cut off in a sigh as he entered her slowly. Halfway in, he withdrew from her again.

"Oh, don't," she said. "You're being horrible."

"Sometimes you're horrible too," he murmured. "Perhaps this is like for like."

"You want to drive me mad."

"In some ways, yes. Do you want me?"

She bit her lip and gazed at him. She wanted him more than anything, but she hated that he made her admit it. But if she didn't admit it, she knew he'd leave her unsatisfied, and she'd hate that more. "Please," she whispered.

"You want me all the way inside you?"

"Yes, please." She twisted her hips, arching to him. He caught her swollen pearl between his fingertips and pinched it until she groaned.

"How does that feel? Do you like it?"

"No," she whimpered.

"But you're awfully wet. Are you wet for me, kitten? Do you want me very badly?"

She hid her face against her arm, and clenched her fists upon the headboard.

"If you don't answer, you won't get what you want." He stroked his cock, regarding her with a speculative expression. "Are you wet for me, Josephine?"

"Yes, I'm wet for you," she said. "You know I am. I don't understand the point of putting me through this agony."

"The point is that you make those lovely noises, and your entire body strains for my touch." He flicked her stiff, pointed nipples, first one and then the other. She gasped at the sharp bursts of pain. "Ask me to take you. Beg me. *'Please take me, Warren.'*"

"Please take me, Warren. Please." She beat her hands against the headboard, and yes, her body strained for his possession. Humiliation burned, but desire burned hotter.

He gave a low chuckle and caught her in an embrace, pushing her legs wider with his knees. She let go of the headboard and clung to him, having reached the limits of her submission. When he pressed inside her she thought she would lose her mind from the hot, tight pleasure, and his lustful force as he buried himself to the hilt. She clenched around him, hooking her legs behind his hips. He took her deep and hard, squeezing her sore, punished buttocks as he moved against her.

"Is this what you wanted?" he asked in between thrusts. "Your husband's cock filling you up?"

"Yes, you knew I did," she said a bit accusingly.

He grinned as he thrust in her again. "We'll have to practice the art of naughty talk at some later date."

Josephine didn't want to practice anything at the moment, except finding her release after so much teasing. Warren drove her across the bed, pinching, sucking, pounding into her, and she clung to him, arching her hips to take him deeper. He withdrew with a growl and flipped her over. She nearly toppled off the bed, but he gripped her about the waist and set her on her hands and knees.

"Don't stop," she cried. "Oh, please touch me. Please hold me."

He kissed her shoulder and her nape, and licked the racing pulse at her neck as he twisted his fingers in her hair. "I've got you. I've no intention of stopping now." He slid his other hand down to stroke her quim, teasing her to a frenzied peak. She ought not to like such abandoned and animalistic activities. What did it say about her, that the more wantonly they coupled, the more pleasure she felt? She clenched around his hot, thick length, begging for more. Begging him to go deeper, and faster. When she finally peaked, he smacked her hot, reddened bottom in time with the pulses of her satisfaction.

It both thrilled and terrified her, the way she gave herself up to pure debauchery, and the possessive urgency of his will.

Chapter Nine:
Confidences

By the time they arrived back to the Baxters' manor, all the house guests were gone. Josephine was glad. She couldn't have faced any of them after the way she'd spent the last few days. Or the last few miles in the carriage before they arrived, for that matter. She thought the evidence of Lord Warren's carnalities must be written all over her, on her lips and hands and bottom and knees. He enticed her to do such bawdy things, things she would never have imagined. What if they knew?

But of course no one knew. Lord Baxter greeted them cheerfully and Lady Baxter gave her a hug and a kiss and exclaimed that she looked very well. Minette squealed at her new lavender gown and hugged her hard, and hugged her brother too, before launching into all the news they had missed after leaving the house party. It was only Josephine who thought of hot skin and whispers, and her husband's hands directing her, his persistent fingers touching her just so. She couldn't seem to *stop* thinking about it, even through dinner and a quiet evening with Minette and Lady Baxter in the drawing room.

The next morning, they said their farewells and set out for his Park Street address in London. She and Minette traveled in the first carriage, while Lord Warren elected to ride his horse alongside. Now and again she could hear his voice over the road noise as he exchanged words with the grooms, or gave one of his boisterous laughs.

When she wasn't straining to hear him, she was staring at the opposite bench, where her husband had bent her over and done lascivious things during their journey from Warren Manor. Her cheeks flushed hot from the memories of kisses and caresses, and wild sexual congress. Minette kept up a steady stream of conversation, mainly concerning her brother. She seemed oblivious to Josephine's fidgeting and her mental preoccupation.

"His real name is Idylwild, did you know that?" asked Minette. "Some people call him Wild instead. I'm sure he's told you by now. As long as I've known him he's been Lord Warren, so of course that's all I call him, which is just as well since Idylwild is a ridiculous name. Nearly as ridiculous as Wilhelmina, but not quite. That's my real name, you know, but I couldn't say it as a child, and what I could say sounded something like Minette, and so that's how I began to be known. I was so silly a girl, and Warren such a saint for putting up with me."

Josephine blinked, trying to follow the tumbling stream of Minette's words. "Did your brother raise you, then? Wouldn't he have been too young?"

"Oh, I had nannies and aunties and tutors and a guardian who was just the thing, but Warren was my brother and I can never..." She stopped, putting a finger to her cheek. "Honestly, I can never remember a time he wasn't looking out for me. He hovered terribly and did everything for me, playing both mother and father. He taught me to read and to dance, and to mind my manners. I even remember him putting up my hair when the maids became cross with my curls."

Josephine recalled his unusual deftness with her hair pins—and her hair brush—and thought perhaps this explained it, along with a great many other things. "I think your brother likes to concern himself with others," she said. "He's very responsible."

Minette laughed out loud. "Warren, responsible? He's been nothing but a gadabout these past few years, but if you've awakened some sense of responsibility in him, I can only thank you for it." She squeezed Josephine's arm. "I know you didn't really want to marry my brother, but I hope things will work out for the best."

Josephine caught a glimpse of him outside the coach, capable and confident atop his dark stallion. He wore his traveling coat and buff breeches rather than his more formal finery, but looked no less handsome. "I hope for the best too," she said. "But we're very different."

"Why, how sad you look. What has my brother done? Has he hurt your feelings? Men can be so clumsy at times."

"He hasn't hurt my feelings. He's only rather…commanding. He does what he likes, and no one can tell him no."

Minette made a soft, sympathetic tsk. "That does sound a bit like my brother."

"He says he's going to arrange a ball when we return to London, to introduce me to everyone and lend respectability to our match."

Minette bounced on the seat as she clapped her hands. "How splendid! I love balls, and it will be just the thing. Warren is such a crack at navigating the social waters. He knows ever so many people and they all like him. He's perfectly right, a grand ball will silence those who might gossip about your quick wedding, and cast your marriage in a less than positive light."

"I don't know." Josephine gripped her hands so tightly together that her fingernails dug into her palms. "Is it necessary to throw some showy ball only because of gossip?"

"Well…" Minette toyed with her fan. "I do think so, in this case. Lord Stafford was piqued to lose you to Warren, and he said ridiculous things about the two of you. Not that anyone believed they were true, but there you are. No, don't frown, I can't bear it. No one thought Stafford's whispers anything more than petty jealousy, but a ball will be just the thing to make him shut his mouth."

Josephine was disconcerted that Minette seemed squarely on her brother's side. From the moment he'd begun talking about this grand gathering, she'd been afflicted with a stifling sense of dread. "I feel terrible that your brother must go to all the expense and trouble of a ball."

"You mustn't worry about the expense," Minette said with a flick of her fingers. "Warren is rich as anything, and as for the trouble, he keeps an army of servants at Park Street who know how to deal with every sort of entertainment. He's probably already written them, so they can get things in hand."

"But I would rather not have this ball," Josephine said. "I really would rather not."

Minette studied her in obvious puzzlement. "Why? Is it that you have nothing to wear? I have ever so many formal gowns, more than anyone needs, and we're the same size. I would be thrilled to share anything in my dressing room with you. Warren has always spoiled me beyond measure. You should see all the bonnets and shoes. I wonder if you could wear my shoes?" Minette hiked up her skirt a bit and aligned her foot to Josephine's. "There, you see? Practically the same. I have a lovely sage green ball gown with matching shoes and gloves and a fringed shawl, and you must have it. I could never have worn it, I assure you. It looks terrible with my coloring but it will look beautiful with your auburn hair and pretty amber eyes. My brother only wants to show you off to everyone, don't you think? No one ever thought he'd get married, that's a fact, but he seems to like you very much."

Josephine wasn't sure about that. They'd only been married a week and he'd already spanked her twice for peevish behavior. She looked out at him again, and an uneasy awareness fluttered inside her, sin-hazed memories of the things he'd done to her *after* he spanked her, things that made her ache and thrill at the same time. She couldn't confide in Minette about that, no matter how easy-going she was. She couldn't confide in anyone about the things Warren did to her.

This whole matter of marital rights had turned her world on its ear, and now her husband intended to throw her into further panic by planning this ball and inviting everyone in the whole world who was more polished and dignified than her.

"Will you help me convince him to wait just a little longer?" she begged Minette. "You're his sister. Can't you make him see that it's too soon for this ball? That I don't wish to be put to such scrutiny? I don't— I can't— I can't bear for everyone to come gawk at us as if our marriage is the curiosity of the week."

"But if you don't let them come, they will exchange tales behind your back, and Warren won't like that." She spoke in her brightest, most encouraging tone. "Really, it won't be bad at all. Warren throws the most famous routs. People come calling like crazy and practically kill one another to get invitations, and then the night of the ball, you wouldn't believe how the carriages line up. So many people crush into the ballroom that one can barely move. There is so much chatter and merriment, and fine food and music…" Her smile faded under the weight of Josephine's frown. "But if you really don't wish to have a ball so early in the season, perhaps it can be put off. I'll try to talk to him."

Josephine squeezed Minette's hand. "Thank you. I'm simply not ready yet."

"He'll understand, I'm sure. Sometimes if I pester him enough, he gives in to me."

Josephine couldn't imagine Lord Warren giving in to anyone, except perhaps Minette, with her impish charm. "I'm so glad we're sisters now," Josephine said, meaning every word. "I've never had a sister and I've always wanted one."

"I've always wished for a sister too." Minette grinned. "We'll have the best time together, won't we? We'll go to the shops together, and take tea, and go calling on our friends. We'll share all our confidences and trials, and when we're feeling down, we'll cheer one another up."

"You have a talent for cheerfulness, I think."

Minette winked at her. "I'm often told I do."

Either the road had improved, or Josephine had finally grown used to the bobbles and rumbles of the carriage, because she began to feel less tense. She took care not to look out at Lord Warren since it only brought agitation, and instead focused on her sister-in-law.

"If we're to be so close, Minette, you must tell me a confidence now, to pass the time. What are your dreams? Who would you like to marry? Is there a gentleman of the *ton* who holds your heart?"

Minette ducked her head, rendered speechless for the first time Josephine could remember since making her acquaintance.

"There is one particular gentleman," she finally admitted, with a bashful twitch of her skirts. "I've admired him forever."

"Oh, how wonderful. Does he know? Have you declared yourself to him?"

"That isn't done," said Minette, giggling. "It's too forward for a woman to declare her love to a man. And anyway, he would only laugh at me. He thinks I'm a silly chit."

"I'm sure he doesn't think that."

"He most certainly does. He's said so plenty of times."

Josephine gaped at her. "I can't believe it. And I can't believe you would admire anyone so rude."

"I wish I didn't admire him, but I do. He's strong and strikingly handsome, and he has this way of speaking that's ever so manly and gruff. He has beautiful, thick, ebony black hair and a fantastic sense of humor, when it's not turned upon me, of course. And he's rich and haughty and is to be a marquess someday. He's perhaps...well...a bit of a rake, but not so very bad that he's outside the bounds. He's only waiting for a wife to make him settle down. But it can't be me. He wouldn't want me, and I'm too young for him at any rate."

Josephine thought this gentleman sounded horrible, and was rather glad he didn't want Minette. "I don't think you're a silly chit at all," she said. "I disagree with this person, whoever he is. I hope you will seek a better match. All the gentlemen seem to clamor around you, so you can afford to be selective. You might even marry for love, if you believe in such a thing."

"Of course I believe in love," said Minette. "Someday I'll find my very dream of a husband. Our eyes will meet and our souls will come together in recognition. Does that sound too much like a romantic novel? Warren says I shouldn't read them, but they help pass the time until my true love presents himself."

"Your true love..." Josephine echoed, thinking Minette both naive and adorably sweet. What a good wife she'd make for someone, with her cheery disposition and firm grasp of etiquette. Minette wouldn't need to be spanked for sulking, or lectured for her shortcomings.

"And he'll be strong and patient, and loving and kind," Minette went on, enumerating all her true love's qualities. "And passionate, of course, when we're alone."

"Oh my." Josephine thought of Warren's lips, and hands, and the thick, hot part of him that invaded her body. Did Minette know of such things? Probably not. She was still unwed, and seemed as innocent as a pale pink rose. Going by Minette's requirements, Lord Warren was a "dream of a husband." He was passionate. He was strong and loving and kind, even when Josephine tested his patience. Even when he turned her over his knee and spanked her, he held her afterward and stroked her hair and comforted her until she felt peaceful again. Josephine looked out the window to find him, but he wasn't within view.

"Now you must tell me a confidence," Minette urged as Josephine's silence drew out. "A secret no one else knows. I promise I'll never tell anyone."

Josephine thought a moment. There were so many secrets she wanted to tell. Like, *I'm afraid of everything.*

I'm afraid of people hating me, but I'm also afraid to be loved.

I dream almost every night about a tiger chasing me, ready to pounce, breathing down my neck.

I'm a baroness, but only of a paltry and run down estate.

I'm afraid of wearing colorful things and being noted, and exposed for who I am. I'm afraid of admitting the reasons behind my fears.

I'm afraid I'm falling in love with your brother.

But in the end, all she said was, "Blackcurrant tea is my very favorite thing to drink." Because that seemed safer, and had nothing at all to do with her heart.

* * * * *

When he was a bachelor, Warren had rarely eaten in his formal dining room. He'd sometimes sat with Minette so she would not have to eat alone, but he'd felt no sense of pride or family, only a nagging wish to be elsewhere, in his clubs or pleasure parlors, or calling on his friends.

So it was a novel experience to sit at the head of the table and dine with Minette on his left side and Josephine on his right, in the fashion of a family man. The food was exquisitely prepared, as always, and the servants seemed puffed up with the honor of the house. He contributed politely to the conversation, although it was dominated by Minette. His wife seemed to have taken a liking to his sister; in fact the two of them joined together to oppose him when he brought up the subject of the ball.

"It's so early in the season," Minette said. "I don't see why we can't wait a while, until Josephine is more settled."

"You know why we can't wait," he replied, looking at both women. "The speculation must be put to rest, for my honor and Josephine's, and Lord Baxter's. And I don't see that a grand entertainment with music and dancing is such a trial, whenever it happens."

He steered the conversation to safer ground, asking Josephine if she was pleased with her new London residence. She answered politely that it already felt like home. He noticed that she didn't eat with much appetite, so he hesitated to bring up his next topic—the procurement of her new wardrobe. Four gowns, no matter how beautiful, would not be enough for a countess's needs. If he had his wish, she'd commission frocks and fripperies in all sorts of sensual colors, dusty rose, sea green, sapphire blue. Such colors seemed most suited to the secret Josephine he knew, the sensual, wild Josephine he coaxed to life during private times.

He cleared his throat and signaled for the dessert course. Now was not the ideal time to recall heated, intimate adventurings with his wife. As the footmen dashed off with the dinner plates, he heard familiar male voices from the hall. It seemed his friends Lord Augustine and the Duke of Arlington had finally returned from Bath.

"There's no need to announce us, old chap," said August to Shelton, the butler. "He knows who we are."

Warren heard Shelton's quiet tones, saw the butler heroically trying to impede August and Arlington from intruding on their dinner.

"It's all right," said Warren. "Let them come. We're just finishing dessert. Would the two of you care to join us?"

His friends accepted the offer, and tucked into an assortment of sweets and cakes as they seated themselves beside the women. Such goings on were typical in his bachelor household, but Warren could feel the subtle disapproval of the servants at this careless etiquette. There was nothing to do for it. Once his friends were back in town, nothing would stop them from coming to see him. August was a dark and brooding sort of rogue, while Arlington seduced the ladies with impeccable manners and rakishly tousled golden-blond hair. They doubtless wished to invite him out for the night, so they might make their usual rounds of debauchery.

"Good evening, Minette," said Arlington to his sister. "I trust you're well?" He regarded Josephine in her ruffled ivory gown. "Is this one of your little friends?"

Warren glared a warning at Minette before she could explode with all the news of the previous week. "Arlington, August, I'm pleased to introduce my new wife, Lady Warren."

Both men turned to stare at him, mid-mouthful. He supposed the news must come as a shock. Now that they understood the lady was not part of Minette's menagerie of friends, they sat up straighter and ceased shoveling poppy seed cake down their throats. A blush crept up about their ears.

"I did not hear you had married," said August. "Congratulations."

"Yes, indeed." Arlington's voice sounded almost normal. "Felicitations to you both."

An awkward silence settled over the table. Arlington was the first to recover and politely address his wife.

"We are honored to make your acquaintance, Lady Warren. Tell us, where did the two of you meet?"

"At Lord and Lady Baxter's home in Hertfordshire," Josephine replied, staring down at her plate.

Warren could see Minette practically in flames to say something. He shook his head at her with another warning glance and offered the agreed upon explanation for their marriage. "We took a great *tendre* to one another at the Baxters' house party and decided to wed at Chapley by special license. It was only a short time ago."

"How wonderful," said August. His dry response communicated that he didn't believe that explanation in the slightest.

"Lady Warren has traveled all over the world," Minette finally burst out. "She is the Baroness Maitland also. She's just returned to England after oh so many years, and we're already like sisters."

August glanced at Minette in amusement. "I'm sure you are."

"Maitland?" said Arlington thoughtfully. "Aren't his holdings in Oxfordshire too?"

"They're very near to mine," Warren said with a nod, "and they're my wife's holdings now, since the tragic death of her parents in India last year."

August and Arlington offered condolences and shoveled in more cake, while Josephine blushed, and Minette made puppy dog eyes at August. Her infatuation with the brusque, dark-haired man was a running joke, although August was kind to her about it.

"Minette," Warren said, when her mooning grew uncomfortably obvious, "if you and Lady Warren have finished, perhaps you would like to retire to the drawing room for a bit of tea."

The gentlemen stood as the ladies took their leave. He could tell Minette would have preferred to stay, but a subtle arch of his brow had her flouncing out with one last lingering smile at August.

The door had barely shut when August braced his arms upon the table and scowled at him. "What on earth? Married? We were barely out of town a week."

The servants brought port, which Warren poured for his friends. "Sometimes a week is long enough. Sometimes one day will do the trick."

Arlington thrust a hand through his thick golden hair and took a drink. "You might have warned us. Sent a note round or something."

"Yes," agreed August. "I nearly toppled over when you said 'here's my new wife,' and her just sitting there like a shiny little dove. For God's sake, you should have come with us to Bath."

"And done what? Fawned over some actress who's slept with everyone and their brother? I have a sister to marry off, you know. There are always single gentlemen at the Baxters' gatherings."

August snorted. "One less, now."

Arlington held up a hand to head off a spat. "You just took us by surprise, old man. First Townsend and now you. That's two out of the four of us, leg-shackled. What's the world coming to?"

"The both of you can sod off. I had no choice, as it happens."

"No choice?" said August. "What do you mean?"

"I mean, it was me, or the blasted Earl of Stafford to ravage her fortune. What was I to do?"

August and Arlington looked at each other. "Was it as grave as all that?" August said. "I'm sorry to hear it."

"You played the hero then." Arlington tsked in sympathy. "At such a price."

Warren shrugged, tracing the swirling pattern carved into the arm of the chair. "I got married, that's all. You and August will have to marry too someday. We've played at rebelliousness and dissolution for a long time, and it was fun, but it's not reality. We're all only sons and we all have a duty to get heirs."

His lecture did nothing to alleviate the somber mood at the table. He poured them all more port.

"She's not so bad, anyway," Warren said, picking up his glass. "I could have done worse, like Lord Rowley's chit with the horse face, or that brainless china doll that August will have to marry."

"I'm not offering for Lady Priscilla," he said with a frown.

"Your father believes otherwise, and so does hers." He cut off his friend before he could argue. "The point is, it's done and I have to make the best of the situation."

"Peace, friend," said Arlington. "You did the right thing. It only takes some getting used to, you know? The notorious Wild Warren, a married man."

"Neither of us was very happy about it. Baxter pressed the match."

"Hard luck," said August. "But things will work out. Remember how Townsey and Aurelia didn't want to marry? Now they make everyone sick, the way they fawn about and gaze at one another."

"Rather the way Minette gazes at you," Arlington said out of the side of his mouth.

"I'm throwing a ball here weekend after next," Warren announced. "I wish both of you would come and lend an air of respectability to the proceedings."

Arlington flicked a look at August. "You're looking to the wrong chaps for respectability but if you want us here, we'll come, eh, Augustine?"

"Wouldn't miss it," he said in the tone of a martyr being led before lions.

"I should explain there was a bit of a to-do at the Baxters' that necessitated a quick wedding. I'd like this ball to silence any gossip about forced marriages and inappropriate behavior."

"Inappropriate behavior?" Arlington's brows rose. "On whose part?"

"Mine, of course," he answered impatiently. "Baxter caught me with Josephine in the woods. Alone."

"Bet he didn't like that," said August.

Warren shrugged. "It gave him the excuse he needed, and honestly, it felt good to put Stafford out of the running. He planned to squander Josephine's inheritance and stash her in Bedlam if she complained." Warren tipped back the last of his port.

"Stafford and those rings," said August with an eye-roll.

"I gather he's not invited to the ball," said Arlington.

"He's the goddamned reason for it. He's been spreading nasty gossip about me and Josephine, like any weak, pathetic man would." A feral sense of protectiveness infused Warren's voice. He had come to care for his wife's well-being, stubborn and moody as she was. Again, August and Arlington exchanged glances, half-ironic, half-concerned.

"We'll keep an eye out for him then," August said. "And plant him a facer when he crosses our paths."

"I'd appreciate that."

Arlington reached in his finely tailored coat to extract an even more finely crafted gold watch. "It's getting on, August. We ought to head out." He turned to Warren. "I don't suppose you'd like to go to the club with us, and Pearl's afterward?"

Warren thought a moment and realized he didn't want to go anywhere but upstairs, where he might molest his wife's luscious body for several hours. "I think I won't tonight, gents." He forced a sigh. "But I hope your adventures prove entertaining."

"Towns and now Warren," August groused, shaking his head as he walked to the door. "It's spreading like some disease, wouldn't you say, Arlington?"

The duke grinned. "Something like that. And you'll be the next one infected, if Lord Colton has his way."

August's voice echoed down the hallway. "I'll not marry Lady Priscilla. I'll find some way to get out of it."

Arlington turned back to Warren before he left. "You're a good man," he said. "I commend you on your selfless act, even though I suspect it was not entirely selfless."

With those words, and another waggish grin, the Duke of Arlington received his hat and gloves from the butler and followed the Earl of Augustine out the door.

Chapter Ten:
Spaces

As Minette predicted, hordes of callers descended on the Warren household after the first ball invitations were sent, sometimes four or five parties at once. Lord Warren made Josephine sit with him in the grand parlor, and relate over and over how they had fallen in love at Lord Baxter's house party, and how blissfully happy they were. If she complained about it, or said the wrong sort of things in company, he took her upstairs and spanked her bottom until it smarted to sit down.

Meanwhile, planning for the ball continued. Josephine overheard the servants muttering about the size of the guest list—five hundred confirmed and counting. Five hundred? The idea of it filled her with terror. She wished some natural disaster would happen before the appointed night, some cyclone or monsoon to deliver her from her fate, but English weather was nothing like Africa's or India's. Josephine thought of running away, at least until after the ball, but where would she go? And how? Even if she could flee to Maitland Glen, it was a hollow wreck of a place not fit for inhabitants, and Lord Warren would only fetch her and make her come back.

At night, he spent hours in her room, distracting her when she fretted about the ball. "There will be too many people," she complained, to which he replied that the Warren ballroom easily held one thousand. "I don't know how to dance," she'd cry, and he'd say something low and sensual like, "Let me show you this dance I know. You do it lying down."

And then he would strip her naked, and caress her, and do things that swept away her senses. Sometimes he tied her to the bed, which seemed designed for that very purpose with lots of sturdy spindles. He caressed her everywhere, her breasts, her quim, her backside, her shoulders, the sensitive hollow beneath her ears, her nape, her hips. He traced her ankles, her calves, and the spaces between her toes. "You're all mine," he'd whisper. Once she was aroused to a fever pitch, he would invade her body in all types of positions, in all types of ways—fast, slow, hard, soft, backwards and upside down while she clung to him and mewled in helpless pleasure.

She suspected such activities weren't proper, but he guided her into them so deftly that she never thought about stopping him until after the salacious acts were in progress, and her body quite engaged in the heated magic of his attentions. *Next time*, she would say to herself. *Next time I will resist him.*

But she never did.

In preparation for the ball, a French dressmaker was called to make alterations to the embellished sage gown she'd acquired from Minette, and to consult with "milord's new *comtesse*" on what other gowns she might like to order for her season's wardrobe.

The appointment did not go well.

Madame Lafleur insisted she must have Josephine's selections right away, as the season was already in progress. Minette tried to help, but Josephine felt pressured and uncooperative, and snapped at Madame that none of the gowns in her fashion plates looked like anything she might wear anyway. It was rude of her, and when Warren began to glower and clear his throat, she knew she had earned herself a punishment. After that she grew positively churlish, and her husband's eyes promised a great deal of retribution indeed.

Directly after dinner he sent her up to her room. As she sat pouting and waiting for her husband to arrive, a maid tapped at the door and brought in a silver covered plate to set on the table by the bed. "By Lord

Warren's instructions," she said, bobbing a curtsy. The girl blushed hotly and would not meet Josephine's eyes.

By Lord Warren's instructions indeed, thought Josephine. She lifted the cover to see what he had sent up for himself. More cakes? An after dinner pudding? What she found instead was a redolent and freshly peeled root of ginger, one end of it carved into a bulb and feathered at the tip. She stared at it in puzzlement, wondering what he meant to do with raw ginger, then turned to find him entering the room.

"Leave it alone," he said. He paused to remove his coat and waistcoat, then approached her in his shirtsleeves. "Do you understand why I'm not pleased with you, Josephine?"

"Yes," she said, wishing she might burrow beneath the bedcovers and disappear.

"Yes what?"

"Yes, my lord. I understand why."

"Turn around."

She obeyed, and felt his fingers tugging at the back of her gown and then the laces of her stays. She felt horribly guilty and vulnerable at times like these, when he stripped her and made preparations to punish her.

"I'm sorry," she said. "I didn't like Madame Lafleur. She was unpleasant and rude."

"No, *you* were unpleasant and rude. Madame Lafleur was only trying to do her job. The job I hired her to do, which is to outfit my countess with an appropriate wardrobe for the season on very short notice."

He drew her gown off, along with her stays, and set the garments aside. Her filmy shift followed next, so her entire back and bottom was bared to his gaze.

"Bend over," he instructed.

"Please... Warren..."

He didn't bother to argue, only pushed her forward with a firm palm planted between her shoulder blades. "You knew when you went too far, when you pushed past the confines of my patience, and still you continued to snap and whine like a sniveling child."

"I'm sorry." It was true. All of it was true. "It's only that I don't want new gowns. I don't want to attend this ball so all the town may come and gawp at us." She said this in the same peevish and whining tones that had gotten her into trouble so many times before.

"I don't want to hear another word about the damn ball, do you understand?" He crossed to the table to fetch the ginger root and returned to hold it in front of her face. "You have pushed and complained and irritated me to the point that a regular spanking won't suffice. This is going in your bottom as an extra measure of punishment, and then you'll be paddled over my lap."

The ginger was going…in her bottom? What on earth was the point of that? She remembered the blushing, bashful maid, and her words. *By Lord Warren's instructions.* Had they known below stairs what he intended to do with it? It had been carefully carved into a phallic shape. She felt ill with embarrassment as he pressed the tip of it against her bottom hole. It wasn't the first time he'd touched her there, for he sometimes pressed his fingers inside her there during the course of their love play. But this wasn't love play.

She tensed as he forced her to spread her legs wider. He held her bottom cheeks apart and inserted the ginger all the way in, until the flange impeded further progress. It went farther inside than his fingers had ever been, and Josephine squirmed uncomfortably. It was certainly a punishment to be humiliated like this.

He left again, and when he returned he held her wooden hair brush in his hand. The cursed thing. She would have to hide it where he could never find it. He pulled her up by the arm and sat on the bed, and arranged her over his lap, a position she was coming to know well. The ginger in her bottom, by this point, had come to feel uncomfortably warm. She braced as he raised his arm to paddle her.

"Oh," she cried. "Wait, it's hurting me. The ginger. It stings!"

"I should hope so." The back of the hair brush cracked against her bottom. She squealed and tensed, and then tried to pull away as the ginger burned her inner passage.

"Oh, please. *Please*," she begged. "Something is wrong. It feels like my bottom is on fire."

"The more you tense, the more it stings," he explained. "If you relax, it won't sting as much."

"But how can I relax—ow!" He gave her an especially sharp crack. "Oh, please. Warren!"

"I perceive you've discovered the point of the ginger. You had your chance to curb your behavior earlier today, and you chose not to. You knew what the consequences would be. Honestly, Josephine, it's been less than a month since we married, and you've had nearly a dozen spankings. You must understand by now that poor behavior will be met with consequences, at least in this house."

"Oh. *Owww!*" She kicked her legs, trying to escape the hot progression of blows. "I know. I'm sorry!"

"Most ladies are pleased to have new gowns and fripperies. I had to marry the one who"—*whap, whap, whap!*—"takes any sort of kindness as a personal affront."

"I'm sorry," she cried. "I should have appreciated your generosity." Sometimes, if she apologized prettily enough, he took mercy on her, but he didn't seem in such a mood today. The ginger stung her bottom relentlessly, but when she tried not to tense, the hair brush paddling felt so much worse. It was an impossible situation.

"Madame Lafleur is one of the best modistes in town," he continued, cracking now at the tender skin between her backside and upper thighs. "One might expect one's wife to be delighted with the prospect of a Lafleur wardrobe. Instead I had to pay Madame extra money to smooth over the feathers you ruffled. She has made Minette's gowns for years and has always had our family's custom. You nearly put that in jeopardy today."

Josephine could barely focus on his lecture, the paddling hurt so badly. "Please, when will you take the ginger out? *Oww.* Please!"

"I'll take it out when I believe you've been punished enough, and not a moment before." She tried to scramble off his lap after an extra hard crack, but was only gathered back again, her arms bent up and across her back. "Nothing so far has made a lasting impression on you. Perhaps the ginger will help."

It was helping all right—helping her take leave of her sanity. Her bottom cheeks throbbed, feeling afire with the unending volley of spanks. She cried and sobbed, begging for respite. Finally, he put down the brush. When he righted her, she got shakily to her feet. She hated this part most of all, when he made her face him in tearful remorse, and promise to do better.

"What do you have to say for yourself?" he asked.

"I'm sorry. I'll apologize to Madame Lafleur for my rudeness. I will send her a note."

"Indeed you will. And you shall do something to put me in a better temper, my dear. Right now, in fact. On your knees."

She wiped away her tears, sinking down and resting her aching bottom cheeks on her ankles. Warren stood and undid his breeches, exposing his stiff, outthrust sex. He took the breeches off, and his shirt too, so he stood before her tall and naked, his male form so daunting and yet so attractive. Defined muscles rippled in his torso as he urged her forward, pressing his shaft to her lips.

She didn't dare balk from this duty, or turn away. No, she had been taught exactly what she must do when he put her on her knees. She kissed and licked the swollen tip, wetting the velvet skin, gathering moisture in her mouth for when he pressed himself inside her. If she couldn't do anything else properly, at least she could do this.

"That's right, my girl," he said, directing her in a thickening voice to lick the base of his shaft, to kiss, to mouth, to caress all the mysterious male parts of him. His legs shook a little as she applied herself to the task. "Open up, now, Josephine. Take me in your mouth."

She obeyed, making her lips into the round, soft shape he preferred. He held her head between his hands, allowing her little choice in controlling the depth of his thrusts. "Kneel up," he said a minute or two later, as he drove deeper. "Now you're putting me in a better humor."

She supposed that was a good thing, but her backside still throbbed from his paddling. She whined softly against the intrusion of his shaft as the ginger root ached inside her bottom hole. Sitting straighter on her knees had intensified the burn again, and she had to concentrate hard to pleasure her husband without nicking him with her teeth. He was so terribly large, and when he thrust too deep inside her, she had to fight the urge to pull away.

But when she managed to take him deeper, he groaned and sighed, and made such noises that she tried even harder to satisfy him. At last he made a rough sound and stopped her. He sat back on the bed, pulling her with him, and spread her thighs over either side of his lap. His shaft reared up between them. He squeezed her hips, lifting her. The ginger set up a new, sharp sting.

"Oh, it hurts," she cried. "Won't you take it out now?"

"I don't think so," he said, settling her down over the head of his cock. She grasped his shoulders to have something to hold onto, some feeling of control as his shaft parted her inch by inch. She felt wet and shivery and sore, and stuffed to the hilt by his manhood and the ginger seated inside her. He seemed to go on forever. When she tried to rise off his formidable length, he pulled her down again. She buried her head against his neck, not certain if she felt good or bad or frightened to death.

"It hurts," she said softly.

"Does it? Or does it only feel...unusual?"

She wanted to cry. She wanted to move on him and kiss him, and offer him her breasts to pinch and bite. He always did this to her, made her feel animalistic, and hotly ashamed of her longings.

"Will you take it out? Please?" It was too much. Too much fullness, too much pleasure. "Please, my lord."

"Why would I take it out? You've two shafts inside you now, haven't you? You've two lovely spaces to put things, not counting your mouth."

He was scandalous. She knew it and yet she participated so willingly, night after night. "The ginger," she said, finding it hard to catch her breath. "It's so hot and stinging. I really feel it there."

"Do you think you'll be a better girl, now that you know how it feels to have ginger in your bottom?"

She wanted to say *yes*, but she knew the answer was probably *no*. At her hesitation, he chuckled and gripped her sore, reddened arse cheeks so she tensed on the ginger again. The burn had lessened, but it was still there. He angled his hips, moving inside her in a slow, sensual slide. She couldn't help but respond by moving her hips too.

He tightened a hand on her waist, guiding her. The other hand withdrew the evilly carved ginger—and then pressed it back in.

She gave a small moan. The ring of her bottom ached now too, a mild sting, but strong enough for that part of her body. As he moved his hips, and his shaft, in incremental movements within her, he moved the ginger in and out too.

"*Ohhh*," she said. She meant to complain but the noise sounded like something else. Like mindless, wanton pleasure.

"Do you like that?" he whispered against her ear.

"No," she insisted weakly.

He made an amused sound and lifted her higher, so he drove deeper. He teased her bottom with the ginger, pushing it in and out again. His fingers traced the welted, paddled skin around it. "I think you like it," he said. "Does it still burn?"

"Yes." It burned and she liked it. He filled her and controlled her and she liked that too, which made her feel ashamed. The servants knew about the ginger, and her husband knew what type of woman she was—what if everyone else came to know? She pressed her head harder against his neck and shoulder.

"Move for me, Josephine." His rasping voice compelled her to do what her body struggled against. She tensed her thighs and rose along his thick shaft, then sank down on it again, excited by the feeling of fullness. The spot he caressed so often with his fingers and his tongue and lips felt swollen to four times its size. She ground it against his pelvis, arching her hips.

"Again," he groaned. "Yes. Keep doing that. Ride me while I punish you with this ginger in your arse."

"Oh," she said. Not *oh no*, as she ought to have. Or *oh stop*. He pressed the ginger in and out, making her thighs and buttocks shiver as she rode him with ever more enthusiasm.

"Someday, I think I'll put my cock inside your bottom," he said. "I'll put my great big cock inside your arse hole and make you ride me just like this."

"No," she whimpered, while she thought with excitement of how that might feel. He grasped her, pressing into both her spaces with hotter rhythm. She ground against him when she could, and reached down to caress herself when she couldn't.

"That's right," he said. "Make yourself feel good. Don't stop until you reach your crisis." His voice lowered a bit. "I won't stop either. Remember how this feels, how naughty and delicious it feels to have something driving in and out of your bottom."

This was depraved. It simply had to be, but she didn't care. The ginger had lost much of its sting, and it stretched and stimulated now, rather than hurt. He pushed it inside her one last time and left it, and grasped her hips and ground her down on him. She clung to his shoulder with one hand and stroked her sex with the other. When her climax arrived, the intensity of peaking pleasure shocked a ragged cry from her lips. She felt as if everything inside her bore down and pulsed, and then exploded. Warren captured her cry in his lips, holding her tight, murmuring *yes, yes, yes.*

Somehow her punishments always ended this way.

Once her racing heart calmed, her husband rang the servants for a bath. They set it up in the dressing room, and the same blushing servant girl poured the hot water into the tub. Josephine was embarrassed. Warren wasn't, and sat about waiting in a flagrant state of undress. Once the maid left, he picked Josephine up and deposited her in the tub, then climbed in with her so the water rose to the edge and splashed over it. She fussed over the wet floors but he drew her back down.

"It's perfectly all right to be outrageous and decadent sometimes, my dear. The floors have survived many decades and will survive many more."

"You are more outrageous than me," she said as he poured water down the back of her hair.

"Perhaps. But I'm working on you, and getting places, I'd say."

His use of the word "places" was no doubt intentional. How could he be so relaxed and unashamed after the things they'd just done?

"You enjoy our outrageous activities," he persisted. He stroked his hands over her breasts, trailing warm water across her skin. "Just as you'll enjoy your new gowns when you receive them, and just as you'll enjoy the ball. These tantrums are silly, as is your resistance. Everyone should see what a beautiful woman you are, and that we are happy together."

She stiffened beneath his touch. "I think you care overmuch about appearances."

"And I worry that you don't care enough."

"What does it matter what people think of me, or you?" she asked. "I'd much prefer to be left alone."

For a while, there was no sound but the faint splash of him bathing her back, and her front, and the place between her legs. "I fear you are as unconventional as your parents," he finally said. "I suppose you wish to board a ship and escape these shores, and sail to every exotic port you can find, so you can behave in any manner you like."

Josephine pulled away and rose from the water. "I certainly do not."

"If you wish to remain in England, you must follow English rules," he said, his voice sharpening in measure with hers. "You mustn't be careless of gossip, for my sake, if not yours." He glowered at her as she wrapped herself in a towel. "I beg you to remember, I married you as a kindness, at great detriment to my accustomed way of life. I have an interest in politics and social reformation, so the regard of the *ton* is important to me. I'm also a peer with a number of material and financial obligations. I can't allow your disdain for societal rules to endanger my interests or my career."

Cold rivulets of water ran down her shoulders and back. "If I'm such a detriment to you, why don't you get rid of me?"

"What a capital idea. Shall I throw you from the tower, or push you out the window?"

She pursed her lips at his jest. "Either would work. Then you could marry someone more suitable, some simpering mouse who follows all the 'English rules.'"

Warren toweled off with considerably less modesty than she did. In fact, he stood quite naked, his broad shoulders and rippling torso displayed to intimidating effect. "Do you truly wish to argue and be disagreeable, and anger me again, Josephine?"

The tone of his voice, coupled with the memory of her latest spanking, prompted a wary response. "No, my lord."

He moved closer and traced a fingertip down her cheek. How could he be so frightening and yet so gentle? "I don't want to throw you from any towers," he said. "I'd miss you terribly when you were gone. I only ask what any man would ask of his wife, that you respect me, and protect the honor of my name. I mean to respect and honor you too. Have I bullied you, or abused you in anger, or ignored your basic needs? Have I forced my attentions upon you without your consent?"

She stared into his piercing blue eyes, and knew he had done none of those things. He'd spanked her, yes, but only when her behavior fell outside the bounds of polite comportment.

He took her arm and turned her around. "Lift the edge of the towel, if you please, so I may inspect the damage to your bottom."

She did as he asked, feeling exposed as he crouched down to examine what he'd done to her.

"It appears you'll survive," he said. "And you won't cut up at Madame Lafleur again, will you?"

There was only one acceptable answer, no matter how cross she felt. "No, my lord."

He released her and launched into yet another lecture. "I suppose you don't enjoy having a hair brush taken to your backside. I'm sorry for it, but you may expect these disciplinary measures to continue as long as your attitude or behavior calls for them. I didn't sacrifice the pleasures of bachelorhood to join myself to a scold and a shrew. I don't require you to become a simpering mouse; I only ask that we show consideration to one another in this marriage."

You're a hypocrite, she thought. Was it considerate to be overbearing, haughty, and self-interested, and constantly paddle your wife? But she didn't want another punishment, so she kept her lips shut tight against those condemnations and obeyed with stiff docility when he ordered her to bed.

Chapter Eleven: Missing

The ball was a day away, and it seemed to Warren that Josephine had finally resigned herself to her new role as his countess. She'd been docile as a lamb during the final fitting of her gown, a lovely work of pale green with voluminous skirts and tiny pearls and flowers on the bodice. They'd spent a few hours in the ballroom, practicing how to dance. She proved naturally graceful at following his lead.

Very much as she did in bed.

Perhaps at some point she'd realize things like bondage, sado-masochism, and sodomy were not standard marital practices, but he hoped by then she'd be too corrupted to care.

No, not corrupted. He didn't wish to think of his wife in terms of corruption. Certainly, he'd had to pay women a great deal of money to perform the services Josephine now happily performed, but Josephine was an innocent to the core, so innocent and earnest and raw that he didn't feel capable of enjoying other women anymore. Most men did stray within their marriages, but for him, her erotic surrender seemed a fantasy unlikely to be surpassed by anyone else.

If only her surrender extended beyond their marriage bed. Though his wife was perfectly aware of the dinner hour, Warren waited with Minette alone at the table, the soup going cold. With the ball the following night, they had much to discuss. He beckoned a footman and directed him to send upstairs for his absent wife.

After a few minutes, the man reappeared.

"My lord, the countess is not in her rooms."

"Well, where is she?" He glanced at Minette. "Do you know where Josephine's gone?"

His sister shook her head. "I haven't seen her since breakfast. I believe she wasn't feeling well. Nerves, you know, about the ball. Perhaps she's gone for a walk in the garden?"

After twenty minutes of searching failed to produce his countess, Warren experienced the first pangs of alarm.

"Where can she be?" asked Minette, her large blue eyes shimmering with tears.

Warren questioned the staff, who couldn't remember when or if Josephine had left. His mind turned with unhappy possibilities. Had she run away? Had she only slipped out for a walk, and had some mischief done to her? The more he considered such a scenario, the more worried he became. His wife was a damned nuisance sometimes, but she was his responsibility and he cared for her. He rather suspected he was growing to love her, a realization that terrified him almost as much as the fact that she was gone.

He sent word to Townsend, August, and Arlington that Josephine was missing and asked if they could join the search. They responded at once and set out to various areas of town to ask if anyone had seen a lady fitting her description. Warren grilled the servants, down to the quietest kitchen maid, and then took to the streets himself, riding through surrounding neighborhoods. Had she called on a friend? Had she walked or taken a hack? Had someone abducted her? Were they holding her for ransom?

I want a cottage, just big enough for me. I want it to be in some quiet town, with a garden and a...a little fence.

Had she run away from him? He had to consider it. *No.* She wouldn't dare. Something had to have happened to her, something unexpected that had detained her. Unfortunately, he was accomplishing nothing wandering about town. Perhaps there was news at home. Perhaps she'd even showed up, out of breath, having gotten lost on an unauthorized afternoon stroll. He turned his horse for Park Street when a familiar voice hailed him in the misty night.

"Ahoy, Warren." The Earl of Stafford rode up, his mouth curved in a half-smile of mockery. "I hear you've misplaced your wife."

He scowled at the man. "If I have, it's none of your affair."

"You look awfully worried. But when you marry a madwoman, what do you expect? Have you checked the docks? The scurvier parts of town?"

"I'll knock you off your horse, you bleeding bastard. See if I won't."

Warren hadn't the time or inclination to stand about trading barbs with Stafford. He continued on his way, only to have the bloody idiot fall into step behind him.

"Go on, then, if you're not going to help look for her," Warren snapped over his shoulder.

"Why should I help? I didn't marry her. You did. You stole her right from under me, and you call *me* a bastard."

"She was never under you," Warren said, trying to erase that imagery from his mind.

"She could have been, if not for your interference. I never would have told you about her if I knew you'd take her from me."

"I didn't take her from you. She was never yours." The sharp words came out like a cracking whip. "We fell in love. Lord Baxter approved of the match, so we decided not to wait."

"Of course, that's the drivel you've been putting around, but no one believes it."

"Speaking of drivel that no one believes, if you continue to disparage my wife's name—"

"I never would," Stafford said, feigning horror.

"If you continue to disparage my wife's name with your whispers," he continued, talking over the man, "then rest assured every future heiress you angle after is going to know the precise nature of all your crimes."

"What crimes?" He flicked his bejeweled fingers. "I'm no worse than you, my lewd fellow. Might explain why your doting wife took herself off to God knows where."

"I mean what I say. Leave off talking about me and Lady Warren, or I'll make it difficult for you to step into any sort of civilized drawing room for the rest of your life. Your finances alone…"

"Really, these threats." But he could see Stafford was shaken. The dissolute earl would be easy to ruin—and it would be hard to marry into money once he was. "Very well." His expression darkened, like a spoiled child deprived of a toy. "I don't suppose anything I can say is as bad as the truth of your marriage, anyway. She's run off and left you, which speaks volumes. When she's not at your big, fancy ball, what will everyone say?"

"Go to the devil," Warren said, and put his heels to his horse.

"Yes, they might say that," Stafford called after him. Warren ignored him and galloped to Park Street, where his friends had convened to wait for news. Townsend and Arlington talked together near the fire while August paced back and forth. He could tell by their concerned expressions that Josephine hadn't been found. Minette sobbed in the corner, too frightened to even fawn over August the way she usually did. Warren comforted her as best he could and summoned Mrs. Everly to take her up to bed.

"No word of Lady Warren?" Arlington asked once Minette was gone.

"None," he replied. "I've been up and down for hours. I don't know where she can be. No one remembers when they saw her last, so I've no idea how long she's been missing." He could hear the hysteria in his own voice. If she was trapped somewhere, or hurt, or frightened… He could hardly bear to think about it.

Townsend sighed and rubbed his chin. "You're certain she's not curled up in some quiet corner of the house? Say, do you remember how Minette used to wander in her sleep? We used to find her in the strangest places. Up in a tree, or in a cabinet, or sprawled out in the neighbor's garden."

"Don't remind me," said Warren. "Thank God, she hasn't done that in years. And I doubt my wife went sleepwalking in the middle of the day."

"Did the two of you argue?" asked August. "Have a disagreement of some sort?"

"Not recently." There had only been the tension over the ball, but Josephine had moved past that.

His friends regarded him with sympathy. "We'll go out and look some more," said Arlington. "You stay here in case she turns up. If you can, get some rest. For all we know, she's hiding in some remote corner of your household, not wishing to be found. In the morning, have the servants search again. It'll be light in a few hours and we can send people door to door, asking if anyone has seen or heard anything suspicious."

Warren knew Arlington only wanted to help—and that he was probably right—but to wait until morning arrived...

"Minette is frightened," Townsend added. "Stay here in case she needs you, and see what the new day brings. If the rest of us hear anything, we'll send for you."

Warren buried his hands in his hair with a groan. Rest? Wait? But he supposed he had no other choice, except to keep riding the dark, empty streets of London, beset by helplessness and fear.

* * * * *

At some point, Warren must have fallen asleep on a chaise in the front drawing room. The crisp tap of a servant brought him to wakefulness. Sun streamed in the tall windows. Warren thought to himself, *Why am I here?* and *Why am I still dressed?* And *Why am I so tired?* Then he remembered that Josephine was missing. He shook his head, trying to focus on what the butler was saying.

"Lord Townsend," the servant repeated. "And Lady Warren."

He sat upright as Townsend walked into the room. The dark-haired man propelled Josephine forward with an arm about her shoulder; she looked as pale and wretched as Warren felt. Relief overcame any confusion or questions, at least for the moment. He strode over to embrace his wife.

"Thank God. Has any harm come to you? Are you perfectly all right?" He took her from Townsend, inspecting her from head to toe.

"I'm fine," she said in a tremulous voice.

"My dear girl." He clasped her close, stroking wisps of hair back from her face. She shivered in his arms, her tears wetting his cheek. He squeezed her hard, then released her and turned to Townsend. "Good Lord, how I worried. Where did you find her?" He turned back to Josephine. "Where on earth have you been?"

When she didn't answer, Townsend spoke up. "She's been at my house. I had no idea, I promise you. I've sent word to the others that she's been found."

Warren rubbed his forehead, staring at her. Josephine began to bawl in earnest, sniffling into her sleeves. "I'm sorry," she said. "I didn't know what else to do, so I decided to hide."

"Hide from what?" he asked.

"She said you were forcing her to attend the ball this evening." Townsend arched a brow at him. "You monster."

Warren narrowed his eyes at Josephine. All his worrying, his sleepless night. His alarm and Minette's fear, and all the hours his friends and servants had spent searching for her. "You went to the Townsends' house to *hide from the ball?*" he asked in a very slow and deliberate way.

"Yes, because I don't want to go." Her trembling voice held a panicked edge. "I don't want to be married to you, if I must do these things. I don't want to be trotted out in front of hundreds of people and forced to act happy for your vaunted career. I want to go live in my cottage. I want to be left alone. I want—"

"You want a spanking," he said, cutting her off. "And I'll be happy to give you one when I regain control of my temper." He beckoned a footman and gestured toward the adjacent doors. "Barnard, will you escort Lady Warren to the smaller parlor and see that she awaits me there?"

He thought she might protest, the foolish girl, but one of his patented glares subdued her, and she allowed the servant to lead her from the room.

His friend, meanwhile, had turned toward the windows, as if he had not just heard this little drama. "I'm sorry," Townsend said after a moment. "I had no idea she was there until the servants tattled. Aurelia had secreted her in her dressing room. Her maid saw toes peeking out from beneath a suspiciously bunched-up row of gowns."

"Blast. I never would have thought. Josephine doesn't even know Aurelia. She's not yet come to call."

"No, she hasn't."

The two friends looked at each other. Warren muttered a colorful string of oaths. "Minette must have had a hand in this. I'll kill her."

"Be calm, man," said Townsend. "Minette behaved wrongly, but I won't let you kill her on my watch. Unless you're speaking in a purely disciplinary sense."

"Oh, I am," he ground out. "That little liar knew exactly where Josephine was all night, while I paced the floor, and she cried and fretted and clutched her curls like London's most talented actress. All of it, a deception." He brought his fist down in a crash against the nearby table top. "Damn it, I don't like being colluded against. Both of them are mad."

Townsend stayed silent as Warren grasped for calm. A fit of temper wouldn't change anything. He took a few steps and sank back down onto the chaise. "It's a hell of a thing when your wife doesn't want to be married to you."

"I remember the feeling," said Townsend. "It's not a pleasant one."

Warren knew that Townsend and Aurelia had had a rocky start to their marriage. He wondered if Towns had ever felt this bleak. "I've only been trying to help her," he said. "You know me. I don't have a sinister bone in my body. I've been everything that's kind."

He chose to ignore Townsend's snort of laughter, and the smile he hid behind his hand.

"Perhaps she just needs more time to get used to her new life," his friend said when he'd composed himself. "More time to get used to being the Countess of Warren."

"How much time does that take?"

"A bit longer than you gave her to prepare for this ball, I suppose."

Warren threw out his arms. "It's a ball, for God's sake, not a damned execution."

"Not to you. Perhaps it feels so to her. I wasn't able to draw much conversation from your wife during the ride here, but I gather she's terrified to face the *ton* tonight. You're so concerned with painting a picture of marital bliss that you've disregarded your wife's feelings. Which rather works against the whole marital-bliss effort."

Warren scowled at him. "You're supposed to be on my side, you bastard."

"I would have been on your side a year ago, but marriage changes things. Which I imagine you already know." He shrugged. "At any rate, I'm sorry I didn't realize sooner that Lady Warren was hiding at

Townsend House. Aurelia will know better than to go along with such a scheme next time."

"Go easy on her," Warren said, studying his friend's determined expression. "She only meant to help my wife."

"Will you go easy on Lady Warren then? And Minette?"

He thought a moment. "No. I suppose I won't."

Townsend clapped him on the shoulder. "I'll let you get to your business, then, and I'll get to mine, so the lot of us can move on." He paused to receive his hat and gloves from the butler outside the drawing room door. "You know, I'm glad I'm not the only married one of us anymore. How did August and Arlington react to the news? Were they alight with congratulations?"

"More like scorn," said Warren. "I think August was angry."

"That's because he sees his own marriage heading down the line. Well, I'll see you tonight. I'm looking forward to the ball, even if Lady Warren isn't. Perhaps I'll even dance with my wife."

"Scandalous. I hope you do. It will give the guests something to gossip about besides my farce of a marriage."

Townsend tipped his hat with a mischievous glint in his eyes. "Sometimes marriages that begin as farces develop into rewarding unions. Give it some time, my friend. Give it some time."

Chapter Twelve:
Punished

Josephine sat trembling, hands clasped in her lap, outside her husband's study. The measured smacking noises within, and Minette's yelps of entreaty, did nothing whatsoever to soothe her nerves. Josephine might have crept off and hidden, if not for the footmen stationed at the end of the hall.

She was glad she had no choice to escape. She deserved to be punished. She only hated that Minette must be punished also for something that was entirely her own fault.

After ten sound smacks, Minette burst out of the study, tearful and red-faced.

"I'm glad you're married to him and not me," she said to Josephine. "He's a horrible, heartless man."

Lord Warren appeared at the door, and Minette took herself off, muttering about tyrannical older brothers while rubbing her bottom through her skirts. Josephine looked up at him, feeling deep remorse and a quailing sense of dread. Why on earth had she tried to run away? Even if it had worked and she got to miss the ball, her husband would have killed her when she came home afterward. Somehow, in her panic, that hadn't occurred to her.

But now it did. She could guess from his taut stance, from the forbidding look on his face, that she was in for a much more difficult ordeal than Minette. His lips were tight, pursed in a stern line. He didn't even speak to her, only motioned her into the study to meet her fate.

He paused after he closed the door, crossed his arms over his chest and looked at her. "Well, Josephine. What have you to say for yourself?" he asked in a deceptively pleasant tone.

She didn't know. She didn't know what she had to say for herself, or what he wanted to hear. Her eyes darted to the large, polished surface of his desk. It was utterly bare, except for the short, thick strap that lay across it. She wrapped her arms around herself and stood with her knees pressed together beneath her skirts.

"I apologize," she finally managed. "I am so very sorry for my foolish behavior. I—I don't know what else to say."

"Oh, well. In that case, I have plenty to say for both of us." His previously pleasant voice took on a biting edge. Oh, this was going to be worse, even worse than she thought. "Do I have it in the right, that you prevailed upon Minette to secret you away from here, and help you hide at the Townsend household until after the ball?"

"Yes, my lord," she said, trying to sound appropriately abject. "I asked Minette for help."

"And caused her to be punished also. You left this house without a word to anyone, throwing lives into an uproar, causing my friends and my servants to search for you all night when they might have been resting in their beds. You involved the Townsends in your scheme, thereby creating anger and tension between Lord Townsend and his wife. You've embarrassed and insulted me by running away like some abused waif because I expected you to attend a goddamned ball. Is that the long and short of it?"

"Well, the thing is—"

"Is that correct?" he interrupted with unnerving emphasis. "Yes, or no?"

"I told you I didn't want to have a ball. You knew how I felt, but you wouldn't listen. What was I to do?"

"What were you to do, my darling? The answer to that is simple. You were to put on your goddamned ball gown, smile at our goddamned guests, and dance a time or two, as any normal English female might do."

His insinuation came through loud and clear, that she wasn't normal. Didn't he understand that was exactly why the idea of this ball made her run away?

"You won't listen," she said, wringing her hands. "You won't listen to me. You don't care."

"Don't I?" He had seemed somewhat calm when he first admitted her to his study, but no longer. The volume of his words rose with each syllable as he stalked back and forth. "Do you have any idea the tormented thoughts that ran through my head while you were gone? I feared you had been abducted, or ravished. I feared you were hurt or lost somewhere. I thought a thousand terrifying things. Does that sound like I don't care? Have you any idea how anxious I felt when you turned up missing?"

The harsh emotion in his voice scared her almost as much as the thick, black strap. "I only planned to stay away until the ball was over, you see. I would have come back."

"Damned right you would have come back." His exclamation made her jump. She backed up as he walked toward her. "You're a married woman and your place is with your husband. I arranged that ball in our honor, for your well-being, to secure your place in society and discourage careless talk. I'm trying to fix things, while you're doing everything in your power to make things worse. It's as if you want to marginalize us. It's as if you want to ensure I'm forever apologizing for you in polite company." He stopped nose to nose with her. "Did you even think about how it would have looked to everyone when you weren't there?"

"I don't care," she said in a high voice. "Don't you understand? I don't care how it looks to everyone. I don't care what people think of me."

"I care!" His thunderous reply echoed off the walls. "I understand that you don't care. You've told me that lie enough times, damn you, but what about me? *I* care, as you very well know! You're my wife. You belong at my side, supporting me, bringing honor to my name. It's not your job to embarrass me in front of hundreds of guests because *you don't care*."

He was furious. Her smiling, easy-going husband had been transformed—by her folly—into a very wrathful man.

"I understand that I shouldn't have done it." She spilled out apologies, only wanting to mollify him. "It was weak of me, and selfish, you're perfectly right. Please, don't hurt me. Don't punish me. I won't ever do such a thing again." She swallowed hard, knowing from his expression that her pleas were in vain.

"I wish I could trust your words, but I don't." He gave her a hard look. "I punished you at Lord Baxter's for sneaking off behind his back, and now you've done it again. You did what you wished, not sparing a thought for anyone else's feelings, and embroiled my friends—even my own sister—in your scheme. Such actions call for a very harsh consequence, because I'll be damned if I have to punish you for this on a third occasion."

She'd lost count of the times he'd cursed at her, and now he was going to punish her harshly, which she surely deserved. Oh, how she wished she could dispute his accusations, but all of them were true. She should never have hidden away and frightened everyone. She hated herself for her cowardice, more than he knew. To explain her past to him, to explain the reasons she did so, might spare her some of his anger. It might even spare her this punishment, but she couldn't bear to speak of the bleak experiences that had made her into the coward she was.

He paused, as if he too wanted her to explain these awful shortcomings in herself, but she could not. With a sigh, he walked toward the desk. "Up to this point, I've only spanked you to calm you down, to refocus your attitude, or to address minor trespasses. This will be a severe punishment spanking and it will hurt considerably worse. Come here, Josephine."

Her insides wrenched and turned over. She felt like she might empty her stomach as she plodded to the desk. She eyed the stout, weathered strap resting on top, affixed at one end with a sturdy handle, marking it as a tool of punishment for despicable miscreants such as herself. "The finest English leather," he said, as he noted her studying it. "For correcting regrettable mistakes. You will bend over the desk and raise your skirts, please."

She could not move. She could not imagine doing something so far outside the bounds of common sense. His temper seemed to have peaked over the course of his scathing lecture. Now there was only this frightening, detached authority.

"Of course, any resistance or refusal to accept your punishment will only make things worse," he said. "Bend over and raise your skirts. I won't repeat it again."

She stepped to the edge of the desk and folded herself over the top. It was precisely the right height for such a use. The rounded edge of the wood supported her hips, and her feet had firm contact with the floor. She reached to her sides and drew up the skirts of her gown. A humiliated flush flooded her cheeks and heated her ears and neck. Her whole body trembled, anticipating the pain to come. The strap appeared pliable and worn, a prodigious punishment instrument.

"I'm not going to tell you the number of strokes." She turned her head as he took the strap and went to stand behind her. He pushed her skirts up a bit higher. The air felt cool on her bottom. "And I'll not bother with ginger, since the pain of each stroke will far outstrip any pain a ginger fig could cause. You may cry and scream as much as you want, but you'll submit to this strapping until I feel you've learnt your lesson."

Her trembling increased as he pressed a hand at the small of her back. "Do not reach behind you and impede me. Do you understand?"

"Yes, my lord," she said. It came out a whimper, and then the first blow fell.

Josephine cried out, trying not to throw her arms behind her. The strap's impact felt like a hot iron laid against her skin. "Oh, no, please, don't!" she begged.

His only response was to increase the pressure of his palm at her back. *Whap. Whap. Whap!* Blow followed stinging blow, with only a few seconds' measured pause between them. Somehow that pause was the worst thing of all, because it showed his control and determination, when she had little of either.

"Oh. *Oww.* I'm sorry. Please!" The words spilled from her, pleas and gasps and quiet begging. Meanwhile, the pain increased, each period of respite allowing just enough relief for the next blow to cause a fresh explosion of pain.

This was punishment, then. She'd been an ignored child, mostly left to do as she pleased. She'd never been severely disciplined for anything. She'd never really understood the reality of "punishment" before, but now she did. She thought back almost longingly on her previous "spankings," which she realized now had been nothing but child's play. Fun and games. Real punishment hurt, and it frightened her and made her feel powerless. It made her feel remorseful too. She knew she would do anything to avoid this in the future.

When she kicked up her legs at the continuing pain, he pushed them down and admonished her to keep them still. "You've no right to resist this strapping," he said. "You earned every stroke. Keep your legs down and your hands flat on the desk."

He had long since surpassed the number of licks he'd given Minette. Josephine supposed that was only fair. In fact, she was being punished for wronging him *and* hurting Minette, who might not even remain her friend after this. She felt so guilty and so bleak, and each relentless blow brought more hot tears to her eyes. She began to weep, all her begging and whining replaced with pure, miserable devastation.

She spread her palms against the desk, her body wracked with shuddering sobs. The strokes were not increasing in intensity…they were only so steady and so unending, each one a hotly blooming pain upon her right cheek or left cheek, or both cheeks at once, or the sensitive skin at the apex of her thighs. Her entire backside burned with a throbbing, aching fire. "Oh, please," she cried out between blubbering sobs and hiccups. "I'm so sorry. I'm so sorry. Please!"

His palm moved higher on her back, holding her still as her body instinctively tried to push up and escape the unending torture. The pause between blows lengthened, each crack resonating with greater force so her entire body shuddered at the pain. Tears coated her cheeks, running into her mouth as she screamed out at each stroke. *Whap! Whap!* She gasped, making frantic, pleading sounds, waiting for the next one. *Whap!* She couldn't bear much more. She sobbed so hysterically she could barely catch her breath. *Whap!* That one was the hardest blow yet. The sting spread out, radiating down her thighs and into her middle. She went limp against the desk, her fisted hands opening and then clenching again beside her head. She screwed her eyes shut. She couldn't bear any more, she *couldn't.*

But no more blows came. She heard him set the strap on the desk. "Stay right where you are," he said. "Don't move."

She lay still, wrung out and drowning in tears. Was there to be more? Was he only having a break? But he didn't take up the strap again, or spank her with his hand, or touch her anywhere except for the place he held her down. She gulped in air, trembling beneath the carefully exacted pressure of his palm at her back. Her bottom felt swollen beyond its normal size, throbbing and pulsing so badly she thought it might burst into flames.

At last he removed his palm, but he wouldn't let her stand. "You shall remain in this position a few more minutes, and think about whether you wish for such a punishment again."

"I don't," she sobbed. "I know I don't."

"Still, think about it. It's important, Josephine. If you haven't learned anything from this, I'll have to punish you even more harshly next time."

A ragged cry escaped her lips. A harsher punishment than this one?

He walked across the study while she lay there. He poured some brandy from a decanter, then returned to pick up the strap and stow it in one of his lower desk drawers. Through all this, she remained with her bottom in the air, skirts bunched around her ears. It was a different kind of punishment, to be stung with shame rather than hot, sharp pain. She wiped at her tears until her cheeks were dry, and closed her eyes.

After fifteen minutes or so, he came to her and rubbed a hand across her exposed bottom cheeks. They still ached, but it was less hot throbbiness and more a deep, nagging discomfort that reminded her she'd just been thoroughly strapped. He lifted her from the desktop, steadying her when she swayed on her feet. Her skirts fell down over her punished backside, both a comfort and added torment as the petticoats scratched at her sensitive skin.

"Now," he said, gazing into her eyes. "You are going to tell me everything that troubles you. Everything." His grip tightened on her arm. "You are to leave nothing out."

"It's just... The ball..." she said miserably.

"No, it's more than that. Something greater is at work here."

"I don't know what you mean."

"Go and sit," he said, indicating a chair near the fireplace. "I'm going to ring for tea while you compose your thoughts, and then we're going to have a very frank discussion, during which you will explain to me the source of your distress and fears."

When she didn't move, he guided her to the assigned chair and settled her into it. She winced as her freshly-punished bottom came in contact with the firm seat. She had endured the punishment to avoid this very outcome, the telling of her secrets, the baring of her soul. Lord Warren's servants were too quick with the tea, so a tray arrived while Josephine was still trying to think of a means of escape, or some falsehoods she could tell to satisfy him.

He brought her a cup balanced atop a saucer, fine Warren china with ivory trim, as if he hadn't just had her in screaming agony. She was sure her face was encrusted with tear trails, and her hair a mussed-up disaster upon her head. He sat across from her with his own cup and gave her a look as if to say, "Talk."

And to Josephine's utter surprise, she did.

"I dream about tigers," she said.

Lord Warren added more sugar to his tea. "Why do you dream about tigers? Did you see them on your travels? I confess I've only seen them at various zoological displays."

His tone was so mild, so conversational, that Josephine continued in a halting voice, relating a story she'd never meant to tell anyone.

"When I was young, we traveled in India a lot. There were English people there, but my parents avoided them, staying away from the colonies and setting up households in the native areas. I always had an *ayah*, a native girl, a nursemaid or minder to look after me so my parents wouldn't be bothered. They had never really wanted a child."

Her throat closed up at the pain of that revelation, which she had known from her earliest age to be true.

In the lengthening silence, Warren asked in that same mild and guiding voice, "Did your parents abuse you?"

"No. They never raised a hand or voice to me, except to tell me to go away. They ignored me and left me in other people's care. I think they always assumed a fever would take me, or that I wouldn't survive the places we went to. They never tried to protect me."

"But you thrived nonetheless," he said with a slight tilt to his lips. "You were speaking of India, and your...i-yah?"

"*Ayah*. I don't even remember this one's name, but she didn't look after me properly and one day I wandered off. I don't remember this. I was told about it later."

"You do have a way of wandering off." He said it so drily she almost smiled. He, however, looked sober. "What happened?"

Josephine stared hard at the arm of the chair. "When it got dark and my parents realized I wasn't at home, and that my *ayah* didn't know where I was, they told all the servants to go looking. I was found..." Her voice faltered. "I was found in a clearing near a river bank, in the company of a...a tiger."

His brows rose. "How terrifying. What did the servants do?"

"They tried to scare the animal away. It paced back and forth by the water, they said, as if it did not wish me to toddle into the currents. When they screamed and threatened it with torches, it finally bounded off."

"Amazing." He watched her expectantly. Of course there was more to the story, to the tragic arc of her life.

"The servants checked me over for bite marks or scratches, and finding none, they took me home to my parents. From then on, the natives called me *baga lika* in their dialect. It meant *tiger girl* or *tiger child*."

"I expect they admired you very much."

She shivered, so her cup rattled on her saucer. "No. They feared tigers, and they especially feared anything unexplainable. They believed, from what they saw, that I could commune with the tigers, that in fact I was half-tiger, and all the villagers regarded me with suspicion. Few of them would work in my parents' house after that. They believed my parents must be powerful sorcerers to give birth to a half-animal child. I suppose my wild tantrums and dirty, neglected appearance did nothing to dissuade them. My hair was very much the color of a tiger's coat at that time, and my eye color..." She glanced up at him with her golden, striated, feline-amber gaze. "In the end my parents were forced to leave that village. I only learned about this later. They taunted me with the story, when they wanted to show me how troublesome I was."

"Oh, Josephine," he said. "I see now why you hated them."

"I'm the reason they died." She bit down on her lip, but she couldn't stay the rush of tears. Lord Warren put down his cup and saucer and came to her, and took her cup when her nerveless fingers threatened to drop it.

"I'm sure that can't be true," he said in a brisk voice, as if he could take this unalterable fact and discipline it to some other reality just as he disciplined her. He knelt before her, his features grim. "If people told you that… If they led you to believe that, they only meant to lie to you and hurt you. Lord Baxter said it was robbers."

"That's the story, but that's not what really happened." She drew in a stuttering breath. "You see, we had been away from India for some time, traveling in the Sub-Sahara. All the while, the tale of the English couple with their *baga lika* had been passed from mouth to mouth so that when we finally returned to India, all the natives seemed to know it, even though we went to a different region and a different village. Again, my parents couldn't find servants for the house. I had to go into the village whenever we needed food or supplies, since we had no help, and my parents were incapable."

"Incapable?"

"They'd become addicted to a number of medicinal substances in their travels. They had become very sick."

"Why didn't you go for help?" he asked. "Were there no English nearby to assist you?"

"If I had gone for help, what would have become of my parents? I was afraid to approach the English, or bring them to the house. I didn't… I didn't want them to see…" Her face screwed up with tears. She'd shed so many tears back then, tears of shame and loneliness. Tears poured out of her now like one of the Indian monsoons. Lord Warren produced a square of linen from his coat and dabbed at her cheeks.

"I knew enough of Englishness and manners to know we were peculiar," she sobbed. "I knew we weren't quality people, no matter what my mother claimed. I didn't dare socialize among the English, and when I went into the village, people avoided me or looked at me like I was a ghastly thing. When I tried to buy meat and vegetables for our house, some of the sellers would turn away and mutter spells of protection. This went on an entire year, and then…"

She took the handkerchief away from him and mopped her own cheeks. She had already told him enough, but she found she had to tell the whole story now, the violent, vile ending that festered inside her and haunted her dreams. "The following spring, bad things started to happen. Livestock died without reason, and insects swarmed and ruined the villagers' gardens and crops. It didn't rain for weeks on end, and the sun baked the land and dried the rivers and streams. The tigers came down from the hills in search of food and water, frightening the people in the village. One afternoon, a tiger attacked a young child and killed her. That night..."

She buried her face in the linen handkerchief. It smelled like him, like sandalwood and freshly pressed clothing. "That night, the villagers stormed our house, screaming of evil and sorcery and the *baga lika*. I ran away. I hid in the woods." That was all she could say. She couldn't speak of the screams and the fire, and that she had left her intoxicated parents behind.

"Of course you ran away," he said, pulling her into his arms. She rested her head on his shoulder, sobbing into the fabric of his coat. "Of course you did. You had to. No one could blame you for that."

"But..." She choked out another sob. "I blamed myself. It was my fault the natives came to the house. I ran through the forest in the dark until I reached the English houses and even then I was afraid to speak to them. But I was more afraid of another tiger finding me, or the villagers. So I went and knocked on a door and told the English that my parents had been attacked. They went to the house and found my parents, and arranged for them to be buried, and treated me with such kindness, but I never told them the rest, that it was my fault."

"Josephine." His voice sounded pained. "Don't say that it was your fault. You can't believe that. The tiger wasn't your fault, and your parents made horrible choices. It's a miracle you're alive, and they... Well, in my opinion, they are better off dead." He leaned back, brushing fingertips across her cheek. "Were you going to keep these wretched memories inside you forever? Why didn't you tell me before now?"

"I don't know."

"I want to punish you again for keeping it from me, all your pain and suffering."

She stiffened, her eyes going wide. "Please, I beg you, no more."

He gathered her closer. "Of course I won't punish you, but you ought to have told me this sooner. I wouldn't have been so hard on you. I understand now why you're so afraid of society's judgment. Why you wish to be left alone. People haven't been very kind to you." He gave a great sigh. "Including me. I'm sorry. I couldn't have imagined such a tragic history, not in a thousand years."

"I didn't know how to tell you. And now, with this ball, and your expectations... I'm so afraid." He massaged her nape as she broke into another barrage of tears. Letting the story out from the dark angst of her soul had been almost as painful as living through it.

"You don't have to be afraid," he said. "We don't kill people here for being different. We don't believe fantastical tales about tiger children and sorcery."

"It's not that. It's the feeling of scrutiny, and disapproval, and having to endure it over and over again."

At some point in her crying breakdown, he had lifted her and settled her in his lap. He tilted up her chin so she had to face him. "You won't need to endure scrutiny and disapproval if you'd only make an effort to go about in society as you deserve. You're a titled, intelligent woman. I know you're afraid, and expect the worst, but no one knows you're that tiger-child, Josephine. No one but you."

"And you," she pointed out, sniffling.

"And me," he agreed. "But I'll never tell. I want you to be happy. I'll help you belong, if you'll only let me. I'll make you into society's jewel. God knows, you're beautiful enough."

As she gazed at him, Josephine admitted to herself, for perhaps the first time, that she would like to feel at ease around other people, particularly his friends and contemporaries. She wanted to live a happy, normal life, she just couldn't picture it. "I don't know," she said, wiping at her tears. "I don't think you can turn me into a proper English lady."

"Boo for proper English ladies. You only need to be tame enough to get by. You can be as wild as you like when it's just the two of us." She shifted as his hand slipped down to her bottom, patting the tender, sore skin. "I can teach you what you need to know about decorum and common courtesy," he said. "It's not a matter of whether you can do it—for I know you can. It's a matter of whether you wish to try."

"Will you spank me if I don't try?" She buried her face against his shoulder. "I don't want to be spanked anymore."

"And yet it seems to prove effective in calming and refocusing you to better behaviors. I daresay this very strict session finally compelled you to open up and tell me some very important things. Not that I enjoy punishing you so harshly." He pressed his forehead against hers. "Won't you trust me to help you? Won't you stop being afraid?"

"Being afraid is what kept me alive."

"There are no wild animals here. No murderous natives. English society can be vicious, but not that vicious. Josephine, your parents made you live a life you didn't want, far from the place you belonged. You want to belong here. In your heart, I know you do."

She had told so many deep dark secrets to him this day, one more slipped out, little more than a whisper. "Yes, I want to belong here. I want to be a proper English lady whom everyone admires."

"Then give me this season to help you. Three months, until August. If you decide then that you still wish to hide in the country, at your manor or mine, I'll allow you to do so, even though it means we'll have to be apart."

A week ago, an hour ago, she would have jumped at the opportunity to be away from him. Now, curled in his lap with her soul bared in revelation, she wasn't sure if she wanted to be alone. Again. "Where will you go if I retire to the country?" she asked in a small voice.

"Well, I'd have to be in London at least some of the year to sit in Parliament, and I must travel to see to my other interests, my holdings and such. It's not ideal to live away from each other, especially if we have children, but if being among society gives you too much pain…"

Children? She pictured holding a sweet, smiling child with auburn hair, or blond curls, and her heart gave a squeeze of aching desire. There was so much to strive for, if she could only be brave. She took a deep breath and let it out. "I suppose…perhaps…I can try to do better. If you'll help me, I'll try to make my way in society, starting tonight with this horrifying ball you've planned."

He pulled her closer and pressed a kiss to her forehead with such tenderness it brought more tears to her eyes. "My brave, lovely girl. No, don't cry anymore," he said, brushing her cheeks dry. "You must trust me. Everything will be well."

Chapter Thirteen:
The Ball

There were doubtless many tasks to accomplish before the evening's entertainment, but Warren went upstairs instead to rest with Josephine in her room. He found it impossible to leave her after the emotional story she'd just shared, and she seemed grateful for his arms around her as she closed her eyes.

But Warren couldn't sleep. He felt like the world's most loathsome ogre for punishing his wife. Of course, such breaches of trust and safety had to be dealt with, but if he had known the reason for her outrageous behavior, he would have gone about things with a lot more sympathy. All this time he'd been bedding her and perverting her, and spanking her for real and imagined faults, and he hadn't even known her. He hadn't understood anything about this woman he had wed.

Well, he would do better. Nothing would please him more than a harmonious marriage with true affection. As he held her and stroked her hair, he vowed to encourage greater trust between them. Above anything, he wished her to feel safe. It was the least he could offer after her nightmarish experiences as a child.

Her lady's maid came tapping at the door a while later. Josephine startled awake in his arms, looking rumpled and groggy, but then she smiled at him. It was a very small, somewhat hesitant smile, but he thought he would always count it among the most beautiful things he'd ever seen.

"You must prepare for the ball now," he said, brushing a kiss against her lips. "Try not to worry about being judged or stared at. Just do your best. I'll be there to help too. All right, darling?"

She nodded. "I'll try not to embarrass you."

"No hiding in the house plants. Rudiment number one."

Her light, sweet laughter assured him they were once more in accord, so he left her to her lady's maid and headed to his sister's room. Minette answered his knock with the expected pout.

"I don't want to talk to you, Warren."

"I want to talk to you," he said, holding the door open when she would have shut it in his face. "You ought to know that as bad as your punishment was, Josephine's was worse. I hope you'll be kind to her tonight."

"Why wouldn't I? I'm not angry at *her*," she said. "I'm angry at *you*. How long will you continue to spank me as if I was a naughty child?"

"You *are* a naughty child, Minette. It was very ill done of you to aid Josephine, and worse, to watch me go out of my mind with worry when you knew perfectly well where she was. I reserve the right to spank you for such behavior until you reach your majority, or until I manage to marry you off into some other man's keeping. And God help the poor sod, whoever he is."

"I can't wait to be married." She flipped back her blonde curls and frowned at him. "I'm certain my husband will be much less a tyrant than you."

"Perhaps he will. At any rate, Josephine is preparing for the ball. I'm sure she'd like to speak with you when you're ready. She could use your support tonight. You've always been wonderful at these sorts of things."

He could see the compliment melt away a bit of her anger. By the time the women came downstairs, they seemed in pleasant spirits once more. They walked arm in arm, heads together in close conversation. Their quick, easy friendship had pleased him, and he was glad to see their camaraderie had survived this unfortunate affair. The two of them were visions in their ball gown finery. Minette wore pale pink, which suited her rosy complexion, and Josephine looked ethereally lovely in green.

He went to his wife and bowed over her hand. "You take my breath away."

Josephine blushed as if his compliment embarrassed her. Perhaps it was a bit strong for public ears. Minette flounced off, muttering again about tyrants as the first guests began to arrive.

"The carriages are in a line around the block," Josephine said. "I saw them from upstairs."

"I suppose when the floor is adequately packed, you and I can begin the dancing. A waltz, perhaps? Some might find it scandalous." His gaze dipped to the enticing expanse of her gown's neckline. "But I don't care."

Josephine fluttered her fan. "I got in trouble for not caring, as I recall."

He saw teasing in her gaze, and marveled at it. "I don't doubt you'll find trouble again, Lady Saucymouth. But pray...not tonight."

He led her into the ballroom as the crowds of guests thickened. It wasn't proper for a husband and wife to hang onto one another at such occasions, but newlyweds might get away with it. He was aware of speculative glances, but many more admiring ones, particularly from his gentlemen acquaintances. He narrowed his eyes at one or two known for extramarital dalliances. He had no wish to share Josephine, and, more surprisingly, no wish to dally himself. More than one lady was disappointed when he didn't respond to their blatantly flirtatious advances.

Near midnight, he and Josephine danced a waltz, opening the way for other couples to join them. The ball was a monumental crush, but a success. Josephine gazed at him in just the right way, whether in guile or innocence, he didn't know. It was a gaze of love cloaked in propriety, a shy, sweet fascination that would put to rest any lingering gossip that the match had been forced under duress. He was afraid he looked at her in the same enamored manner, judging by Townsend's bemused looks.

While Lady Townsend made her way over to visit with Minette and Josephine, Warren stood and chatted with his friend. "Have you seen August and Arlington?" he asked. "They were supposed to come."

"They'll be along." Townsend shifted as guests packed closer around them. "Seems you've already got all the people you need. I saw Baxter a little while ago, looking pleased as punch that his ward is so happily married."

Warren snorted. "Good thing he wasn't around last night."

The two men escaped the crush, climbing to an open balcony overlooking the festivities. "Look at them." Townsend pointed to Minette, Josephine, and his wife. "Have you noticed? Not one of the three has sat down the entire evening."

"The sore bottom club. Poor lambs." Warren leaned on the railing. "Poor conspiring lambs, who shall know better next time."

Townsend laughed. "I wouldn't count on it. It makes me nervous to see the three of them together. They could be plotting revenge."

A couple of gentlemen came to bow over Josephine's and Aurelia's hands and ask for a dance, breaking up the trio. Minette stood a moment alone, and then a familiar, dark-haired gentleman came to offer her a dance too.

"Oh, look, there's August with Minette," said Townsend. "I told you they'd be here. Arlington's probably over by the food."

Warren frowned as the two of them headed to the dance floor. His sister stared up at his friend as if he were a god. "I wish he wouldn't encourage her," he said.

"Who, August? He has no interest in your sister, believe me. He's only being polite. Should he have left her standing alone?"

"Yes, probably. Someone else would have come."

"It's a childish infatuation on Minette's part, nothing more. She'll leave it behind as soon as one of these other dunderheads manages to capture her attention. Honestly, did we ever act like that?" He pointed to some of the younger men, more than one of whom gawked artlessly at Minette in August's arms.

"No, we never acted like that," said Warren. "We only went to balls when we had to, and swore to one another we wouldn't accept a shackle until we were fifty. How foolish we were."

"Not foolish, just young. Like Minette." Townsend turned his back on the dancing blur of guests. "I perceive Lady Warren is in better spirits. You didn't have to drag her down the stairs?"

It was his friend's offhand way of asking if things were all right after the morning's drama. Warren thought how very many things had happened since then. A harsh punishment, and even more difficult revelations on Josephine's part.

"I understand better now why she was afraid," he said. "And I didn't have to drag her. She promises she's going to give the season a go."

"I'm glad to hear it." His friend looked back down at the guests. "It was good of you to marry her. I hope everything works out for the best." He gave a short, sharp laugh. "If Aurelia had wed you as she wished, what would have become of poor Baroness Maitland? She'd be at home polishing all the gaudy new rings Stafford purchased with her inheritance."

"I'm glad now that I wed Josephine." Warren watched her dance around the ballroom with Lord Grimshaw, smiling, head held high, all to please her husband. "As for Aurelia, that snarl's in the past. She ended up with the right person."

"It's early to say, but I think Josephine ended up with the right person too."

Warren stared hard at the banister. "I don't know, Towns. I don't know if I'm a decent husband sometimes. I'm better than Stafford but... I don't know."

"You don't know what? Stafford is a perverse, self-centered arsehole. He has no conscience. You're nothing like that."

Warren's chest felt tight with shame. Josephine had been an innocent when he married her and he'd taken full advantage, asking her to do things most gentlemen would only ask of a whore. A perverse, self-centered arsehole? Perhaps he was that too. He took a bit too much pleasure in spanking his wife's bottom, that was certain.

"It's not the same, old chap," Townsend said.

"What's not the same?"

"The activities you're thinking about. The things that are making you go red about the ears." His lips curved in a smile. "I know your brand of perversity, and it's not the same perversity of Stafford's ilk."

"But...the things I ask of her... She's a lady," he said, his voice harsh and tight.

"Is she a willing lady?"

"Of course she is. But only because she doesn't know any better. She wasn't raised in a traditional fashion, to harbor feminine inhibitions, so I've taken advantage, just as someone of Stafford's ilk would."

"Stafford sees women as objects to use, vessels to hurt and manipulate for his own pleasure. I know you, Warren. What you do with your wife is not the same."

"It feels the same to me sometimes."

"Listen." Townsend leaned closer to him and lowered his voice. "Don't tear yourself to pieces. I do everything with my wife." He raised a brow. "Everything. It's perfectly all right."

"Everything?" He regarded his friend, thinking of prim, pure Aurelia. "What do you mean, everything?"

"Everything," Townsend drawled, with slow, deliberate emphasis. "For Aurelia's honor, I won't go into specifics. I'll only say we engage in a delightful array of marital activities, and it pleases us both. If you'll recall, you were the one who goaded me to demand what I desired."

"I was drunk then, and mostly asleep."

"But you were right. As you know, Aurelia was raised very traditionally. She's been bred to propriety from the cradle, and yet she enjoys…"

"Everything?"

"Pretty much. Yes."

Warren let out a low whistle. "How I admire you right now."

"Don't admire me," he said impatiently. "Just wipe that guilty look off your face. You're nothing like Stafford, because you care about your wife and you want what's best for her. If you and Josephine enjoy unusual intimacies in your marriage, then get down on your knees and thank the heavens for it. I certainly do."

The idea of getting down on his knees, and heaven, brought some rather lurid images to Warren's mind. He turned to seek out Josephine among the dancing couples. He imagined stealing her from her partner and crawling beneath the ruffled skirts of her gown, pushing her back and tossing them over her head…

Townsend grinned and nudged him on the shoulder. "Everyone's watching you stare, so you might as well go down to her already. I daresay no one will bat an eyelash if you choose to dance with your wife an outrageous number of times."

A flush heated his cheeks, to be caught staring so avidly. "We're supposed to be silencing gossip, not inviting more," he said, tearing his gaze from Josephine.

"You're supposed to be silencing the wrong kind of gossip, and giving the *ton* something more pleasant to prattle on about. If it helps, I'll go reclaim my wife as well. We'll play reformed rakes, transformed by love and marriage. Come, Warren, add more yearning to your gaze."

Warren grinned. Easy enough to add more yearning. He couldn't wait to take her upstairs, away from the music and whirl of society, and be alone with her again.

* * * * *

Her husband never said so, but Josephine knew he would come to her afterward. She waited up in her dressing gown, peeking out the window at the last of the retreating carriages. Her feet hurt from dancing nearly every dance, many of them with her husband. Her face ached from forced smiles, and her brain hurt from trying to come up with answers to the inane conversation of her dance partners. She had tried to be a gracious countess for Warren.

And he'd told her he was pleased. The last time he danced with her, he'd bowed his head close to hers and murmured "What a very good girl you are," and the tone of his utterance had reminded her of private and exciting things. His touches, his kisses, his authority, even the punishment he'd given her earlier. She'd clung to him rather too closely for propriety as he'd guided her through dancing figures, but he hadn't seemed to care.

She turned at a firm tap on the door. A moment later, Warren entered the room. He wore breeches, but nothing else of his formal finery. His defined chest muscles shone in the candlelight, and she had an image of him dancing in the ballroom as he was now. How the ladies would have stared! He had been the handsomest gentleman there, in her estimation. Remarkable, that he was hers.

She felt the strangest impulse to smile at him, to flirt, to be coy and drop her lashes as she'd seen other ladies do, but she didn't know if she might look ridiculous. Instead she stood still as he approached her. A shy smile trembled at the corners of her lips.

"Lovely Josephine." He embraced her, pressing his forehead to hers. "I've wanted to kiss you all night." He did so now, gently at first, teasing her mouth open with patient pressure. "Darling," he said in the midst of this play. "How beautiful you looked in your gown. How gracious and dignified you were."

"You too," she whispered, leaning away. "You looked very splendid in your black silk, like an estimable gentleman."

"We fooled them all, then, didn't we?" He laughed, swinging her into the *one-two-three* steps of an abbreviated waltz. She heard a softer, lighter sound of merriment and realized it was coming from her. He pulled faces, humming the music and imitating some of the most notable guests until she grew breathless from laughter.

He stopped, out of breath himself, and swayed with her in the middle of her room. He held her hand in his, palm to palm, against his heart. "Do you remember the night we met, Josephine? At Baxter's ball?"

"Yes, of course. I found you very strange."

"The feeling was mutual, but I still wanted to dance with you. Did you want to dance with me? Even a little? Tell the truth."

She gazed at him, remembering how she'd shrunk from his size, his heat, and his solidity. He had frightened her more than anything. She still felt agitated when he was near, but it was a different sort of agitation now. "I—I was rather afraid to touch you that night. Or even look at you. Much less dance with you."

He gave his pirate's grin, dirty and lopsided as a listing ship. "What if you had known then that you would go to bed with me?"

"I would have run screaming from the room."

He laughed hard at that, and let go of her hand. "Come with me. There's something I've wanted to show you. Nothing to make you run away screaming." He thought a moment. "Well, perhaps."

She opened her mouth to protest but he was already drawing her along to his suite of rooms opposite. His furnishings were as bold and masculine as hers were frilly and feminine, all black and deep blue with gold edging that caught the candles' glow. His bed was gargantuan, big enough across for four people. He tossed her into the middle of it, then went to fetch something from a chest.

"You must forgive me," he said. "I enjoy playing with you far too much."

"Forgive you for what?" she asked warily.

Again, his extravagant laugh. He brought a small, nondescript box to the bed with him, and the canister of slippery oil he used when he

156

fingered her bottom. A flush rose in her cheeks. He set these aside and kicked off his breeches, and fell upon her, easing off her dressing gown and shift, and spreading her hair upon his pillow. His bedding smelled fresh and starchy, and rather intoxicatingly like him.

He touched and teased her beneath the covers, kneading here and pinching there, exploring all the places that most delighted her. He sucked at her nipples so her whole body trembled with arousal, and then used his knees to spread her thighs. "Keep them open, darling," he said. "Stay open for me."

"Oh…" She always felt nervous when he did this. He shushed her and placed a palm over her most heated place. She arched her hips against the contact, feeling the familiar slide away from propriety to wilder cravings. "Oh, please stroke me there," she whispered.

"Of course. I love stroking your pussy." His fingers played over her folds, seeking her most sensitive center and coaxing it to life. As he explored her, he dropped kisses along her neck and shoulders, light, teasing kisses punctuated by the occasional lick. Sometimes he took her like a thunderstorm, pounding and holding her hard, but this was more like…a summer rain. Humid, lazy, relaxing, and so wonderfully warm she felt she might melt right there in his arms.

"Warren," she sighed. "Come inside me, please."

"Soon, lovely. But first you must do everything I say."

Oh goodness.

"Turn onto your tummy. No, you're not going to be spanked. Don't tremble so. Why would I spank you when you've been so good?"

She buried her face in the mattress as he cupped and squeezed her bottom, still sore from her punishment earlier. "You spank me all the time just for the fun of it," she pointed out.

"Do I?" He gave her a couple of crisp smacks. "Like that, you mean?"

"Yes." It hurt her bruised cheeks, but she squirmed at the sudden heat flooding her middle. How wanton and licentious she'd become.

"You want me inside, I know." He rubbed her shoulders and her back. "Your little quim aches for me."

"Oh…" She sighed in agreement, too ashamed to look at him.

"And your bottom's still marked up from this morning." As he said it, he pinched one of the lingering welts. "Let's play with your pretty arse a bit. But no spanking, I promise."

She barely knew how to go on when he bespelled her like this, with nothing more than his intention and his shocking words.

"You beautiful thing," he said, dropping kisses along the back of her neck. "I want to be inside you always, everywhere." As he said this, he slid his fingers down to her quim and breached her. He moved one finger deeper into the slick proof of her arousal, then slid it upward, back and forth across her bottom hole. She tensed as she always did when he touched her there.

"Easy," he said. "Don't fight it. Let me inside, my love."

He pushed his fingertip against the tight bud. She made a soft, anxious sound.

"I know, I know. You're always this way at the start, but then I make you feel good, don't I? Let me show you what I've got for you."

He fetched the box and the lidded canister. She turned on her side and he showed her an oblong, ebony bulb of sorts, nestled in a bed of pewter-colored silk. It looked smooth and finely worked...and a bit frightening.

"What is it?" she asked.

"A training tool, I suppose, for perverts and libertines. I thought we could make use of it." As he spoke, he reached for the canister and dipped his fingers inside, coating them with the slick, fragrant oil. He took the bulb from the silk-lined box and rubbed the oil all around it. "Does this remind you at all of the shape of the ginger?"

Josephine had hoped that wasn't where this "training tool" was intended to go. Oh dear.

He smiled at her flustered look. "Don't pull faces. I promise this won't sting like the ginger. On the contrary, I believe you'll feel quite transported with pleasure before we're through."

"I don't know. It looks awfully big and hard."

"Well, you ought to be used to big and hard things by now. Turn over again and lift your bottom. Keep your hands out of the way."

Her wavering protests were ignored as he turned her and made her arch her backside in a lewd fashion. Again, he breached her bottom hole with his fingertip. It went easier this time, with the slick stuff to prepare the way. She lay very still, grasping the sheets in her fists. Why did she surrender so easily to his indecent trespasses? She supposed it was because, as he said, there was always pleasure before he was through.

Next, she felt the cold, hard tip of the bulb at her backside. She squirmed a bit, until a sound from her husband stilled her. *You ought to be used to big and hard things by now.*

Oh, but this was so strange. It felt like stretching, and pressure. As he eased the shaft into her, he moved his other hand up and threaded fingers into her hair. When he pulled it, tugging her head back, she felt the pain in her quim, all the way to the wet, aching core of her sex. He tugged harder, in slow degrees, until she could barely control her jerking hips. At the same time, he pressed the ebony shaft deeper and deeper until he finally drove it home. She felt its fullness and presence inside her, held in place by its prominent flange.

He released his hold on her hair and pushed her back over. He spread her open with his knees as she clenched on the solid intrusion. "How does that feel?" he asked, gazing down at her with his vivid eyes.

When she didn't answer, he parted her pussy and stroked across her sex, manipulating that little button that made her squeeze even harder around the shaft impaling her. She felt overwhelmed with sensation. She couldn't say anything but a shocked, "Oh."

"Is that a good '*oh*' or a bad '*oh*'?" His lips curved up in a grin. "It's not so bad, is it?"

Josephine shook her head. It didn't burn like the ginger, that was true, but the bulb felt hard and unforgiving. She found herself tensing upon it again and again, unable to stop the instinctive inner movements. Warren leaned back, his huge cock held in his fist. "Are you ready for me?" he asked with an edge of tension. "Do you want me inside you now too?"

"I don't know." She already felt so full. She eyed his prodigious girth. "I'm not sure that…both…"

"Yes, both," he said. "You can take it, Josie. It's going to feel so good."

Josie. No one had ever called her by a pet name before. She thought she rather liked the sound of it. Her husband moved forward, rubbing his cock against her slick entrance, and then began to press inside. She'd had only the vaguest sense of her nether anatomy before marriage to Lord

Warren, but she had a much greater understanding of it now. She worked to relax, to accept his thick length alongside the stout bulb seated in her other passage. He went slowly and carefully, so there wasn't any pain, only a great deal of stretching and accommodating. She felt a hot sense of surrender, a fearful kind of pleasure in the act.

"Yes, that's it," he said when he was fully seated. "I like this very much. You feel so exquisitely tight."

She squeezed her muscles and he gasped, withdrawing halfway again. He eased forward, making a guttural sound. His entire body seemed to vibrate as he arched over her. "Such a good, naughty girl," he whispered. He caressed her with one hand while he braced himself on the other. Each time he touched her breasts or nipples, or stroked her neck, or nibbled her ear, she squeezed on him again, thinking how much better it felt each time.

The fullness was turning to something else altogether, some delicious bliss at being so coarsely and deeply possessed. As her arousal surged, his talented fingers slipped again between her legs. Oh, he had only to touch her there. She threw her head back and groaned at the dexterous pleasure of his touch. Her nipples drew tight, forming pointed peaks. When he pinched them—oh, so brutally hard and so tightly—she nearly lost herself.

"Yes, my dear," he crooned. "I know. I told you it would feel good. Oh, God." His words cut off in a stifled curse as she squeezed on him again, her muscles taking over, seeking her body's desire, seeking to grip and caress and stroke. He drove her to the top of a peak and then over it, so she threw out her hands to clutch the covers. Ecstasy consumed her, a beautiful, encompassing aftermath capping a summer's storm. He pressed deep within her, so hard and so fast that another series of spasms sent her shuddering from head to toe.

He collapsed on top of her. She ought to feel discomfort—he was still quite hard, and she was still quite full inside—but all she felt was a great reluctance for him to leave. After a few moments, he withdrew from her as carefully as he'd pressed in. She waited for him to take out the ebony bulb too, but he didn't.

"How does it feel now?" he asked. "Does it hurt inside you?"

"No," she answered after a moment of consideration. "It only feels very naughty and scandalous."

This seemed to please him. "Naughty and scandalous. Very good. Only imagine how scandalous you shall feel when I put my cock inside your tiny backside. Not tonight," he said when her eyes went wide. "Tonight you must rest. But sometime soon I'll let you see what it feels like. We'll work up to it. Would you like that?"

She took a deep breath. "Well... If you think it's possible."

He chuckled and cupped her chin. "It's possible, I assure you. In the meantime, let's leave the bulb in your bottom a while longer so you can become accustomed to how it feels."

His words sounded wonderfully provocative, and his arms were bracing and warm. Sometime soon? Perhaps by then she would regain her senses, or perhaps by then she'd be even more willing to please her wicked husband. She'd survived his ball, hadn't she?

She looked into his eyes, wondering how far she would go to retain his affections. The way he looked at her this moment, she thought she would go quite a ways, in whatever direction he told her. Into forests full of tigers, or ballrooms full of haughty ladies and gentlemen. Into bedrooms where strange and singular things happened.

He had a way of making her face her deepest fears.

Chapter Fourteen:
Lessons

Josephine agreed to order gowns, shoes, hats, fans, and gloves in dozens of colors. She could not imagine why, except that Lord Warren preferred her to be stylish and bright.

When she wore her new clothes about town, to rides in the park, or shopping with Minette, people noticed and smiled at her—an entirely new experience. Many ladies complimented her on the recent ball, thanking her for the invitation and promising to call at Park Street soon. Josephine smiled back at them, even though, inside, she quailed in fear of being discovered as an imposter. The *baga lika* hiding amidst the quality, disguised in her fashionable gowns.

Perhaps that's why she'd grown progressively fonder of her husband. He was the one person around whom she could be herself. He knew everything about her, even the most awful secrets no one else knew. He knew she was flawed and afraid, and that she was responsible for such a gross crime as her own parents' death, although he insisted it wasn't her fault. Sometimes she almost, *almost* believed him. At the very least, she considered herself preternaturally unlucky, the type of person who might cause mayhem at any moment if she didn't exercise the utmost control.

And so she tried to control herself, and she practiced being the wife he wanted. She practiced smiling, she practiced walking, she practiced nodding just the right way, and she practiced holding her head with the proper degree of loftiness. She practiced addressing dukes and earls, and marchionesses and viscountesses, and practiced dining in the most polished manner of refinement.

She practiced conversation too, most often with Minette, who was always pleased to chatter on for an hour or three. They walked in the garden or sat at embroidery together, and Minette conversed so effortlessly, knowing exactly what to say and how to carry herself, and how to address servants in the exact right tone. Josephine marveled at it and did her best to copy it. She wished she was half as easy and carefree as her sister-in-law, to always do everything with such élan.

Lord Warren helped her practice conversation on other days, when Minette was off somewhere with her acquaintances. Her husband always used much more sadistic methods. Today, for instance, he held her upon his lap on a chaise in the smaller drawing room, her back pressed to his front, her skirts pushed up to her waist and out of the way to bare her legs. He twirled a riding crop between his fingers; three pink marks already decorated her thighs.

"What is the proper response when a dowager complains of poor digestion?" he asked.

She gazed warily at the crop's flicky tip. "One might suggest she avoid fibrous foods and other roughage of that sort. Ouch!" She jumped as the rectangular tip connected with her left outer thigh, leaving a fiery sting.

"The words 'fibrous' and 'roughage' should be avoided in polite conversation, darling. They'd send most dowagers into a swoon. Try again."

"Offer her some lemonade? Ouch! *Damn!*" The word slipped out, because he said *damn* all the time and she'd picked up the habit. She clapped a hand over her mouth but it was too late.

"Polite women don't curse," he said with another flick, this time on her right thigh. She squirmed from the sting but he only tightened his grasp at her waist. "I believe you're getting worse at this instead of better. Everyone knows lemonade is terrible for digestion. A dowager would only go on about sour stomachs, and where would you be then? I'll give you one more chance to come up with a reasonable answer."

"Or what?"

"Or you get the crop on your silly little behind. Think."

"I'm trying to think," she said. "But it's not very easy, with that horrid thing hovering over my kneecaps."

"I'm not striking anywhere near your kneecaps," he chided her. "And believe me, there are much worse places I could crop you if I wished to be horrid."

As he said this, he stroked the tip up the inside of her thighs, to the simmering spot at her center, the spot that always wanted to be touched ever since she'd married him. *Oh, please, my God, not there.* He stroked her with the edge of the crop, back and forth, as threatening as he pleased.

She flushed, trying to close her legs. He forced them open again. "What have I told you five times already? Leave them apart."

"Someone will come in. One of the servants will see me like this."

"No, they won't. And if they did, they would only understand what I already know. That you are a very poor conversationalist in need of constant correction."

Her burst of laughter transformed to a yelp as he cropped her very, very near that most sensitive place. "You mustn't," she begged. "You really, really mustn't strike me there."

"On your pussy? Say it. *Please don't strike me on my pussy, my lord.* Put a bit of begging into it."

More laughter bubbled up in her throat, mingling with fear and surging lust. "Please don't strike me on my...my pussy, my lord." *Damn* was easy to say, but *pussy* was harder. It was a naughty, ribald word, like calling his thing a cock. Thinking of his cock did nothing to calm the lustful urges blooming inside her. She could feel him stiff and hard within his breeches, pressing against her back. "Please, I'm sure it's not at all proper to spank me there."

"On your pussy?" he prompted.

"Yes, on my pussy," she said, shame-faced.

"I'll spank you wherever I like, as often as I want."

Why did it excite her when he said such things? He parted her legs wider, so she felt even more helpless and vulnerable. She moaned, turning her face against his neck.

"What is it?" he said. "Does your pussy need a strict cropping? Is that why you're so squiggly and squirmy?"

"No." Her outraged no sounded rather similar to a *yes*. "You're supposed to make me feel good there, not bad."

"We've talked about this before. It's more exciting if I make you feel good and bad at the same time."

This session was quickly diverting from its original purpose. "What of the dowager and her indigestion problems?" she asked. "Shouldn't we be focusing on that?"

"Who cares about dowagers and their goddamned digestion? There are other things that need to be taken care of right now, like your naughty pussy."

"Oh, no. Warren!" She protested as he stood her up and walked her over to a nearby chair with great padded arms. He lifted her skirts and made her sit with her bottom on the upholstery's rough, embroidered surface. That accomplished, he tugged at her legs, forcing her to drape one knee over each arm of the chair so she was spread wide open.

"Please," she whimpered. "This is so wicked. I'm afraid of what you're going to do to me."

He stood and looked down at her over his straight, aristocratic nose. "Perhaps you ought to be a bit afraid. It's going to hurt like the devil."

Josephine made as if to get up but he pressed her back again with the tip of the crop. "Be a brave girl for me, and I'll reward you afterward. Arrange your legs as I positioned them. Wider."

She eased her bottom forward so she could hook her legs securely over the chair's arms as he wished. As a result, her most private core was on flagrant display. "You say I must be proper," she groused, "and then you make me behave in this manner."

"For me only," he replied. "You're never to behave this way around anyone else."

As if she would. Her whole body flushed and shook with embarrassment as well as fear. He took up the crop again, trailing it up and down her inner thighs, to the tender juncture between her legs. She gathered up her skirts and buried her face in them. Oh, it was so humiliating, the way he made her feel! The tip slid against her womanly slickness, to that place so sensitive the tiniest contact made her gasp.

She peeked up at him from behind her rumpled skirts and petticoats. "Please. Warren…"

"Please what?"

"Please don't hurt me."

He drew back the crop and delivered a direct flick to her aching button. "Oh, my mercy," she gasped, burying her face in her skirts again. "Oh, please, no." It hurt, of course, but it also felt shockingly good. She was appalled at herself, at her indecent urges and cravings. *Don't stop*, she thought secretly. *Please don't stop.*

"Oh, please stop," she cried aloud as he flicked her again, and again. Her world was dark and shameful, her face hidden from view, but she knew he saw everything. He gave a sharp stroke to her left thigh, and her right. She cried out and drew her legs in closer to her body, as if she might close herself up tight.

"No," he said. "Put them where they were."

With a sigh, she draped them back over the chair's arms.

"Scoot forward. Open yourself to me. This is what you need, Josephine. To be disciplined and taught a proper lesson." He slid the crop's long leather handle through the tingling folds of her center. "Look how you respond to it. More than anything, that tells me this is what you need."

She gritted her teeth as he continued to crop her pussy and her inner thighs, sometimes standing before her, and sometimes behind her or at her side. He flicked her until she was frantic, not from the pain of it, although it was sharp and stinging enough, but more from the arousal of feelings. He was her husband, exercising marital rights she'd never imagined existed, and she did nothing to stop it. She hugged herself tight and kept her legs open for his torturous ministrations even when she must strain to do so. How long would this go on? Why did he want this? How could something so terrible feel so exquisite?

And what about the dowagers' digestion, for God's sake?

She dreaded being discovered in this ignominious state by the servants, but no servants came, or even knocked. Josephine thought they must know very well what was going on within the lord and lady's drawing room, from the rhythmic thwacks of the riding crop and her wailing cries. Perhaps they listened at the door, scandalized. Perhaps they busied themselves elsewhere so as not to hear. After Warren spanked her or disciplined her, the servants would never meet her eyes, except for her pale, freckle-faced lady's maid, who blushed furiously for hours afterward.

"Oh, it hurts," she whined, wiggling her feet. "I think you've stung every inch of me twice over."

"But you're not nearly finished," he said, raising his brows. "Your pussy wanted cropping, but it wants something else too."

"No, it doesn't want anything else," she insisted. "It's really perfectly content."

"Is that so?" He held the crop a moment, kneeling before her. She peeked over the tangle of her skirts just as he leaned to touch his lips to her nether folds. "Oh...damn," she burst out, as he sucked at her swollen button. "Oh, Warren, you must...not..."

He leaned back a bit, enough to swat her thighs again with excruciating firmness, and then he went back to licking and kissing her pussy, flicking his tongue against her in the same way he'd flicked the crop against her. She grasped his hair, transported by his voluptuous talent. The sensation was so intense she could hardly stand it.

"No, no," she whined, but again, it sounded more like, *yes, yes.*

"You know what I'm waiting for," he murmured against her skin. "When you give it to me, I'll stop."

Stop what? The licking? Or the hurting? The implement assailed her again, sharp flicks wherever arousal pooled. She kicked her legs, thrashing beneath the crop, or was it his mouth? He hurt her, then soothed her, then hurt her again, while her heightening need threatened to undo her. She balled her skirts in her fists, pressed silken material to her mouth. Oh. *Ohhhh.* It felt so fine when he licked her there, in that deft and steady way.

She keened through her teeth when the climax overcame her. She felt his hands tighten on her inner thighs as he teased her, on and on, drawing out the pulses until they gentled and let her breathe again. Her thighs and quim stung, but they tingled with ecstasy too.

Warren stood and tore at his buttons, pushing back his coat and waistcoat and opening his breeches. He impaled her roughly, just as she was, legs spread and hooked over either arm of the chair. The position admitted him deep, as he stretched her even wider than she was already stretched. He bucked against her, his scent overtaking her senses, his hot breath against her ear. The pleasure that had already wrung her out began to resonate again, building along with the frenzied pace of his thrusts.

"Oh, Warren, that feels…very…good…"

"*You* feel very good, my naughty girl. Yes, take all of me. Move your hips for me."

She clung to his shoulders and his hair, grabbing what she could to bring him closer and deeper inside her. She growled, or perhaps it was him. He went rigid, pressing fast and hard within her in the throes of his completion, and Josephine cried out in a second, shattering release. Somehow, she found the energy to unhook her knees from the chair and wrap them about him instead.

By slow degrees, she became aware of the sun coming in through the parlor curtains, and the vases of flowers, and the tea tray from earlier, still sitting on the table across the room. They were downstairs, in broad daylight, and her husband buried to the hilt within her. She would always be improper, she realized, at least in this.

But she wasn't sorry, and she was trying very hard not to feel ashamed.

"Goodness, Josie." Warren took her face between his palms and kissed her nose, her eyes, her cheeks. His talented tongue made a foray up and down her neck, and then back again, to end in a kiss beneath her chin. "My goodness."

That was all he said for a while, which was more than she could say in her breathless satiety. At length he moved away from her, so she could sit primly again. He dressed, tucking and smoothing and buttoning his many buttons, then knelt and helped her arrange her wrinkled skirts. Little good it did to compose her appearance, when she was still wet and sore underneath.

He put his hands on her knees and squeezed a little, flashing one of his handsome grins. "I don't know how you'll ever learn to converse properly when our lessons descend to such depravities. How naughty you are, to distract me so."

"You suggest this episode is my fault?" she asked hotly. "You're the one who does lessons with a riding crop in your hand, and my skirts tossed up about my ears."

"How else are you going to learn? By the way, the answer to any dowager's complaint about digestion is a delicate and concerned tsk, and a wish that she should be feeling better soon. Do you think you can remember that for next time?" He picked up the crop and flicked it against her ankle, still grinning.

She forgot everything when he smiled at her that way.

* * * * *

Over the next few weeks, Warren settled into the role of husband and disciplinarian with great contentment. He nurtured Josephine, taking pains to amuse her and squire her about society. No one could have the impression now that he didn't care for his wife. In point of fact, he lusted after her quite shamelessly, and continued to do coarse and immoral things to her body. He liked that aspect of their marriage quite a lot.

He liked that the pinched, tense lines had mostly disappeared from around her mouth, and that the dark circles had faded from beneath her eyes. He liked that he was used to the sound of her laughter now. He liked that she was trying so hard to behave as his perfect wife, and liked spanking her when she didn't quite manage it. He liked everything about her.

Perhaps he even loved her.

Was it love that made him draw her closer when they did carnal things together? Was it love that enticed him to spend most nights in her frilly, feminine bed rather than skulking back to his own? Was it love that made him glare at any gentleman who looked at her too long as they strolled in the park? He knew he didn't want to live away from her. He had promised she might hide away in the country if she couldn't bear to go on in society, but he wished he hadn't said such an outrageous thing.

So he took her about town whenever he could, to the theater and the park, and to dinners and social events, to help her grow more comfortable. He danced with her at balls, and flirted with her right in the open, until it became the thing to do. Other gentlemen began to flirt and dance with *their* wives, causing the frowning matrons to wave their fans and declare it an unseemly display. Such was society—one had to keep a sense of humor about it, or go stark-raving mad.

And he didn't wish Josephine to go mad. She had endured too much grief and hardship to lose her wits now. He told her so sometimes, when they had raw, whispered conversations about her fears and what she hoped for the future.

God, please let them have a future. He'd come to care for her so much.

"Warren? Are you listening to me?"

Minette tugged at his sleeve. He'd been staring moon-eyed at his wife again, in full view of every dandy in Hyde Park. "Pardon me," he muttered. "What did you say?"

"I said that Lady Chastity has accepted a marriage proposal from Lord Goss. Isn't it romantic? They've been friends forever, since they were eleven or twelve."

"That does sound romantic," he said with a wink at Josephine. He escorted both women on his arm, although the arm with Minette endured considerably more pulling and jostling.

"They won't have the wedding until next year, although Chastity wished it to be sooner. But she has so many things to order, and so much to plan. They're to have a big nuptial breakfast at her father's estate in the country, with flowers and swans."

"Swans," Josephine exclaimed, because he had taught her that one must balance conversation, and not stay silent too long. "How pretty that will be."

Minette launched into a breathless recitation of her own wedding plans, where she might have swans and flowers, and oh, rainbows if the weather could be made to cooperate, and white bunting all over the place. Josephine smiled as Warren tipped his hat to Arlington, who trotted toward them atop his horse.

"Good day to you, Lady Minette, Lady Warren," he said, greeting them with ducal politeness. "And Warren, well met. I was just about to leave before the midday crush."

"You'd better go soon, then." As he said it, a great group of Minette's friends bore down upon them, trailing prune-faced chaperones. Some of the young ladies looked wistfully upon the "Viking duke," who was the *ton*'s most desirable bachelor at present. Arlington, of course, made sure to be well away before the group arrived.

Warren waited with Josephine as the young people crowded around Minette. They had a special invitation to view the Royal Menagerie at the Tower, and they wished for Minette to accompany them. "May I?" she asked, turning to Warren. "Oh, please. How I have wanted to go!"

Warren and his friends had taken Minette to see the menagerie a year or so ago. She doubtless didn't remember because she'd spent the entire time gawping at August rather than looking at the exhibits. "I suppose you may go, if your friends' chaperones don't mind an extra ninny to look after."

"I am not a ninny," she said, tapping the brim of his hat with her fan. "And you must come too, you and Josephine. It'll be delightful, peering into the cages at all the exotic beasts."

"I don't believe I want to go," said Josephine, her hand tightening on his arm. "If there will be animals there."

"And you call me a ninny," Minette teased. "Of course there will be animals there. That's what a menagerie is, all kinds of curious creatures. Bears, lions, monkeys, even huge elephants lumbering about. There are tigers too, snarling and stalking to and fro, with great piercing eyes and claws as big as a man's head. Honestly, Josephine, you should want to go most of all, because you've lived in so many wild places. Come with us, won't you?"

"No, Minette," he broke in. "She doesn't want to go." In fact, since Minette had brought up the tiger, his wife had gone quite pale. "Go along with the other young people. Josephine and I shall go quietly home like old married folks."

"Oh, but..." She began again to entreat Josephine but his furrowed brows silenced her. "Very well. I'll have Lady Julia's carriage bring me home when we're done, and I'll tell you about my adventures. And then you'll wish you'd gone!" With those words, she hooked arms with Lady Julia and another friend and set off across the park.

"Did you wish to go?" Josephine turned to him in dismay. "I'm sorry. I ought to have asked you."

"There's no need to feel sorry. Caged animals give me the chills." He took her hand and squeezed it. "It gave you a start to hear about the tiger, didn't it?"

"A little bit."

"Would you like to go sit down?"

He drew her to a bench, away from the growing crowds. She sat beside him with her hands clasped in her lap and gave a little sigh.

"I feel I've disappointed my friend. Minette has been so kind to me." Her hands clasped tighter. "Perhaps I ought to have gone as she wished."

"Minette will be fine in the company of the other young ladies. The lot of them will soon be surrounded by admiring suitors, and none will give a whit for the animals."

Josephine smiled. "Your sister cares nothing for suitors. Her heart is already given."

"To whom?"

"To Lord Augustine, of course."

Warren laughed. "That silly *tendre*. Well, I'm afraid she's going to be disappointed there. August's under pressure to marry Lord Colton's daughter. Family politics and matters of that sort. I expect he'll give in and offer for her before Christmas."

"Minette will be crushed."

"No, she won't. She knows as well as any of us that a match with August would never work. He sees her as a little sister. *My* little sister. I wouldn't allow him to court her even if he wanted to."

"Why not? He's your friend."

Warren snorted. "Exactly. I know where he's been and what he's done, and what he likes to do. And right now, thanks to you, I'm trying very hard not to picture him doing such things to my sister."

"You mean the sort of things you do to me?" she asked in a curt tone. "How protective you are, except when it comes to your own wife."

"Hmm." He frowned and pulled at his gloves. "I protect you. I protected you when I married you, didn't I?"

She wouldn't look at him. "I suppose."

"You sound churlish, my dear. Shall I borrow Arlington's riding crop and take you behind a copse of trees to correct the problem?"

Her gaze flew to his, and then over toward the Duke of Arlington, who rode with a large black crop tucked beneath his arm. She shut her mouth, sufficiently threatened against further peevishness.

"Speaking of Arlington," he said, touching the back of her hand. "He's giving a garden party next week, and he's invited us. It's to be outdoors, with dancing and games, a fun and frivolous affair, but still the sort of thing one might bring one's wife to."

She peered over at him. "Does His Grace hold garden parties that one might *not* bring one's wife to?"

"I'm not going to answer that." He'd been to some parties at Arlington's that would have sent the devil running for cover, but that didn't seem salient to the present conversation.

Josephine sighed, looking out across the park. "Do you think I'm fun?"

"What do you mean?"

"I mean…" She bit at her lip. "You are very fun and frivolous. I think you always have been. I wonder if you wished for a fun and frivolous wife to take to these fun and frivolous parties you and your friends enjoy."

"I like my present wife very much, thank you."

"You know what I mean," she said impatiently.

"I'm afraid I don't. Are you asking if I wish you to be more fun and frivolous? I tend to believe we balance one another out. I have a tendency to lackadaisical behavior, while you're a more sober sort." He didn't know if that was the right thing to say, but he hoped it was. "Do you wish I was a more serious person, like you? In the end, we are who we are, and we're married for life, so we must make the best of it."

"Is that what you're doing?" she asked. "Making the best of it?"

Warren turned and scanned the park. "Where is Arlington with that damned crop?" He turned back to her and took her hands. "I care for you very much, and I like you just as you are."

"That's not true. You spank me all the time for displeasing you."

"Because you can be damned ornery when you feel like it. I love you, Josephine," he said, and realized he meant it. "Do you love me?"

She stared at him. "You love me?"

He frowned, all the angst of his confession swirling inside him. "Why are you answering my question with another question? You wonder why I spank you so much. Do you care for me, Josie?" That seemed a safer tack. "Do I make you happy? I'm trying to."

At last she squeezed his hands with a tremulous smile. "I do love you. Sometimes I can't believe you really love me, with my poor manners, and the way I irritate you."

"Sometimes I can't believe it either," he teased. "But I enjoy spanking you immensely," he added in a lower voice. "So I suppose it all squares up in the end."

Josephine tried to look outraged, but then laughed along with him, and he realized that yes, he hadn't lied. He loved her, and he ought to have told her so before now. What a humbling development, to fall in love with one's wife. His gentlemen friends would never stop ribbing him, just as they ribbed Townsend.

Warren decided he didn't really care.

Chapter Fifteen:
Choices

Warren held the sugar bowl for the Dowager Countess Overbrook, who happened to be one of the more influential dragons in society. Even better, the lady was his mother's older sister, and had dandled him on her knee when he was an infant. Such fond connections could prove useful, particularly when you were trying to secure your wife's position within the social tier.

"Are you comfortable?" he asked. "Are you sure you won't have another cake?"

"Oh, no. I've had quite enough. You know, my digestion is not what it was. I make it a rule not to overindulge."

He had counted nine cakes upon his aunt's plate at one point, but he gave a delicate and concerned tsk, and wished that she should be feeling better soon. After that, they fussed with chairs and place settings so she might not be too much in the sun. When she settled, she gave a great sigh of contentment.

"Indeed, one cannot fault the Duke of Arlington for his elegant garden parties," she said in her warbling voice. "His Grace's events are strictly upper crust."

"Yes, Auntie. Of a certainty," Warren agreed. The matron's line of vision did not include the front lawn, where a grabby game of Blind Man's Bluff was underway.

"And you, young Warren," she said, turning to him. "I must say you've turned out very smartly. Your mother would have been proud of the man you've become."

"How kind of you to say."

"She would have liked your new wife too. I heard from Lady Fairglen that your countess grew up an unclothed savage in the jungles of Africa, but I told her straight away that I'd not believe such nonsense, nor allow her to repeat it to anyone else. 'No,' I said to her, 'my nephew would never marry such a woman, even if she is a baroness.' She is a baroness, isn't she, dear Idylwild?"

He twitched at his hated given name, but he supposed his aunt had the right to use it. "She is the Baroness Maitland, it's true. Her holdings are near my land in Oxfordshire. And I assure you, she was raised to English ways, although her parents were inveterate travelers."

"I cannot fathom what inspires proper English people to strike out and travel to such godforsaken places, when they might stay safely at home."

"I suppose it's plain English grit and our society's glorious history of exploration." He said this with a straight face.

His aunt shone with approval at this bold announcement. "Well, I suppose there is much to be said for good English gumption. I cannot see your lady's suffered for her absence. She's obviously as cultured as you or I."

Warren accepted this compliment on his wife's behalf with true gratitude, for it meant society was coming to accept her as he'd hoped. Josephine was well on her way to earning the regard of her peers. She played her part perfectly, having pleasant conversation with the younger set of married ladies, mingling about and smiling as he'd encouraged her to do.

He wished to go to her, but he was rather entrenched with his dowager aunt. He looked around and met August's gaze. He made a subtle gesture—*help me!* In their wilder days of wenching and drinking, they'd developed an entire silent language based on degrees of glaring and secret flicks of fingers or wrists, or angles of their heads. August came obediently over to ask Warren if he would like to make the acquaintance of Lord So-and-So, and he agreed that he would very much like to meet this completely made-up fellow, and so he had the excuse he needed to bid farewell to his aunt and her aged friends.

"Thanks for rescuing me," said Warren, when they were far enough away. "How goes it? Did Arlington bribe you to come here?"

"No. I came for the cakes and tea, of course, and the scintillating conversation."

"As bad as all that, eh?" Warren frowned. "I suppose your china doll is here?"

"Yes, she is." His words gave no hint of his deeper feelings toward Lady Priscilla, either positive or negative, so Warren dropped the subject. They moved onto less fraught topics: August's new horse, recent debates at Parliament, and all the notable goings-on at their favored gentlemen's club. Warren was vaguely aware of guests strolling about, children laughing and shouting, and young ladies flirting with their suitors in the breezy, idyllic garden. Minette paid particular attention to a ginger-haired chap, cheering him on when the active game of Blind Man's Bluff game gave way to an even more active cricket match. Then he realized he hadn't seen his wife in some time.

"I say, where has Josephine gone?"

"Lost her again, have you?" August chuckled. "Not sure these wives are worth the trouble."

"Oh, they are," Warren said, looking around. "With any luck, you'll understand one day. Blast." He turned back to his friend. "I'm off to find her."

"Need help?"

Warren shook his head. "Not this time. She can't have gone far."

Even so, it took him twenty minutes to locate her. He couldn't very well shout for her, or charge about asking if anyone had seen her, and so he had to stroll around in a perfectly casual manner until he saw her rum pink gown peeking from behind a Greek temple folly down one of Arlington's paths.

He went to her, calling her name when he was close enough. "Josephine. Are you hiding?"

"No." She emerged, looking sheepish. "Well, yes. A little."

"Is there such a thing as hiding 'a little'?" He took her hand and squeezed it in a fit of pique. "You worried me. I didn't know where you'd gone."

"I'm sorry. I know Arlington is your friend, but I couldn't bear it any longer. Everyone is so snobbish and affected in manners. The women's prattle..." She shuddered. "Warren, you can't understand how cloying it is."

"I certainly can. I sat with my aunt and her friends for nearly an hour, for you, Josephine. To have them on our side."

"Our side? Are we at war?"

"I don't know. Perhaps we are." He let go of her hand and leaned against one of the smooth marble columns. Inside the miniature temple, Arlington had installed a whipping pole, along with a chest of aromatic oils and equipment to punish naughty ladies in the manner of a lewd Greek god. Warren might have done so to Josephine, if they weren't within yards of polite society.

"It's not the thing, to go wandering off during these sorts of functions," he said. "It makes you look sullen and impolite. It invites others to gossip and wonder what you're up to. It's one thing to go off with other ladies, but you mustn't stroll away alone."

"I know."

"Then why did you do it? Townsend and Aurelia found themselves in an unwanted marriage after going off alone into the woods."

She gave him an arch look. "So did we."

Warren straightened and crossed his arms over his chest. "All the more reason not to go off by yourself. Someone might see it as an invitation and join you here and make inappropriate advances, and nothing you could say or do would save your reputation."

"Of course my reputation is all that matters."

He narrowed his eyes at her. Why must she make him out to be the ogre? They weren't his rules, and it wasn't his fault they had to attend these parties. "I thought we agreed you were going to make a go at society. That you were going to give it a chance."

"I have." Her voice sharpened, rising with the color in her cheeks. "I've been trying but it's so tiresome. It never ends."

"The season ends in August, Josephine. It's not much longer. A few more weeks, and the social whirl will die down. Come, let's return before someone sees us quarreling out here."

"We wouldn't be quarreling if you'd only let me have a few moments in peace to collect myself. But, apparently, that is not permitted." She gathered up her skirts and flounced ahead of him, onto the path toward the house.

Again, he considered dragging her inside the temple and fixing her to Arlington's whipping pole, but it would only fuel gossip when he returned her to the company all rumpled, with tears in her eyes. He caught up with her and took her hand. After a small battle of wills, she permitted him to place it upon his arm.

"Behave yourself, for God's sake," he muttered. "You've been doing so well."

"I'm tired of doing well. I'm tired of everything. I'm tired of talking about recipes for lemon tarts, and fashions from Paris, and which damned ball is the one to be invited to this week."

He arched a brow at her rough language. "Perhaps we ought to head home, if you find the company so tedious that you must curse."

"Are you going to spank me there?"

"I believe you've earned a spanking, yes."

"For cursing?" She blinked at him in outrage. "You curse all the time."

"It's not only the cursing. You promised you would try to behave as a proper lady and countess. You promised to let me help you."

"I don't like the way you help me. Your spankings hurt, and they don't work to change me anyway."

"Whose fault is that?" He refused to continue arguing with her, not now when they were in sight of all the guests. "Go and sit with Minette and her friends for a while if you wish to be cross. They're merry enough that they won't notice. Only stay where I can see you," he said as he released her. "And Josephine?"

She looked back at him with a frown.

"Next time you head into the woods alone," he said, "rest assured I shall join you with a freshly cut switch."

* * * * *

They didn't leave at once. In fact, her husband made her stay at Arlington's affair for two more hours, while she seethed and twitched, and fretted over her coming punishment. At last, an impending rainstorm broke up the gathering and sent everyone home.

Later, as Josephine prepared for bed, a maid tapped at the door and delivered a silver tray Josephine had come to know well. She wondered what Warren would do if she took the ginger from inside and hurled it out the window. He'd undoubtedly be cross, and send to the kitchen for more. He seemed to have access to an endless supply.

If she protested loudly enough, would he cease doing these things to her? Did she want him to? It confused her, how she despised and yet desired his "punishments." The authority in his voice, the intensity in his gaze, the tension in his body as he arranged her over his lap. She had come to be excited by these things, even the ginger. She wanted these awful, indecent things, while polite aspects of society seemed beyond her grasp.

She could only conclude that she was an awful, indecent person. How else to explain her frustration with social niceties, and her boredom at balls and parties? But if she wanted Lord Warren with his grins and seductive depravity, she had to find a way to do the other things he wanted, like smile and be polite, and behave as a hoity-toity countess should. Otherwise she'd have to stay in the country, away from him, lest she threaten his all-important standing in society. In her absence, he'd be obliged to take a mistress or satisfy himself with other women; a man of his appetites wouldn't stay quietly at home if there was no one at that home to see to his needs.

By the time he showed up, she was nearly in tears about it. She let him think they were tears of penitence and remorse, as he stood her before him and delivered a lengthy lecture on manners and expectations, and all the woeful things that might happen to her reputation if she didn't play by the rules.

She only half listened. By now she'd heard a thousand variations of this theme. The weather worsened as he droned on at her. Hard droplets of rain pelted her bedroom windows and rumbling thunder provided an air of menace to the proceedings. She started to cry in earnest, miserable, silent tears that he occasionally wiped away.

"It's not your frustration I'm punishing you for, you understand? I'm not punishing you for feeling angry or sad."

"I know. It's because of what I do."

"Precisely. It's your actions, your choices. You didn't need to hide away at the garden party. If you wanted to escape the ladies' prattle, you might have gone to cheer at the game, or gone to the refreshment table, or visited with me for a while."

She nodded. She knew. Of course she knew.

"And when I came to fetch you, you were unnecessarily cross with me. You knew it would mean a spanking and you sniped at me anyway."

He didn't yell or scold, only stated the damning facts in a calm voice that made her feel ten times guiltier. "I know. I know," she said, wiping at her eyes. "I knew it was bad behavior, but I was just so tired."

"You'll be more tired still when this is over. Something to think about next time." He gave her a long, hard look and stood from his chair. "You will take off your dressing gown and shift, please, and bend over the side of the bed."

She undressed as quickly as she could with her hands shaking and her legs trembling, and her vision blurry with tears. As she bent over the bed, she saw him taking off his coat and waistcoat, and turning back his sleeves. He went to the tray for the ginger, the root carved as usual into a rounded bulb with plenty of feathered edges. She buried her face in the covers as he parted her bottom cheeks in a humiliatingly perfunctory way and inserted the rounded ginger. This wasn't the kind of touch that aroused. Oh, why couldn't she behave?

It always took a few minutes for the ginger to really start burning, which is why he made her wait there, clutching at the bed linens and dreaming of escape. The storm grew even more violent, with lightning flashes illuminating the dim room. Her bottom clenched around the fullness of the ginger, and all too soon the smarting, tingling sensation grew into a steadier ache.

When she started to moan and wiggle her bottom in anguish, he pulled her up and sat on the edge of the bed, securing her over his lap. Like most of his punitive spankings, there were no soft smacks to start with, to accustom her to the pain. No. The first one hurt, the second one hurt, and every spank afterward hurt. She gasped over his lap, knowing this was only the beginning, with much more to suffer. It already hurt so much!

The ginger's sting grew more acute, rising a degree in temperature each time he made her tense upon it. Her tears of guilt and sadness became tears of torment, as he punished her without any softness or sympathy. The smacks rained down, his hands hard like stone. Palms and fingers that touched her so gently now punished her with their rigid strength.

"Oh, I'm sorry," she cried. "I'm so sorry."

"I'm glad to hear it," he said, though he didn't stop spanking her. "You must learn proper behavior at social gatherings. You must learn to hold your tongue rather than say words which are neither pleasant nor respectful. And of course you must"—*smack*—"stop"—*smack*—"wandering into woods."

"I know. I'm sorry."

He'd taught her by now that she might say *I'm sorry* as much as she liked, but not *no*, or *stop that*, or even *please, please stop*. Because he would never stop, not until he decided she'd had as much punishment as she deserved. He made her feel so powerless—stripping her, putting ginger inside her, holding her firmly over his lap. She squirmed, but only so far. She cried, but only so hard.

Because some part of her needed this reassurance that he wouldn't give up on her.

"I'm so sorry," she wailed as the spanking picked up pace. When that happened, they were nearer the end than the beginning, not that it was much of a comfort. He moved from the throbbing center of her cheeks to the less punished areas lower on her bottom, alternating so each part stayed equally achy and hot. He was so skilled at punishing her to maximum potential, which was not at all a good thing. *Ow, ow, owww.*

He didn't stop until her entire backside felt flaming and used up. He lifted her off his lap and made her stand before him once again, only this time she was shivery and naked, and so sorry she hadn't just swanned around the party, and smiled, and simpered on about various topics the way she ought to have done. Were they worth it, her petty acts of defiance, when they only ever led to this? The storm seemed to have positioned itself directly over Park Street, for the thunder and lightning continued unabated, rattling vases and windows and lighting up her husband's face.

"Do you feel punished?" he asked at last.

She sniffled through the lingering waves of pain. "Yes, my lord."

"And yet I think I must exact some further form of atonement for your disrespectful behavior earlier. I am not quite satisfied."

Oh, no.

"I'll give you a choice," he said. "You may endure a second punishment session with fresh ginger, and a hair brush this time."

She shuddered. The dreaded hair brush! "Or?"

"Or you may have the ginger out, and have my cock inside your bottom for a good buggering. Both options will teach you a lesson, as well as put me in a better mood."

Those were her choices? They both sounded horrid. She gazed at him, feeling more naked with every second that passed. Her arms crept up to hide her breasts.

"No," he said. "Don't cover yourself. You know the rules."

"But I'm ashamed. And I'm afraid." She made fists at her sides to keep her hands still. "I don't want either one of those things, and they won't make me any better."

"They might." He stared at her, uncompromising discipline and stern will. "You're still resisting it, Josephine. It's time for you to accept your reality, your future. You're going to be a proper lady. If you fight me on this, I'll fight back in the only way I know."

"By punishing me. By making me bend and obey!"

"Yes." Thunder punctuated his sharp avowal. "Now, I've offered you two choices, of which you may choose one. I will mention that the second may possibly bring you pleasure. The first will not."

"But the second one will hurt!"

"So will the first one, my dear."

Josephine thought over her options. A paddling with the hair brush would really hurt, especially when her bottom was already sore. And fresh ginger? But to submit to the other...

"I can't choose," she said. "I'm too afraid. I don't want either one."

"Then I suppose I must make the decision."

"Yes, you're the one with all the power," she cried. "I suppose you will choose whichever will hurt and humiliate me the worst."

A corner of his mouth turned up. "I'm less concerned with hurt and humiliation and more concerned with getting you under control. Bend over the bed again."

"I don't want to."

Of course, that didn't matter. He bent her over himself and pushed her arms up over her head. "Do not move from this position, darling, unless you wish to experience both choices one after the other, and additional consequences too. Keep your palms flat on the bed."

She winced as he took out the ginger and disposed of it. Her breath came fast, rasping in her throat. She did feel out of control, and she didn't like it. "What are you going to do?" she asked.

"If you'd made a choice, you'd know. As it is, you'll have to wait and find out."

Oh, he was so maddening. She tried to stand up but he pushed her back down.

"You'd better stay as you are," he said.

He wasn't sending for ginger, or getting her hair brush, so she knew he planned to take her bottom. He removed his clothing and set it aside for his valet while she shivered and shook against the bed. She eyed his thick member as he kicked off his stockings and went to fetch the oil. My God, he was so large. Even with the oil, he would hurt her.

"Keep breathing," he said as he returned with the canister. He opened it and smeared a good amount of it around her spasming bottom hole. It soothed the lingering sting of the ginger but didn't do much to calm her fear. He pressed a finger inside her, inserted it deep, and then added another. She whimpered at the uncomfortable stretching. Two fingers felt achy and intrusive, and he was larger than two fingers by far.

"You know, on second thought," she said, "I... I would rather have the hair brush."

He pressed the fingers deeper. "You had your chance to choose, and gave the choice to me, and I've decided to bugger you into submission. It's difficult to be rebellious with a cock buried in your arse. Now relax, for God's sake. Let go of the covers and put your palms flat on the bed the way I told you."

She felt his thighs press against the back of her legs. He unfolded her fists by force and arranged her hands beside her head.

"I won't be rebellious anymore, I promise," she pleaded.

"No, you won't be, after this."

He eased his fingers inside her again, in and out. She tried to wiggle away but his legs and body held her trapped. "What if you hurt me?" she asked. "Please, I'm so afraid."

"It may hurt a bit at first. But just as with the bulb, if you relax and give your body time to adjust, you may come to find the sensation more tolerable. Even pleasurable, if I think you deserve to be rewarded." He withdrew his fingers and added more oil to her tensing backside. "Let's see if you can be a good girl rather than a rebellious one, and open up for my cock."

Oh my word. There had to be other, more civilized ways of putting down a wife's rebellion. He might decrease her pin money, or make her go without dinner until she apologized. This was so coarse, so invasive and frightening. She trembled as he pressed the tip of his shaft to her slickened opening and pressed forward a bit.

She scrunched her eyes closed. It *hurt*, rather too badly to be borne. Her timid whimper rose to a cry as he persisted. Her entire body tensed.

He rubbed the small of her back and made a soothing sound. "I know. It aches, doesn't it? This is the hardest part. Your little ring has to stretch, but you can do it. You only have to relax and let me in. Relax. Relax..." He pressed forward a bit more and she bit down on her lip. Just when she thought she must complain and fight him, he stopped and held very still, and waited that shallow distance inside her.

"It won't hurt any worse than this," he murmured. "It has nothing to do with depth, only the initial entrance, and you'll soon be used to that. Keep breathing. Palms flat, my love. You're in fists again."

She had gathered the bed linens into clumps. She straightened them out only to have something to distract her as her backside clenched around his thickness. She dreaded how it would feel when he began to move. Would she be able to bear it? How much pain could she tolerate before she broke down and begged for the hair brush?

But as he inched ever so slowly forward, she realized he was right, that the pain was no worse the deeper he went. If anything, it had eased somewhat.

"Oh," she whispered.

"Is it better now? At least a bit?"

"Yes," she answered. "But it still feels...scary."

"Sometimes it's good for naughty wives to feel scared." He moved inside her a bit more, the smooth, oily lubricant easing the way. How bizarre it felt. A bit like the ebony bulb, or the ginger, but there was so much more firmness and presence. He eased out a little, and then back again, and she thought she had never experienced anything so curious in her life. It didn't feel pleasurable, exactly, but it felt very...filling. It felt wicked and licentious.

She wanted more.

She arched her hips as he moved forward again, slowly sliding within her. "You like that, my little seductress," he said in a thick voice. He ran his palm up to her nape, holding her down and driving deeper. "I like it too. I like that my naughty wife is submitting to a firm buggering for her own good."

When he said things like that, she didn't know what to think, except that something was wrong with her, because it made her feel hot and lascivious and full of lust. She made a low, begging sound as his hands clamped on her shoulders.

"Yes, I won't stop until you've had enough," he said in a tone of assurance. "Until all that rebellion is forgotten."

She couldn't remember anything about rebellion anymore. She tensed her bottom, thinking how warm and strong her husband felt as he invaded her backside. She shouldn't want this. She *didn't* want this, but...she did.

As she pondered this strange form of "punishment," he wrapped his hands in her hair and jerked her head back. She gave a little yelp and his grip loosened, but still, his rough action unleashed something inside her, some hot, fast drumbeat of primeval desire.

"You may pull my hair again if you'd like," she whispered, too embarrassed to say such a thing aloud.

He did pull it again, and this time, he leaned down to bite her ear, not hard enough to injure her, but hard enough for it to hurt. She moaned like a wild, trapped creature as he trailed sharp bites down her neck and caressed her in the roughest, most provocative manner. He gripped her pussy and encouraged her when she jerked her sensitive button forward against his palm. When she thought he might make her come then and there, he stopped and played with her nipples, sliding his hands between her breasts and the bed to twist the sensitive points.

"Oh, my. Warren!" she gasped. It hurt so badly she cringed, but it was the delicious type of hurt he was so good at. Meanwhile, he drove in and out of her bottom, pressing deeper each time so her muscles gripped the rock-solid intrusion. These firm, deep thrusts didn't hurt in the least, not anymore. In fact, they were coming to feel quite good.

"Please touch me again," she begged. "Please touch me there."

"Where?" he asked. "Use the word for me."

"Touch my pussy, please." Her entire middle felt hot and heavy, and desperate for more. He slid his hand down between her folds and found her favorite place, and manipulated it as he slid in and out of her.

"Yes, yes, please," she blathered over and over. "Yes, yes, yes." He rode her so firmly that her toes lifted from the floor and her hips bounced against the edge of the bed, but she didn't care. She was so close to completion. If he'd only keep... touching... her... there....

She reached her peak with a wailing cry. He turned her face and kissed her as she panted for air, her body wracked by wave after wave of pleasure. Now he was the one reaching for his climax, groaning, straining, driving against her. His body tautened and he went still, buried mercilessly deep. Then he bucked, muttering an oath and lifting her toes quite away from the floor before he sighed and collapsed atop her.

Josephine sucked in air, lying limp upon the bed. She had gathered up clumps of sheets again, but this time she buried her face in them with a feeling of floating. Her body still pulsed around his rigid length. Warren laid his head beside hers and stroked her hair.

"My good girl," he said after a while. "My very naughty good girl."

She let out a ragged breath. "How can I be good and naughty at once?"

"Don't worry about that. Are you in a better temper?"

She wasn't sure if she was in a better temper. She was still too shocked by what he'd done—and the fact that she'd very much enjoyed it. She felt exposed and wicked, and yet satisfied. She felt very close to him in an intimate way. "Will you want to do that again?" she asked.

"Right now?" He laughed and caught her chin when she tried to hide her face. "It wasn't so bad, was it?"

"It was better than more ginger and the hair brush."

His smile tickled her cheek. "Perhaps we'll save this sort of congress for your most rebellious moments. It seems to have calmed you considerably, as any good buggering should."

She wiggled her bottom as he pressed within her. He growled and clapped his hands over her hips.

"Don't tempt me to begin again. Be still." After a moment he withdrew from her slowly, leaving her empty inside. He tossed her up onto the bed and curled around her, cradling her in his embrace. "I'm not sure we can truly call that punishment, although I am feeling better. In fact, I'm feeling quite happy. I barely remember your wrongs from this afternoon."

Josephine remembered them, but they probably seemed more appalling to her. She was tormented by all her mistakes, big and small. She wanted to make him happy, she truly did, because she didn't want to lose him. She was glad he punished her for poor behavior, because it gave her the incentive to behave correctly in future situations. It reminded her that he cared.

"Thank you," she said. "I do feel calmer."

He rubbed a palm across her bottom and gave her a light, brisk spank. "I'm always happy to help."

How light he could be, after reducing her to such depths of emotional darkness. She hardly understood him, except that he loved her and always seemed to know the best things to do. "You're a very good help to me." Her voice trembled a little, until she strengthened it. "I know that you care, and that you're trying to make me better."

"Not better. Happier." He leaned over her, capturing her gaze. "I want you to be happy with yourself. I want you to become that fine, esteemed lady you've always wished to be."

"Yes, I know. I...I love you."

He'd said it to her before, many times, and she'd dutifully said it back, but she'd never really meant the words in her heart and in her soul, not until now.

He gazed at her with his deep blue eyes. "I love you more than words can say. You know that, don't you? You're my beautiful, brave girl."

She lay beside him and vowed to live up to that praise, to keep improving herself for his sake, even if the only thing she improved was her self-control. Self-control would help her do and say all the things she had to for propriety's sake, and that would be enough to help him retain the necessary standing among his peers. He would be happy, and if she was with him, she'd be happy too.

They roused themselves to wash up and then tumbled back into bed together. The storm had blustered out, leaving behind faint, faraway rumbles. She snuggled into his chest, feeling very safe and very warm.

"I never knew marriage could be this way," he said as he held her close. "I never knew I could feel this way about another person."

I hope you'll always feel this way about me, she thought. *I'm not sure I could survive it if you stopped loving me.*

The storm outside had gone, but the storm within her raged as violently as ever. That night, she dreamed of dozens of stalking tigers surrounding her, and knew she mustn't fail her husband—or herself.

Chapter Sixteen: Self-Control

By pure force of will, Josephine managed to keep herself out of trouble for the next few weeks. Any spankings she received were of the more playful variety, to keep her focused, and she didn't mind those very much. Her love for her husband grew, along with a novel sense of contentment in her situation. The season's whirl became more bearable with Warren's encouragement, and by mid-summer, the hustle-bustle of parties and merriment tapered off. Soon, the gentry would begin their yearly exodus from London as the season drew to a close.

In the meantime, society's families cemented betrothals, threw final balls and dinners, and made their plans for fall and winter visits. Some would attend house parties with friends, while others would retreat to their sprawling manors to hunt, drink, and play cards.

A few men sought Warren's permission to offer for Minette, but she would have none of them, and Josephine was secretly glad, because she had come to depend on her vivacious friend's company, especially as the great Parliament dinner loomed. The most powerful and influential members of the House of Lords closed the season every year with a private dinner party. Invitations were exclusive and hard to come by.

Of course Warren received one, the insufferable man.

The day of the dinner dawned sunny and bright. Josephine was obliged to report to her rooms in the afternoon, to dress in her most elegant ivory-and-pearl ensemble, and let the maid do all sorts of decorative curling and arranging of her hair.

Minette stayed with her as she fretted, and patted her hand. "Don't be nervous, all right? Yes, it's a big dinner, and yes, all of Warren's colleagues will be there with their wives, and yes, everyone will be watching you especially, since you and Warren have recently married—"

"Minette, you're not helping."

"You didn't let me finish. I was going to say that in the end it doesn't matter, because they all think Warren is the most proper and estimable fellow, and they've come to think the same of you. You've become so much better at conversation and dancing, and you're so graceful when you walk, and you have the prettiest figure for gowns, everybody notes it. You know all the different titles and how to address people, and how to ply your fan, and how to toss your head just the right way when you talk." As she said this, Minette demonstrated with impish detail, perfectly imitating the *ton*'s most lofty ladies. "So you see, it shall all be fine, and you mustn't worry about anything. My brother is so proud to have married such a highly regarded woman. He's been in a tizzy for weeks, just waiting for this dinner to arrive."

Josephine rested her head in her hands. She knew her sister-in-law meant to be helpful, but every word made her more anxious about the evening to come.

Self-control. You'll only need to use self-control, and be the perfect wife. This would be her chance to win everyone over and fix her place in society as his worthy partner. She only needed to be...perfect.

"Oh, my word," she sighed, raising her head. "I think I need more tea."

"No, my dear. You'll bloat beneath your stays."

Josephine frowned and sent the tray away with the maid. Her stays already felt tight, perhaps because of nerves, or the extra cakes she ate to forget her woes.

"There, sister, you look absolutely beautiful," said Minette, tugging one of Josephine's curls. "You mustn't worry. Warren will tell you what to do and who is most important to talk to. They'll mostly be stuffy old men and haughty ladies, but keep your conversation to homemaking and weather and none of them will take offense. Just smile a lot." She pinched her cheeks. "Smile. Smile!"

Josephine smiled into the mirror. She looked rather ill.

"I wish you would go in my place," she said. "Everyone loves you. You've such a gift at conversation."

"Of course I can't go," laughed Minette. "Warren wouldn't take his sister when he has a wife. What gossip it would cause, and Josephine, everyone loves you, too. Don't you understand that? Everyone finds you fascinating and beautiful."

Beautiful? Josephine touched the delicate diamond and pearl necklace Warren had given her for her birthday the week before. The pale gold filigree was worked to look like ivy, and it caught the light just so whenever she moved. It suited the dress perfectly, and it was beautiful, but she felt like a fake. She had never worn jewelry or fine gowns until she came to England. As much as Warren hoped to improve her, her uncivilized past would never go away. It would always be a secret shame inside her that no jeweled necklace or fancy gown could disguise. She was shoddy and second-rate, like her laughable, run-down "holdings" in Oxfordshire.

She rubbed her temples and shook her head. She ought not to be in such a mindset, not before this important gathering. Of all the fetes she'd attended at Warren's behest, this evening's would have the most direct effect on his political career and aspirations. When she went down the grand staircase to meet him, she rallied her courage and pasted on a smile. It became a genuine smile as her husband pretended to falter in a swoon.

"You're too ravishing to be borne," he said. "You look like a goddess. You'll outshine the queen."

She halted on the last step. "Will the queen be in attendance?"

"Probably not, but if she was, we'd have to drape a cloth over you or something."

"Warren, you're as silly as Minette sometimes."

He took her hand and pressed a kiss to her cheek. She breathed in the scent of him, masculine and crisp, with a hint of shaving soap. His ornately tied cravat was high and starched, glaringly white against his formal black coat and waistcoat. His blond curls shone in the light, so pretty on Minette, but fully masculine and handsome on him. He looked incredibly dashing.

From above, Minette clapped her hands. "The two of you are a sight. You must sit for a portrait in those clothes. Promise me! How stunning you both look."

They said their goodbyes and climbed into the coach waiting outside the door. All too soon they arrived at the Duke of Lansing's sprawling mansion a few streets over, where the dinner was to be held. "Every year a different fellow hosts the festivities," said Warren. "I suppose one year it shall be our turn. No, don't blanch, my love. It won't be anytime soon."

She looked up at the grand edifice of the duke's home, and then down the street at all the majestically appointed carriages of London's upper crust and almost choked at the idea of hosting such a gathering. She hoped it was ten years in the future. Twenty years.

"You know, the Duke of Lansing is Aurelia's father," he said. "She grew up in this house, if you can believe it."

Josephine could make no reply to that, since she was occupied staring at the crowds and the lights. Even Warren looked on the grand granite facade of the duke's city home with an air of wonderment. It was that outrageous and ornate. A fancy colonnade ran the length of the house, and great clusters of guests stood about looking haughty and important.

"I daresay Aurelia will be here tonight with Townsend. Arlington has been invited too, so you'll have some familiar faces."

"I don't feel well," Josephine said, gripping his arm.

"Now, now. You mustn't panic. I have faith in you. Be your charming self and everything shall be fine."

Her charming self? What of her panicking self? Or the self that required regular spankings to be tamed?

He led her into the mass of aristocrats, gentlemen and ladies with coronets and medals, and ostrich-feathered turbans, and glittering rings and jewels. Her ivy necklace, which had seemed so ostentatious in her dressing room, seemed nothing more than a trinket compared to the thick ropes of gold and gems around these ladies' necks. A tall, thin man raised a quizzing glass to regard her. She didn't know whether to smile or look serious as he gawked at her.

"My goodness," she murmured in Warren's ear. "Please don't let go of me."

He didn't, not once, as he introduced her to a never-ending parade of people. Some of them she recognized, but some of the older aristocrats did not socialize as much, or at least attend the balls and parties they did. They all scrutinized her with curiosity, but most were polite. Stafford was there, looking pompous and jealous, and perhaps a bit awed by how different she looked now that she wasn't hiding in black. "He wishes he'd married you," Warren whispered to her. "Pitiable fool."

Aurelia's father, the host, seemed even more pompous than Lord Stafford. He wore a ducal coronet and robes and seemed quite puffed up with his own importance. If she and Aurelia had a moment alone, they might have had a giggle about it, but her friend was occupied on her husband's arm. Josephine did her best to copy her regal bearing, and blank her expression to one of refined hauteur.

Self-control. It's just an act. You can do this, for your husband's sake.

All was well and Josephine felt relatively secure until they were called inside to be seated for dinner. This task took three quarters of an hour, since people were still talking and exchanging introductions. They milled about in the soaring ballroom, which had been outfitted with two long tables set for two hundred guests. Everyone pored over the seating cards, laughing and talking before they located their assigned seats. It was considered gauche to seat husbands and wives together, so she had expected to be separated from Warren. She just hadn't realized they would be separated quite so far.

She was near the head of one table, across from Lady Astbury and between Lord Merryworth and some other older gentleman. From a few seats down, Lord Townsend gave her a fortifying smile. Warren was halfway to the other end of the table with the Duke of Arlington, while Aurelia was seated near her mother and the Earl of Stafford at the foot of the second table. Josephine could just catch a glimpse of her husband beyond the table settings and large candelabras. He smiled and winked at her, completely at ease. Yes, she must be at ease also. She only had to dine and make polite conversation about nothing. How difficult could it be?

For a time, it wasn't difficult at all. Lady Astbury and Lady Burke, in her immediate vicinity, were avid conversationalists—it would be unkind to call them gossips, although that was what they were. They kept up a steady stream of banter about goings-on in Parliament, and the best parties of the season, and the most notable matches between families. Josephine recalled that Lady Burke's son had courted Minette, and so when the lady asked after "Lord Warren's sister" in a chilly tone, Josephine assured her she was very well, and thought her son must have been one of the men Minette refused.

From there, the conversation turned to plans for travel. Lord Merryworth, whom Josephine suspected was tired of listening to Lady Burke and Lady Astbury, fixed his gaze upon her. "I believe we have a very experienced traveler in our midst. Lady Warren, is it true you grew up on an undiscovered island in the Pacific?"

Well, that was a new one. She smiled and shook her head. "I'm afraid you've been misinformed. I grew up in Africa and India, among other places. It's true I've traveled a lot. My parents were never inclined to stay in one place."

"Oh, you must tell us stories of your outrageous experiences," Lady Burke exclaimed. "Africa and India! I cannot imagine the things you've seen."

"I'm sorry I have no outrageous stories to tell," she lied. In truth, she had seen thousands of outrageous things, most of which she wished she could forget. "We lived there very much as you live here, with English customs and English ways."

There were faint murmurs of approval. Of course, it was only well and good in their mind that one would not live as a savage among savages when one was finely bred. If they knew the truth of how she'd grown up, they would snub her to the grave.

"Do you miss the wayfaring lifestyle, now that you've returned to England?" another gentleman asked. He, at least, didn't seem bent on mockery, but genuinely interested. In fact, several more faces had turned their way.

"I don't imagine Warren is eager to take you back to those places," another man said in a booming voice.

Josephine forced a smile. "We're exceedingly happy here in England. I don't miss traveling, no."

"But where on earth did you live?" asked another lady. "In huts, or tents? Where does one live in those places?"

"They have houses there," said Josephine. "Not as grand as this one, but they have them."

A few of them chuckled at that. An elderly gentleman next to Lady Astbury asked if Josephine spoke any primitive languages, to which she replied, truthfully, that she did not.

"But how did you communicate with your servants?" Lady Astbury asked. Her unctuous tone set Josephine's teeth on edge. These privileged aristocrats had no idea about the larger world or what it was like in the places she'd lived. Servants? Sometimes even food and water was not a guaranteed thing. Of course she couldn't say such things without shocking everyone.

She had no idea what to say.

"I suppose if one wanted to order servants to do various tasks, one could make one's wishes known without formal language," said another man.

"With a whip," jested the elderly gentleman. "That's how we did it in the king's navy, when we landed on some misbegotten shore."

Everyone laughed at this. Josephine put down her silverware and met Lord Townsend's gaze with a beseeching look. He tried twice to steer the table's discussion in another direction, to no avail.

"I've been to Africa and India both," said the portly gentleman with the booming voice. "You must have your husband bring you to Westmoreland, Lady Warren, where you may see my many hunting trophies."

"What are hunting trophies?" she asked, imagining medals or plaques or some such thing. Polite laughter sounded all around her.

"Hunting trophies are deceased wild animals," said the man next to her, "skinned and mounted on the wall."

"Yes, animals I've shot," the booming fellow said proudly. "I brought down my first wild beast in Africa many years ago. Such vistas, such beautiful, wild land. My friends and I went looking for lions and giraffes and such. Amazing creatures, when you see them in their own habitat."

Josephine took a sip of wine as those around her exclaimed how exciting that was. Exciting, to slaughter Africa's wild animals for sport? She'd seen giraffes on the plains, and lions. And tigers too, in India...

None of these people had hearts, she was certain they didn't. She wished she could push back her chair and go to Warren and beg him to take her home. He could spank her, bugger her, whatever he liked, anything but this vile conversation.

"There was an elephant the third day we were there," the man went on. "We separated it from its group and I'll tell you, it took a dozen or more shots to bring the thing to its knees."

"I say," Lord Townsend interrupted in a sharp voice. "Perhaps you will upset the ladies with this sort of talk. Especially over dinner."

"You shot an elephant?" cooed Lady Astbury, not sounding upset at all.

"Yes, my chaps and I. It wasn't an easy thing. But best of all were the tigers we shot in India. You couldn't believe how big they were, and how sleek and fast." He threw back his head and gave a poor imitation of a tiger's snarl. Josephine balled her fists in her lap to keep herself from throwing her glass in his face. "I've a tiger skin on the floor of my study now," he went on, "and a great, vicious creature it looks. We shot one of the biggest males in the pride, or whatever their groups are called. Packs?"

"I believe a group of tigers is called a streak," said Lord Merryworth. "Perhaps Lady Warren will know."

Josephine couldn't do anything but stare at her plate and seethe in silent hatred.

"Did you know a group of martens is called a richness?" she heard Lord Townsend ask. "I learned that at Oxford, along with a great many other useless things. Say, Merryworth, you're an Oxford man too, aren't you?"

Josephine was grateful for his efforts at changing the topic, but the other ladies and the pompous man—Lord Westmoreland?—couldn't seem to let it rest.

"I believe you must have ventured into a jungle to find those tigers," said Lady Astbury, leaning across her soup to bat her lashes at the man.

"Oh, yes, we did. Humid, ghastly places, jungles. Nothing like the wide, rolling fields of England."

"It sounds so dangerous," said Lady Burke, simpering as if she were not a woman of sixty years or greater.

"It was, I warrant, but I was a young man full of myself, and I had no fear."

"Because you had rifles, you and all your cohorts." Josephine snapped her mouth shut as soon as she realized the sharp words had come from her.

"Well, I wasn't going to bring the beast down with my bare hands," the man joked in the silence following her remark. "I'm not that brave."

"I don't think you're brave at all," she said in a heated voice. "And I don't think you ought to be bragging about killing a majestic, wild creature that only wished to be left alone."

Now everyone was staring. Lord Westmoreland thrust his chin out a little as he leaned back in his chair. "Now, Lady Warren, I gather you have a soft spot in your heart for animals, but tigers are vicious beasts that hunt and kill without remorse. The world can do with a few less, in my opinion."

"They hunt and kill for survival, not for sport, which is more than I can say for you," she replied, scowling at the odious man. "And what of the poor elephant you shot a dozen times? They're gentle and peaceful. I can't believe you killed one for the mere fun of it, and that you'll crow so proudly about it here, among civilized company. Hunting trophies, indeed. I suppose it makes you feel very important to tread over your tiger carpet, but I find the idea of it revolting in the extreme."

She realized the room had gone quiet, and that, at some point, she had taken to her feet. Lord Townsend stared at her, wide-eyed, as if she'd lost her mind. None of the other gazes she met were friendly, and Lord Warren was too far away to save her from this debacle, even if he could.

There was no way she could sit back down and continue to eat as if nothing had happened, and there was no way to disappear into the floorboards, so she did the only other thing she could. She lifted her skirts, turned toward the door, and fled.

Chapter Seventeen: Falling to Pieces

Josephine found her way outside, brushing past a footman onto the now-deserted grand colonnade. What a monumental mistake she had made. What a disaster, to cause a scene before everyone, before Townsend and Aurelia and Arlington, and Lord Stafford, and all her husband's most powerful friends.

She buried her face in her hands, trying to catch her breath. She had to get away. She had to go hide, and cry, and tear at her hair in frustration. All her hard work to fit into society, destroyed in one undisciplined outburst. Why couldn't she be like Aurelia, sitting so calmly and politely? Or the other ladies, so confident in their manners?

She knew why. She didn't belong with these people and she never would. She was a shabby baroness of a shabby manor in the country, raised in ghastly jungles amidst vicious beasts. She was the dreaded *baga lika*, and she'd never be anything more, no matter her husband's riches or political career. She stumbled forward, looking up and down the line of carriages for one she recognized, but there were too many to count. She reached to pull her wrap closer around her and realized she had left it behind.

"You can't do anything right," she said to herself. "Stupid, stupid girl."

"Josephine!"

She turned at her husband's voice. He'd emerged from the house with her wrap bunched up in his hands, and covered the ground between them in great, angry strides. "Josephine Bernard, you utter madwoman. What on earth were you about, attacking the Earl of Westmoreland in front of two hundred of his peers? Have you completely lost your mind?"

She angled herself away from him. "I want to go home."

"Oh, you're going home. You're certainly not going to rejoin the dinner after you made such a spectacle of yourself. Here."

He thrust the wrap toward her, and helped her bundle it over her shoulders while lecturing her in a scathing voice. "I can't imagine what you meant by that display. Standing up and shaking your finger at Westmoreland as if he were some errant schoolboy. My dear, he is the head of Parliament's foremost political committee, not to mention a senior member in the ministry of finance and reform."

"How was I to know that?" She bristled. "He shoots tigers and lions and elephants for sport. Only to kill them! To make carpets for his study!"

"Plenty of gentlemen kill for sport. It's not your place to judge. It's your place to sit quietly and look pretty and—"

"And simper in a sweet little voice what a marvelous hero he is? I can't do it. I can't bear this anymore. I hate all of these people."

"Hush." He put a finger over her mouth as her voice rose in volume. "That's all we need to complete the performance, is you standing out here raving at the top of your lungs." He looked back over his shoulder. In the darkness, Josephine imagined the guests spying on her, pulling back curtains to gape and twitter and tsk at the daft countess. She shivered in revulsion. She couldn't bear to feel this way ever again.

"Come along to the carriage." At some point he must have signaled it, for the correct one came rolling to the front of the house. "I don't know why you couldn't bite your damned tongue for propriety's sake. All English ladies do it. It's not that hard. You might have told me later, amongst ourselves, that Westmoreland annoyed you. I would have agreed with you. You might have privately expressed your anger, even your outrage, and I wouldn't have faulted you for it, but no, you must rail at him before everyone. You must make a great dramatic scene."

"I didn't mean to," she cried. "It's only that they wouldn't stop talking about my exotic travels, and giving me those looks, like I'm some half-dressed native sitting at the table."

"You're the only one who sees that," he said, throwing up his hands. "You believe it about yourself and so you think everyone believes it. They were talking about hunting, for God's sake, not you and your blasted tiger, or the way you grew up. I thought you had left all that behind by now. You looked beautiful tonight, every inch a civilized and dignified lady, and then you opened your goddamned mouth."

She stared at him, at his pursed lips and his hard blue eyes. She hadn't believed him capable of such cruel words, such heartless disregard for her struggles. She had only been trying to please him. "I won't talk anymore, then," she said, fighting tears. "I won't say a word ever again, not to you or anyone."

"I wonder how long that will last," he scoffed.

"Forever. I'll go away. Then you won't have to listen to my 'goddamned mouth' ever again."

He took her arm hard, almost painfully. The groom stood by the carriage steps, pretending not to notice. "Listen to me, dearest," he said through gritted teeth. "You are going absolutely nowhere, except home to await me in your room."

"You said I could go away if I wanted," she reminded him a bit hysterically. "You said I could hide in the country."

"And you said you would try to do better, so you wouldn't have to," he snapped. "Is that what you did this evening? Tried to do better? It didn't seem so to me, when you were throwing a tantrum in front of my entire set, even Lord Stafford, for God's sake. Was that your intention, to humiliate me to the worst possible degree in front of everyone I know?"

She shook off his grip and pushed him away. "I want to leave you," she shouted. "I hate you for making me go to these things when it's obvious I'm not happy. I hate you for making me smile and lie, and pretend to be content. All you care about is what other people think, and your precious political career. Why should you care about my feelings? I'm only your wife."

"Josephine," he said in a warning tone. "That's enough."

"I want to leave you," she said again, her voice rising over his. "I want to go away and live on my own, away from these people you call your friends."

He clasped her arm harder, pulling her right against him. "You're not leaving me, you understand? I never should have said that, because I won't allow it."

"You can't stop me. I'm a baroness with my own land and fortune."

His derisive snort hurt even worse than his grip on her arm. "Your land and fortune? Good luck with that, darling."

She stuck her chin out. "I have enough to get by. Enough to live quietly and comfortably, which is all I ever wanted to do. And you'll be happy to be rid of me."

He scowled down at her, not answering. What did she want him to say? That she was wrong? That he needed her and loved her? Tonight's events proved beyond a doubt that he'd be better off without her. He probably wished at the moment that he'd left her to Stafford. Stafford ought to have been her fate.

"Why can't you just let me be who I am? An inappropriate and awful person whom no one likes?" Her voice rose to a shriek. "I won't change, not ever. This is who I am and who I'll always be. I'm going to Maitland Glen and I'm going to stay there, and you can't stop me."

The groom witnessed all of this, blank-faced, the door in his hands. Warren's expression broke her heart. He felt no pity, no sympathy.

"You are ridiculous when you get this way." He hustled her up the steps and into the carriage's dark interior. "I can't even speak to you in this state. But rest assured we'll continue this discussion later."

She had very little trouble understanding the tone of threat in his voice. This continuation would doubtless include some sort of severe punishment. Anxiety rose and constricted her throat.

"I don't want to discuss anything," she said. "I'm going to Maitland Glen."

"Like hell you are. You're going home to wait for me, as I instructed you. In the meantime, I have to go back in there to try to fix the damage you caused. I'll have to tell everyone some made-up story about why your nerves were frayed to the breaking point, so they can talk about that rather than your melodramatic tirade."

"People shouldn't kill tigers," she yelled as he backed down the steps. "Even pompous Lord Wester-whoever-he-is."

"Westmoreland. Damn you, Josephine," he yelled back, slamming the carriage door.

She was shut in darkness, cradled in the cushioned luxury of her husband's largesse. Silence resounded after their heated exchange and her arm throbbed where he'd gripped it. She felt as if she were falling to pieces, one trembling limb at a time.

Why had he said such things to her? And why had she shouted back at him that she wanted to leave him? It wasn't true. She only wanted him to accept her, to see her as more than some form of career currency. She needed him for his laughter and his smiles, and the way he encouraged her, but she'd failed him, and the truth was, she always would. She was a wild, pathetic creature like the poor elephants and lions that man had killed. Like the tiger on his study floor...

She knew she would dream of tigers tonight, toss and turn in terror-filled nightmares. Escaping that ballroom had been like running out into the jungle, fearful for her life. The feelings of danger and hysteria had been right there, vivid as the day her parents died. She put her head in her hands, chasing away the memories. Perhaps she ought to go back to India or Africa, where at least she wasn't expected to fit in. But such travel was out of the question, at least for now.

There was only one place she could run to in England, one place that was completely her own, where she could hide from her pain and feelings and love for Lord Warren. Once she was there he would understand it was best, and perhaps he'd let her remain there.

It was her home, her only home, no matter how shabby and run-down it was.

* * * * *

Warren knew he shouldn't be at the club. He ought to be home working things out with his wife, but he was too disturbed by the wretched things they'd said to each other. Hated him, did she? He rather hated himself.

He'd sat down to a game of cards with Stafford, for no other reason than to punish himself for his actions. He was losing badly, but he deserved it and so he kept throwing down money and playing more hands. Finally Townsend showed up and extracted him from his spiral, inviting him to a quieter parlor for a drink.

Why not? He was already spectacularly drunk and hoped to be even drunker before he stumbled home to pass out. Towns caught him when he tripped and almost pitched to the floor. Not very dignified, falling down drunk. Certainly no more dignified than Josephine bawling out Westmoreland, but Warren was a man, and therefore permitted to publicly act like an arse every once in a while.

"Steady on," murmured Townsend, leading him to a deep, upholstered bench. "You're losing your touch, Warren. You used to be able to drink all of us under the table, and still get the prettiest ladies."

"Because my cock is impervious to spirits," he said.

"Maybe a little quieter," replied Townsend, glancing around. "Was it necessary to drink yourself into a stupor over this?"

"You were there. You tell me."

Townsend grimaced. "They hounded her a bit, I think, and that's why she snapped the way she did. I tried to change the subject several times, but you know Westmoreland when he starts blathering on."

"Someone told me she called him a fat old hound."

"She didn't. People are exaggerating, as they always do when something sensational happens. Westmoreland won't hold a grudge."

"Yes, he will." Warren groaned, burying his head in his hands. "Why's the fellow got to go around shooting wild animals and bragging about it to my wife, anyway? She apparently loves the damn things."

"She has a good heart."

He grasped his friend's sleeve. "She's good all over, and don't let anyone tell you otherwise. She's a magnificent woman."

"Of course." Townsend gently disengaged his fingers.

"I married her because I had to, but I wouldn't have anyone else now. She lets me do things to her that even Odd Sally—"

Townsend shushed him. "Let's not talk about that here. Blast, you're tipsy as a wheelbarrow." He took away Warren's half-filled glass of brandy before he could drain the rest. His friend asked the attendant for strong tea and Warren swore at him. Meddling friends.

Townsend swore back at him, oath for oath. "It's time to stop wallowing in liquor and cards and put your mind to fixing this mess," he said when the attendant left them. "My wife did what she could to defend Josephine afterward, but you know how ladies are. If you don't do something to stem the tide of gossip, they'll still be talking about this next season."

"By next season, Josie will have done a dozen more outrageous things for people to talk about, and Westmoreland will hate me forever."

Townsend gave him a sharp look. "Does Westmoreland's regard mean more to you than your wife?"

"Westmoreland could be prime minister," Warren slurred in his defense. "She oughtn't to have ripped up at the man."

"But she did, and what's done is done. Do you care for her? Enough to forgive her?"

Warren felt old and tired. And guilty. Poor Josephine, his tiger girl.

"I shook her and yelled at her out by the carriage," he said. "I swore at her. She dreams about tigers, Townsend. She cries sometimes in her sleep. It's even worse than Minette and her wanderings."

His friend watched him. Warren wasn't sure he was making any sense but it was all too clear in his own mind. He'd been a horrid, selfish bastard. All he had cared about was himself, his need for her to be accepted, to be social and outgoing when it wasn't in her nature. *Why can't you just let me be who I am?* Inappropriate and awful, she had said, but it wasn't true.

"She wants to leave me. She wants to live at Maitland Glen." He put his head down on his arm and slumped upon the bench.

"I'm sure she doesn't want to leave you," said Townsend. "She was only upset."

"She ought to leave me. I'm a bastard of a husband."

"You've been a good husband to her. You've been faithful. You've tried to help her." He nudged his arm. "Listen, we all make mistakes. I've done things to my wife I'll always regret, but she forgave me. I've tried not to do them again, but I probably will one day, and I pray she'll forgive me again. That's love, Warren. It's not always pretty."

Warren levered himself up. He must look a sight, mumbling and slobbering drunk. He took some of the tea, thinking of life without Josephine. She hated him. He believed that she did. He also believed he deserved it.

"I don't want her to leave me." He put his cup down with such force he nearly shattered the thing. "I'll tell her she can't."

"That sounds reasonable. Only…say it a bit more romantically, with a softer edge."

"But I've already promised she could, if society didn't suit her. I said she could stay in Oxfordshire. What am I to do?"

August arrived, looking rather dissolute in his shirt sleeves, with his thick black hair in need of a comb. "Good evening, gents," he said by way of greeting. "Warren, is it true your wife called Westmoreland a loathsome pig at the Parliament dinner, and upended a tureen of soup in his face?"

Warren looked at Townsend and then August in dismay. "Really? That's the story now?"

August sat next to Warren on the bench and slung an arm about his shoulders. "Never mind. I understand you're to be congratulated."

Warren shook his head. "I'm not to be congratulated."

"Your wife's not pregnant?" At Warren's irked look, August sobered. "Goodness, what a lot of talk going around tonight, and all of it nonsense. I had so hoped she called him a pig, anyway, and doused him with hot soup."

Warren kneaded his temples. He signaled for more brandy but Townsend waved the man away before it could be presented.

"You rotted bastard," said Warren. "I need another drink."

"You need to go home to your wife," he replied calmly. "It's four in the morning."

"What am I going to say to her?"

Townsend thought a moment, as August wandered off. "I suppose you must say things to change her mind. Things to make her love you again and want to stay."

But by the time Warren arrived home, he hadn't the choice to say anything at all. She had already departed in his traveling coach, leaving behind a succinct note.

Dear Warren,

I've gone to Maitland. I should never have said I hated you, because that isn't true. I just don't think I can be the wife you need.

There was no signature, only a bit of a mark that might have been a smudge, or the dried drop of a tear.

He let the paper flutter to the ground. She'd left him, the vexatious woman. Her and her melodramatic flights. Enough was enough. He wasn't going to allow it.

He'd never let her go.

Chapter Eighteen: No More

The carriage rode through the night and on through morning, manned by a small group of servants who insisted on accompanying her in spite of her husband's certain wrath. Two coachmen, a groom and a maid, and another outrider she suspected was armed. She had hoped to sneak away with one groom perhaps, and a maid to help at the house until she got settled, but they were not at all inclined to allow that.

"Lord Warren would have our heads, ma'am, if anything happened," said Prescott, the outrider. They seemed to understand, with servants' subtle intuition, that she would go to Maitland Glen either way, and thought it better to look after her than risk the master's ire should she come to harm.

But she thought they set a laggardly pace, and stopped a great many times, the better for Lord Warren to catch up with them. They were, after all, *his* servants, and it was his carriage and horses that conveyed her, with the gowns and shawls and slippers he'd purchased her stowed in the back. The maid had long since fallen asleep on the opposite bench, her head bobbing against the pile of Josephine's hastily assembled belongings.

She wasn't running away again, Josephine kept reminding herself. Her husband had promised she might live in the country if she wished.

She was only removing to her own home and her own legal property, which was certainly within her rights. But when she tried to sleep, she couldn't manage it, even exhausted as she was. As the carriage plodded along, her senses strained for the sounds of approaching hoof beats, for Warren's yelling voice demanding she come home.

For his home was her home. She knew it, only she didn't deserve it. She didn't want it. If she told herself so enough times, she might believe it. This, too, kept her from sleep. The endless battle with herself, the search for some peace in her soul. She had no peace, not like the maid, who slept so easily. Not like the groomsmen and outriders who adapted to each duty with a dignified sense of honor. As the coach rattled along at its snail's pace, she realized she had never been running away, only seeking this peace which eluded her.

At length she must have finally slept, for she dreamed that a tiger joined her in the carriage, the tiger from her childhood in India. Somehow she knew it was that specific tiger curled beside her, warm and furry on the cushioned bench. She stroked her fingers through its rough-soft pelt, crying a little, feeling scared and lost. Then they weren't in the carriage anymore, but back in India beside the river. When she walked toward the sparkling, fast moving river, the tiger placed itself before her, impeding her. "No," it seemed to say, "I won't let you," although it only said this with its eyes.

When she grew tired of trying to get around it, she lay down in the curve of the great beast's body instead, feeling its chest move in and out in a calming rhythm as it breathed. It felt so real, the tickle of its fur, the forest smell of it, the heated whisper of its breath. Its great paws lay beside her hands. "I'll care for you, *baga lika*. You don't have to be afraid."

Suddenly the tiger beside her wasn't a tiger at all, but Lord Warren, speaking in his steady voice. The tiger's forest-amber eyes transformed to Warren's piercing blue ones. The paws were his hands, holding and guiding her, and the whisper of breath his gentle kisses. "You mustn't," he said against her lips, turning her from the water. "You mustn't go that way."

She startled awake, gasping in the carriage's dim interior. She could still smell the hot, earthy fragrance of India. The forest air clung to her skin and filled her lungs. She coughed, trying to clear it.

"Milady?" said the maid, sitting up in alarm. "Are you well?"

209

Josephine burst into tears, caught between the present and her strange dream that had felt so real. "Warren," she whispered.

"Milady? Oh, dear me, don't cry." The maid produced a worn handkerchief from her dress sleeve and held it out with shaking hands. "What can I do to assist you? Shall I— Shall I tell the driver to turn around?" But the carriage was already slowing, the groom calling to the outrider. The maid looked out the window at Josephine's manor rising stark and humble from the surrounding fields. "I think we're there, ma'am."

Josephine mopped at her cheeks and nodded. The sun had risen high in the sky, flooding the carriage and hurting her eyes.

Home.

Josephine composed herself as well as she could, only to soothe the agitated maid. She was one of the kitchen girls, not accustomed to serving "milady," but brave enough to accompany her on this wild flight. "Yes, we're there," Josephine said, and her voice sounded remarkably steady. She handed back the maid's handkerchief as the carriage jolted to a stop. More voices, and the carriage door opened.

Josephine emerged into the light of an English afternoon, stiff and somewhat abashed. She hoped her eyes weren't too terribly swollen and red. A stately, formally dressed servant sketched a bow. "Welcome to Maitland Glen, Lady Warren. I am your steward, at your service."

"My steward?" Josephine stopped at the bottom of the carriage steps.

"I am overseeing the improvements. This is Mrs. Hatchley, the head housekeeper."

Josephine had expected to find a boarded-up, deserted manor, not improvements and a steward and housekeeper on staff. She nodded to Mrs. Hatchley, who was already taking the maid in hand and coordinating the unpacking of her things. Questions, so many questions. Josephine still felt half asleep.

"Mr..." She looked at the polite manservant. "I don't know your name."

He bowed again, even lower this time. "Mr. Hargrove. Lord Warren hired me to oversee the improvement and provisioning of your home. It's been my honor to serve you."

His bowing and scraping confused her almost as much as the bright flower beds flanking the house, and the new, brass-trimmed door, and the

210

smartly polished windows. "Lord Warren is improving the house?" she asked.

But of course he was. Why, he must have known all along that she wasn't going to make it in London. From the looks of it, he'd set the project in motion weeks ago.

"How...? When...?"

"The work commenced in early May, my lady. Only the best craftsmen in Oxfordshire, you may be sure. My lord wanted the best of everything for your honor. When the main house renovations are done, he intends to add on to the east wing. Perhaps you've seen the plans?" He seemed at last inclined to acknowledge her utter confusion, awkward though it was. "I perceive this all comes as a surprise. Would you care to step inside and see what's been done?"

The grooms had already taken the carriage off to unhitch the horses in working, refurbished stables. *Improvements.* Lord Warren had commenced improvements on her house without even telling her. He had presumably paid for all of it from his own funds. Her dream poked at her as she walked toward the house. Lord Warren, and her tiger. *I'll care for you. You don't have to be afraid.*

The outside had been patched and repaired, made pretty and respectable, but the inside took her breath away. The walls were plastered in handsome modern finishes, topped with ornate molding. The floors were completely redone in varnished wood and tile. New furniture filled out the rooms, soft sofas and elegant bureaus and tables, and carpets so thick she nearly tripped as she walked upon them.

"Not much has been done upstairs," Mr. Hargrove said, as she stared upward at the polished, refurbished chandelier. "Lord Warren expressed a wish that you might choose your favorite rooms, and decide on chambers for guests, and dressing rooms, and a nursery." At this last, the older man blushed. "We were not expecting your visit for a couple more weeks."

A couple more weeks. Warren had planned to bring her here at the end of the season, had expected to. He had known all along things wouldn't work out. The idea both comforted and devastated her. This beautiful, small property. He'd made it livable for her, not just livable but lovely and grand.

She swallowed hard. "Lord Warren is not with me. I decided to come earlier."

As she said it, she heard the sound she had strained so long to hear, the sound of hoof beats through the open door. There was shouting and a ruckus in the newly paved courtyard. As she moved to the front of the house, she heard Lord Warren berating the London servants.

"If I want you to take my wife somewhere, I'll goddamn tell you as much," he bellowed. "She may be Lady Warren, but I'm the master of the house."

She put a hand to her lips. Tears threatened again. He'd come after her, but oh, he was so angry. She watched as he stalked around the side of the entryway. His boots and breeches were covered in dust, his coat only half done up. He looked disheveled as he kicked through the neat beds of flowers and faced her.

Sun slanted across his features, and in that moment, she saw the tiger's eyes in his gaze. She saw the protector in him plain as day, so she could only stare in bewildered recognition, wondering how she'd never noticed it before.

"Won't you come inside?" she asked when she found her voice. "Won't you come see? It's so beautiful, what you've had them do."

His glare drilled into her. Despite her fear at his obvious fury, she felt a hot and awful joy.

He crossed his arms over his chest and let them down again. "I don't trust myself not to abuse you if I come inside."

She spread her fingers on the newly installed door frame. "I know you would not abuse me."

"But I'd spank you awfully hard. No, perhaps I really would abuse you this time. I'm feeling rather at the end of my tolerance."

The servants disappeared, every one of them. The bustling business of the lord's arrival had transformed into a tense and lonely silence, with only the two of them to untangle their affairs. She could barely raise her head to look at him.

"You cannot continue to run away from me," he said after a long moment. His voice held steady but his blue eyes blazed. "I told you last time that it couldn't happen again."

"I didn't run away. I told you I was coming here. Why, you had it prepared it for me."

"Had it prepared—?" He blew out a breath. "It was to be a surprise. I wanted you to have a home you could be proud of, a home we could share. I thought perhaps we could spend holidays here, or have secret getaways from the larger manor. I thought we could bring our children when the weather was pleasant." His voice rose along with the color in his face. "I wanted to make you happy. I've tried to make you happy." He took a step closer, emotion contorting his features. "My God, why did you leave me? Why do you hate me when all I want to do is help you?"

She reached out to him, terrified of his anger, but more terrified at the vulnerability in his gaze. "Won't you please come inside? You must see what they've done. It's too magnificent."

The blaze in his eyes darkened to a fire. "Certainly, I'll come inside with you. If that's what you really want."

Warren worked to master himself as he followed her into the manor. After his drunken night, his shock at her departure, and his wild ride here, he was not at all sure he would treat his wife with proper respect.

But she hadn't treated him with proper respect. He gave a cursory glance around the bottom floor, at the staircase and gleaming floors, and the tall windows admitting ample light. He was so angry with her, so furious. How dare she invite him inside this house like a bloody queen, when he was the one who'd restored it?

For her.

He'd restored it because he wished to please her and make her love him. He wished her to feel more worthy in society, being in possession of a fine home. Little good his efforts had done. He took her arm and drew her into the westernmost parlor, which was the most private, and firmly shut the door.

She pulled from him and backed away, no longer the gracious queen of the manor.

"You're afraid now? You invited me in," he said. "You might have kept me outside. This is *your* land and *your* property." He flung the words at her in an immature tone.

"I didn't want to keep you outside." She stood by the window, her hands clasped in front of her skirts. "You're my husband. I wish us to be civil."

"You weren't civil last night. Come here, Josephine."

She turned her head the slightest bit. It seemed a pitiful and yet erotic gesture. He was frightening her, and worse, he meant to. "Come here," he repeated in a louder voice.

"What are you going to do?"

"I'm going to do what I ought to have done last night, and what you surely deserve today. I'm going to spank you until you can't sit down." When she didn't come, he went to get her, pulling her resisting form to a nearby chair. He sat and flung her across his lap. "You remember the last time you ran away?" he asked in a hard voice, tossing up her skirts. "What happened to you then?"

"No," she cried. "Don't do this."

"I wish I didn't have to." He corralled her wrists and held them against her arching back. "I thought that punishment would have been harsh enough to prevent a repeat performance."

He began to spank her, sharp, stinging blows meant to teach a lesson, or perhaps only disperse his emotional pain. He ought not to be spanking her in this mood, but he didn't know how else to proceed without falling into a pile of brittle-edged pieces.

"I didn't run away," she gasped, crying out at each firm smack. "I didn't."

"You did." He gave her another volley of wild wallops. "You snuck away in my carriage like a thief in the night."

"Because you wouldn't let me go. You wanted me to be better, but I won't ever be better. *Ow, ow, ow!*" Her bottom was flame red already, reminding him of the severe strapping he'd given her the last time. And what had it changed?

"Please, don't," she cried again, struggling to get away from him. "I'm sorry. I'm so sorry I've failed you time and again."

He paused, sucking in a breath. Failed him? He wasn't so certain now who had failed whom. He released her, pulling her upward into his lap. *Oh, Josephine, what do I do? Where do we go from here?* She smelled of sunshine and flowers, and everything he needed. He buried his fingers in her hair and pressed his lips to her breasts, her shoulders, her throat. She held onto him, wincing as he twisted his fingers in her curls.

"Damn you," he whispered. "God damn you." He kissed her, a punishing kiss, violent and feral. It was a kiss to reclaim her, to subdue her. He wanted to lock her in a tower until she understood how much he loved her. How to make her understand? Not through force and anger, and constant recrimination. What a blundering arsehole he'd been.

He broke away and pressed his cheek to hers. "I never wanted you to leave. Never, not in a thousand years. I love you. No matter what I say, no matter what I do. God, I'm an idiot." He spread his hands on either side of her face, cupping her cheeks between his palms. She had been so brave; she had tried so hard to please him in so many ways. "You haven't failed me, Josephine. I've failed you. I've tried to make you into something you're not, something you should not be. I've watched you struggle and be very unhappy, and I kept pushing you anyway to be what I wanted, when you are already magnificent and unique. I wonder if I haven't been as bad as Stafford, causing injury to you."

"You haven't," she said, shaking her head. "Don't say such things. You saved me when you married me."

"No. I've hurt you." He brushed his palm across her round, pert bottom cheeks, now sore with the evidence of his temper and will. "I've hurt you time and time again. Someone ought to save you from me."

She put her head down against his shoulder, and he realized she was crying. He shoved her face against his neck, punishing himself with the heat and moisture of her tears, the very evidence of how much he'd damaged her. He could have cried too, for all the pain he'd caused. "I've been selfish and demanding," he muttered in a self-reproachful litany. "I've punished you for things that aren't your fault."

"No. Well, perhaps. But you saved me from a miserable life with Stafford. You listened when I poured out the bleak, awful feelings in my heart. You saved me from loneliness. You can never understand how lonely I was." She raised her head and looked into his eyes with a faraway sort of gaze, before she really seemed to see him. "I'll never forget that you saved me. That's why I love you so, and why I wish... I wish I could be the sort of countess you need."

"The sort of...?" He *hated* himself. "I don't give a damn anymore what sort of countess you are. I love you, Josephine. When I came home and realized you'd left, I barely knew how to go on."

"I thought you'd be grateful. Last night I humiliated you in front of every one of your friends. I never say or do the right things. I'm not proper or ladylike the way I should be, and I doubt that will ever change."

He groaned, holding her tighter. "You're impossible, you really are, but I can't bear to be away from you. I think I'd rather go about in society with a wife who isn't quite tame. Eccentricity is occasionally accepted, especially if it is dispensed with the proper élan. I think half the guests at the Parliament dinner admired you for cutting up at Westmoreland. You were so showy about the whole thing."

A laugh escaped her, a strangled, smothered giggle she buried against his coat. "I'm sorry. It was very bad of me. I hardly remember what I said."

Then he was laughing too, great belly laughs erupting from the shambles of his soul. "It was terrible of you. And so terribly hilarious. I warrant no one has ever dared give Westmoreland such an earful about anything. They say you scowled at him through every word."

"I'm afraid I did."

He couldn't stop laughing now, and embracing the wild and inappropriate creature in his arms. This wonder, his half-tame wife. He tilted her head up and kissed her, a kiss for acceptance and passion, and merriment, and love. She wound her arms inside his coat and around his back, holding him near. "I didn't want to leave," she whispered against his mouth.

"Then why did you, naughty girl?" He grasped her nape to hold her still for more kisses. She moaned as he pulled back and gave her a stern look. "No more running away from me, Josephine. Not for any reason. Do you understand me? No more."

"No more," she promised as his grip on her neck tightened.

"You belong with me always, at my side. My countess. My lover. My wife."

She clung to him, making small, anxious sounds as he whispered kisses down her neck. "But..."

He paused. "But what?"

"But what if I'm never accepted? What if I harm your social standing, and your career?"

"Then we shall carry on as we may, and make the most of things for our children's sake. I'm sure between the two of us, we can create attractive enough boys and girls that a bit of family eccentricity won't ruin their chances at a match. If they have even half your beauty..."

Her tears had never fully gone away, and now he saw them start anew, a great gush of guilt and misery. Well, she wouldn't be cured of her misgivings in a day. He'd spend a lifetime reassuring her if he had to, a lifetime convincing her that she was wonderful and beautiful, and perfect just as she was.

"Don't cry, dear love." He stroked her hair for long moments, brushing away her tears, wishing he could brush away all the thoughts that troubled her too. "Shh, all will be well. Who's to say our children won't wish to avoid society too? There will be Maitland Glen for them to escape to, and Warren Manor. And that cottage I still intend to build." He sat straighter and tipped up her chin. "You see, I've thought about things last night, and all the long journey here, and I've realized that making society happy is not as important to me as taking care of you. What truly matters to me, what I truly wish to do in life, is to make you as content as you've made me. Yes, my career has always been important, my friends, my social standing, all that, but they were important *before* I met you. Since then, you've changed me, and you've changed my priorities too."

She reached up and put her hands on his cheeks. "I've changed you?"

"Can you doubt it?" His laugh came out thick and clumsy, weighed down with emotion. "You didn't know me before, but I assure you, I'm quite a new man. And I much prefer the man I am with you. I used to be a devil of a rogue, caring only for myself and my interests. It seemed fun at the time, but looking back, it was a sad sort of existence." A thought occurred to him, ridiculous but wholly accurate. "You've tamed me, Josie, all the while I was trying to tame you."

It seemed hilarious again, to both of them. Her tears disappeared into one of her ungoverned fits of giggling, the sort he hoped would increase with each week, each month, each year they spent together. This business of taming his wife was a blasted nuisance, and Warren thought he was more than done with it. Let her be wild in her rebellious way, if that was who she really was. He'd be there to look after her and shelter her from the worst consequences, as her tamely domesticated keeper.

Baga lika. She awed him, with her strength, her heart, and her perseverance. At some point, he would have to research the native translation for "tiger wife." But not now.

Right now, he had to take her someplace private, with a large, comfortable bed.

Chapter Nineteen: Love Like This

They ended up at Warren Manor, because the upstairs rooms at Maitland Glen were not yet finished. The staff at his manor home hadn't expected them from London for a couple weeks, but they put together a fine dinner anyway, and the rooms were always kept in readiness for unexpected guests.

And, of course, the manor offered certain disciplinary necessities that Maitland Glen lacked.

Josephine waited upon a chair in his bedroom, her knees pressed primly together. Her brows went up when the maid tapped at the door and delivered a covered tray.

"What did you think?" Warren asked with a half-smile. "That you'd escape with no consequences whatsoever?"

"You spanked me once already," she reminded him. "Quite hard."

"An over-the-knee spanking, for less than a minute. No, the past two days' shenanigans deserve a proper consequence to disperse any lingering tensions. You agreed it was necessary. Have you changed your mind?"

She stared up at him. He could see the dread she felt, and the longing also. They both understood these intimate acts of discipline calmed her and brought them closer together. She lowered her face, a blush creeping across her cheeks. "I haven't changed my mind. I deserve to be punished. I'm sure Westmoreland will want to know that you've put me in my place."

"Westmoreland would probably like to take a sturdy birch rod to your bottom, but luckily for you, it's my job to discipline you, not his."

She gave a little shiver as he walked to the corner where he'd secreted a schoolroom cane. Her eyes went wide.

"May I change my mind about the necessity of punishment?"

He tapped it against his palm. "I'm afraid not. I'm sure you believe I'm being too strict, but I don't think a hand spanking or a hair brush paddling will suffice in this case, with two such outrageous infractions. Even the strap..."

As he named off these implements, her shivers increased. "I've never been caned. Will it hurt even worse...worse than the strap?"

He looked her up and down, wishing to communicate gentle trust, while simultaneously scaring the tar out of her. "You may inform me afterward which you believe hurts worse."

Of course he wouldn't cane her full out, as his schoolmasters used to do when he was a reckless and disobedient pupil. He'd make it hurt just enough that she would feel expiated, and when she felt better, he would too.

"Come along then." He tapped the high expanse of his bed. He preferred to dole out the stricter punishments in here, rather than the ruffled bower where she slept. It was a mind game of sorts, a way to make her even more anxious. She approached the bed and bent over it in a provocatively reluctant way.

Damn her, he was already hard, solid as a rock within his breeches. He rearranged his surging length and drew up her skirts, placing the cane beside her where she could see it.

She promptly turned her head the other way.

He tsked at her. "No, I put it there intentionally, so that you must look at it and think about what a naughty troublemaker you've been. You ruined the Parliament dinner party, didn't you? And threw two households into upheaval with your overnight flight. Three households, counting this one, where they didn't expect us for another fortnight. I imagine they know below stairs what the ginger is for."

She turned back to the cane with a soft, worried sigh, her blush deepening to the back of her neck. So charming, her sensitivity. By the time he'd worked the rather thick plug of ginger into her bottom hole, she was blushing indeed. That done, he set about undoing the back of her gown and divesting her of every stitch of clothing before bending her back over the bed. He took off his own coat and waistcoat next, putting them aside for his valet with slow deliberateness. His cravat came after, the pin set into a jewelry box.

All the while Josephine stared at the cane. He was certain it looked terrifying in her eyes, and yes, it would cause her some discomfort.

Speaking of discomfort... He left his breeches on, lest he traumatize her further by his flagrant state of arousal. Josephine was squirming already, making uncomfortable noises as the ginger took effect. What a delightful target, that squirming bottom. How he'd love to release himself and plunge inside—

Punishment first, he chided himself. *You lustful beast.*

He took up the cane and stood beside her, placing a hand upon her lower back. "You're to be still," he said in his strict voice. "Palms flat on the bed."

"Yes, my lord." Her shaky words emerged, muffled, from within the sheets.

"We'll have eight good strokes, and then we'll see where you're at."

She bore the first stroke rather well, he thought. A sharp yelp and a little jerk. A line of pink bloomed across her buttocks as she processed the fiery sensation. "Count for me," he reminded her, tapping upon one tensing cheek.

"Oh," she gasped. "One."

He made her wait a bit for the second. She clenched upon the ginger in her bottom, making hot little panting noises as she wiggled and squirmed. He laid the second stroke above the first, and the third just below. She counted with obedient determination, her whole body tense as a rail.

"Four," she cried out at the next stroke. He'd laid it directly atop the first one and she arched up, sobbing, "Oh, please, I'm quite sure I can't bear any more."

"Bend over. Palms on the bed," he reminded her. "I'll add strokes if you don't take your punishment the way you've been taught."

"But Warren! It hurts so badly."

"I don't doubt it. Now, we're halfway there. Will you bend over and take the remainder of the strokes, or shall I tie you down and add a few more?"

"May I only rub my bottom for a moment?" she begged. "And remove the ginger, just for this one spanking? Oh, my lord, please?"

"It's to be ten strokes then," he said. "Two extra strokes for whining and dithering."

Josephine made a meek sound of protest but she bent over the bed and even offered out her smarting bottom.

"That's better," he said approvingly.

"Five," she wailed as the caning recommenced. "Six! Oh, it hurts. It hurts! Perhaps you had better tie me down after all."

"There are only four strokes remaining. You may have a short break to gather yourself if you really need it. To let some of the pain disperse."

"Oh, yes, please. I would like that."

He lifted her from the bed and put her on her knees. "You can pass the time by showing me just how sorry you are for your naughtiness." He undid the straining front of his breeches, releasing his rigid shaft. She stared up at him, blushing, rather tearful, her bottom still tensing from the pain of the last two strokes. She accepted him in her mouth so eagerly he almost went off right then. "Stop," he groaned. "Go slowly. Tease at all the places I've taught you. And don't think to distract me from finishing the rest of your punishment, because you won't manage it. This is only a rest."

Oh, how easily he could have been distracted. He could have let her pleasure him for days and not grown tired of her earnest efforts, accompanied by the occasional whimper of discomfort from the ginger in her arse. She was so beautiful like this, surrendered and submissive. "Yes," he said, stroking her hair. "A little break, then four more strokes."

She whimpered again. Such a lovely sound, especially when she was on her knees. When his control was near to bursting, he told her to stop and bend back over the bed. She obeyed, her hands tensed into fists. The ginger's flange nestled between her cheeks, that extra, secret punishment for very naughty penitents.

"You remember which number we're on?" he asked.

"Seven. *Ow!* That was seven, my lord." She buried her face in the sheets again. On eight, she danced on her tiptoes and made a sound that was very unladylike indeed.

"There now," he said, staring down at his aching cock, still thrusting obscenely from the front of his pants. "We might have been finished with the punishment, mightn't we? If you had better self-control."

"I have terrible self-control," she said. "I know it."

"Then you must endure the last two."

He made both strokes as hard as the others. No going soft, not him. She would know, and it would somehow discredit the whole punishment, to not dole out what she'd earned. She squealed and cried, and counted, and squeezed on the ginger so she bawled even harder and begged him to take it out.

"Not yet," he said, putting down the cane. Eight distinct lines crossed her backside, since he'd laid two of the strokes atop another. He traced each one to be sure there was no broken skin. She winced every time he touched her, and shimmied her bottom so he almost lost his mind.

"I think it's time you had a firm rogering," he said, barely holding his voice steady. "To further fix you in your place."

He didn't wait for any comments of disagreement, or consent, only took her hips and plunged inside her, burying himself so deep his pelvis contacted her sensitive, caned cheeks. Her body held him tight, a perfect, fitted vessel for his aching manhood as he pounded into her. He enjoyed taking her like this, when she was sore and conflicted, for if she clenched around his cock the way she liked to, she clenched around the ginger too, constantly crossing the line between pleasure and pain.

"Are you going to be a good girl now?" he asked. "Have you learned your lesson?"

"Oh, yes, I have. I'm going to be so, so good," she said in a tumbling whisper.

She probably hadn't the least idea what she was saying, which was both charming and erotic. She was close to falling apart, he could feel it. By this point, he could tell just by the way she breathed. He didn't want this to be over quickly, this surrender, this reconnection to each other, but then, they were going to be together forever. They could do this every day. Twice a day if they liked, and twice nightly.

Forever.

"Oh, Warren," she cried, pulling at the sheets. "The way you make me feel..."

"Does it feel good? Move with me, love." He thrust so deep and hard inside her slick warmth that they both collapsed forward onto the mattress. He leaned on one elbow so he wouldn't crush her, and wrapped the other arm around her, holding her close and working inside her with all the passionate lust he felt. Her legs slid against his as she neared her climax. "Yes, that's right," he urged her. "Yes, feel me inside you. My good girl. My strong girl."

He licked her nape and then bit it, not hard, but enough to send her over that edge into shaking, shuddering ecstasy. She cried out with an elated sound that sent a shot of pleasure to his balls and thighs. He stiffened over her, pumping all his life and love into her as she bucked beneath him. Exquisite sensation wracked him, leaving him exhausted and bathed in a feeling of bliss.

"Josephine..." He lowered himself atop her, covering her from the curve of her nape to her toes hanging off the edge of the bed. He couldn't get close enough to her. She'd survived so many perils to reach his side, to become his wife and his lover. He wanted to shelter and protect her from any more harm, even if it meant changing his own goals and dreams. He'd uncover *her* goals and *her* dreams and they'd go forward together, always as close and connected as they were now. From now on he would be the husband she deserved, accepting her as she was. He'd give her no more reasons to run away and hide.

He made all these vows silently, in his head, but to her he only said, "I love you, I love you," over and over, kissing her shoulders and jawline and the delicate curve of her neck. She laced her fingers through his and whispered that she loved him too.

Her love, which he'd never sought, had come to mean so much to him, had indeed changed him from the inside out, into a completely different sort of man. She'd changed him into a person he was proud to be. In the warm intimacy of their embrace, they soon succumbed to exhaustion. They roused themselves at some point to liberate Josephine of her ginger, and to wash, and then both of them crawled back into his bed. She lay drowsy and limp beside him as he pulled up the covers.

"Warren," she murmured as he hugged her close. "Do you know what?"

"What, love?"

"On the way here, there was a tiger in the carriage with me."

"A tiger? My goodness. I hope he behaved."

Her lashes flickered, half closed. "It was only a dream."

He kissed her lightly, once, twice, unable to resist. "You mustn't be afraid of tigers anymore," he said as he drew away. "Not even in your dreams."

"I wasn't afraid." She drew her fingers down one of his bristly cheeks. "Because the tiger turned into you."

"Did it now?"

"Yes." Her breathing softened and slowed as her fingers went still. "I love you, Warren."

"I love you, too, dearest."

She said nothing else, only snuggled right against him, until he felt her fall peacefully to sleep.

* * * * *

Josephine woke and slept, and woke and slept, and ate a bit, perhaps around breakfast time. She had quite lost count of the hours, caught up as she was in her husband's touches and caresses, and the intimacies he demanded with his secret, lascivious smile.

At last she rose and stretched, and went to the window to see about the clatter in the courtyard.

"Oh, your sister has come with Mrs. Everly," she said over her shoulder. "And August and Arlington too, it appears."

He crossed to stand beside her. She couldn't help noticing his manhood was ready for action yet again. "Perhaps you should stay away from the window until you've dressed," she said with a pointed glance.

"Impertinent comments will get you nowhere. Except over my shoulder."

She let out a half-shriek, half-yelp as he upended her and gave her bottom a teasing spank. "They are right downstairs," she protested, flailing her arms. It was a long way from his shoulder to the floor.

"Not yet," he said, grasping her tighter. "They're still in the courtyard. Minette will be chattering on and on to the butler and housekeeper about every detail of the journey, Arlington and August will be taking some refreshment, and the servants will be unpacking their things, if they've come to stay. We've at least half an hour before they demand our presence." He gave her bottom another sharp slap, right over the tender stripes from her caning. "But half an hour isn't long enough to do anything very exciting."

He righted her, and she leaned against him, pressing her cheek to his chest. "I suppose there won't be quite so many spankings now," she said, "since you intend to let me be more eccentric."

He stroked light fingers over her bottom. "I don't know. The spankings do have a calming effect on your nature. I suppose you might need one every once in a while."

"Every few months, perhaps?" she said, looking up at him hopefully.

He snorted. "Every few days, I should think. Unless you intend to go completely tame."

She wasn't sure if he was teasing or not. She wasn't sure she wanted him to be. From the open window, she saw Minette fluttering about, talking to her companion and directing the unpacking of the carriage.

"I suppose Minette worried after I left," said Josephine. "I didn't tell her my plans. I didn't want to get her in trouble again."

"She gets in plenty of trouble without your help. But yes, I'm sure she worried when she learned you'd gone. I think everyone worried when word got around that you'd rung a peal over Westmoreland. The three of them have probably come to be certain I haven't wrung your neck." He gave her nape a playful squeeze.

She smiled and tugged at his hand. "After you scolded me at Lansing's, you said you would go back inside and make up some story to excuse my behavior. What was it? In case someone brings up the topic?"

"Why, I didn't have the chance to make up anything at all. The wives had already decided you were in an 'interesting condition,' since this apparently causes ladies to behave in all sorts of erratic ways. And the tale must have made perfect sense to their husbands, because they all asked when the joyful event was to occur."

"Joyful event?" Josephine was lost. "What is an 'interesting condition'?"

"A pregnancy, my dear. A child. I'm afraid I let them go on believing the story because I couldn't think of a better one in the moment."

Josephine looked away from him, deep in thought. "A child?" She tried to remember the last time she'd had her monthly. It was past due now, surely. "Perhaps it's not such a made-up story after all."

He went very still. "What do you mean?"

"I mean... I wonder if perhaps..."

His eyes went very wide. "Never tell me you're breeding, Josephine. Not after the things I did to you last night, and this morning. My God!"

She put her hands on his chest to calm him. "I don't know for sure. And if I am, I'm certain everything is all right. Although we might reconsider the idea of spankings every few days."

Warren remained white-faced. "I suppose I'll have to consult a physician on the matter. 'Tell me, is it all right to spank my wife when she's breeding? How often would you recommend?'" He sputtered out a laugh, and then his mouth relaxed into a grin. "A baby, Josie. Imagine. A little girl or a little boy. We'll have to air out the nursery wing, and finish the renovations at Maitland Glen. We'll need clothes and toys and bright places for the baby to play."

"We have some time." She smothered a smile at his excited planning. "I believe babies take many months to appear. And you mustn't tell anyone yet, until we confirm it."

"But everyone already believes it's true. The gossips will expect a baby in the spring. Not that we care about gossips anymore," he said quickly when she frowned at him. He lowered his voice to a lighter, more sensual tone. "If you're not with child, I suppose we had better start trying for one right away."

"I think you more than did your duty in that regard last night. And this morning," she added, raising her eyebrows. "But we can keep trying if you like."

They both turned to look outside. Minette, August, and Arlington had already gone into the house. "We have only a quarter hour now," he said, turning back to her. His eyes glinted. "It will be a rush."

"We'll manage." Josephine squeaked as he swept her up into his arms and carried her to the bed. He laid her back and crawled atop her, spreading her thighs. Had this frightened her once? Now she couldn't wait for him to ease inside her, inch by delicious inch. She clung to him as he filled her.

"Oh, it feels so good."

"You feel so good," he said, kissing her and nibbling at her lips. "Yes, arch for me. Show me how much you want me." She writhed against him and smothered her helpless cries of pleasure in his shoulder when the servants came tapping at the door.

"We'll be down presently," he called out in a rough voice. "Give us ten... Well, perhaps twenty minutes." He sucked in a breath as she squeezed on his thick length. "We've some very important and sensitive matters to attend."

"Yes, my lord," came the servant's reply.

Josephine licked the scratchy underside of her husband's jaw. "How dutiful you are," she teased. "And how I love you for it."

He answered this praise with an especially forceful thrust. In the end, nearly an hour passed before they made it down to greet Warren's sister and his gentlemen friends, but none of them seemed put out, except perhaps Lord August, who by now had endured nearly two whole days of Minette's adoring company.

"Josephine," Minette cried, flying across the room to embrace her. "I heard the news. It's all over town! I heard it from Lady Bexford who heard it from Lady Geoffrey who had it from Lady Mary Elaine that you're in the family way. I'm to be an auntie soon, am I? Is it really true?"

Josephine smiled shyly at her husband and then back at Minette. Lord August and the Duke of Arlington stood a bit away, looking embarrassed. Josephine placed a hand over her middle, where Warren had only recently kissed her and whispered achingly tender things. "I certainly hope you'll be an auntie soon," she said. "You'll do very well at the job."

Minette practically levitated with excitement, clapping her hands. And in her heart, Josephine didn't think she was raising false hopes. Somehow she knew Warren's child was growing within her, just as she knew Warren's love lived within her now and always. *Half tame, but fully loved*, he had whispered as he caressed her. *Oh, Josie, I love you so.*

The five of them proceeded to the garden to talk and take tea in the light of the breezy day. How far Josephine had come from that evening in Lord Baxter's ballroom, when she'd hidden among the house plants, hoping not to be found. How far Warren had come too, from his dissolute days. He had found her and changed her whole life, and she had changed his too. They were going to have a child together, perhaps many children, all of them cherished, happy, and safe.

The gentlemen laughed, the cakes were delicious, and Minette glowed under Lord August's occasional regard. Warren sat by her side, touching her hand now and again and sharing secret smiles. This was so much better than a lonely cottage somewhere.

It was so much better to belong, and to be close to him.

It was so much better to be loved.

THE END

A Final Note

I hope you enjoyed this second story in the Properly Spanked series. If you missed Townsend and Aurelia's story, be sure to read *Training Lady Townsend* to hear their emotional tale. There are two more books still to come in the series: *My Naughty Minette*, and *Under a Duke's Hand*. You won't want to miss any of this spankalicious saga, so be sure to subscribe to my newsletter at annabeljoseph.com for news about upcoming releases, or follow me on Twitter (@annabeljoseph) or Facebook (www.facebook.com/annabeljosephnovels) to hear updates on my works in progress.

Many thanks to my beta readers, Linzy Antoinette, Tasha L. Harrison, J. Luna Scuro, GC, and Doris. Thanks also to my editors Lina and Audrey for their generosity and guidance in making my books the best they can be. And as always, thanks to you, my readers and supporters, for your reviews, your emails, your artwork, and your recommendations to others. Thanks for being part of the Annabel Joseph world.

Coming Soon: My Naughty Minette, the third story in the Properly Spanked series

The Earl of Augustine has always thought of Lady Minette as a sister, but when a nocturnal adventure goes horribly awry, he's forced to make her his bride.

Now his friend Warren is furious with him, the jilted Lady Priscilla is spreading ugly gossip, his father's illness is worsening, and Minette is...well...being Minette. Flighty, exuberant, and utterly irascible, she wants a true marriage, when all August can see is the impish girl he rescued from scrapes as a child.

But Minette has idolized Lord August for years, as long as she can remember, and she's determined to make their union a passionate and fulfilling one. She launches caper after caper in an effort to capture his attention and awaken lustful and masculine hungers. Unfortunately, all she seems to accomplish are repeated disciplinary sessions over his lap.

Can she make August realize she's the love of his life in time to save their crumbling marriage—and her smarting backside? Or will he hold her at arm's length forever, refusing to acknowledge the powerful emotions she stirs in his heart?

If you liked To Tame A Countess, *you'll also enjoy* Lily Mine *by Annabel Joseph*

When Lily wends her way down the country lane to Lilyvale Manor, she hopes the coincidence of names bodes well, for she is in dire straits. She's been disowned by her London family and finds herself desperately in need of a job.

Lord Ashbourne is equally at ends, his fiancée having jilted him for a commoner and run off to the Continent. Her powerful society family is determined to delay the breaking scandal in order to save the younger sister's prospects. When a servant leads Lily to his parlor, James is astonished to discover how closely she resembles the missing lady of the manor.

He hatches a plan, convincing Lily to play his absent "wife" to keep the gossips at bay. He reassures her it will be in name only, but soon enough, playacting turns to real attraction, and friendship to aching, mounting desire. The strictures of society and unforeseen tragedy combine to test the pair's forbidden love, even as they are driven ever closer into one another's arms...

This novel contains spanking, light bondage, and light BDSM elements.

Also Available:

The Comfort series by Annabel Joseph

Have you ever wondered what goes on in the bedrooms of Hollywood's biggest heartthrobs? In the case of Jeremy Gray, the reality is far more depraved than anyone realizes. Brutal desires, shocking secrets, and a D/s relationship (with a hired submissive "girlfriend") that's based on a contract rather than love. It's just the beginning of a four-book saga following Jeremy and his Hollywood friends as they seek comfort in fake, manufactured relationships. Born of necessity—and public relations— these attachments come to feel more and more real. What does it take to live day-to-day with an A-list celebrity? Patience, fortitude, and a whole lot of heart. Oh, and a very good pain tolerance for kinky mayhem.

The Comfort series is:
#1 *Comfort Object* (Jeremy's story)
#2 *Caressa's Knees* (Kyle's story)
#3 *Odalisque* (Kai's story)
#4 *Command Performance* (Mason's story)

About the Author

Annabel Joseph is a multi-published BDSM romance author. She writes mainly contemporary romance, although she has been known to dabble in the medieval and Regency eras. She is known for writing emotionally intense BDSM storylines, and strives to create characters that seem real—even flawed—so readers are better able to relate to them. Annabel also writes vanilla (non-BDSM) erotic romance under the pen name Molly Joseph.

Annabel loves to hear from her readers at
annabeljosephnovels@gmail.com.

Printed in Great Britain
by Amazon.co.uk, Ltd.,
Marston Gate.